Homeless

Homeless

Ms. Michel Moore

www.urbanbooks.net

Urban Books, LLC
97 N18th Street
Wyandanch, NY 11798

ISBN 13: 978-1-62286-995-4
ISBN 10: 1-62286-995-8

First Trade Paperback Printing July 2016
Printed in the United States of America

10 9 8 7 6 5 4 3 2 1

This is a work of fiction. Any references or similarities to actual events, real people, living or dead, or to real locales are intended to give the novel a sense of reality. Any similarity in other names, characters, places, and incidents is entirely coincidental.

Distributed by Kensington Publishing Corp.
Submit orders to:
Customer Service
400 Hahn Road
Westminster, MD 21157-4627
Phone: 1-800-733-3000
Fax: 1-800-659-2436

Homeless

by

Ms. Michel Moore

CHAPTER ONE

"It's all fun and games, right? You thought you could get something for nothing, and no one would care? You thought I was gonna really put on a cape and save your pathetic ass? Hell naw; not me! Shit don't work like that; not today, yesterday, or fucking tomorrow!" Lonnie's deep husky voice grew more sinister with each passing word. His purposely weathered cracked hands shook as his grip tightened around "number four's" quivering throat. He was caught in his unstable emotions; withdrawn from the god-awful realism he was putting into motion.

"Please! Please! I'll do anything you want, just please, stop. I'm begging you. I have kids, please," she repeatedly pleaded with the man from the homeless shelter she'd recently grown to trust. "If you want the pussy, you can have it! You can have it, I swear! I'll do whatever!"

"Look, you're a nothing-ass crack whore; nothing more and nothing less. You don't deserve to live anymore. Begging, asking for handouts, acting as if the world owes you something just because you call yourself all of a sudden getting clean. Fuck all that. I'm doing society a huge favor, you tramp! And for the record, please don't mention them babies you don't even have custody of! The ones you threw away like garbage just so you could go suck some random, diseased-infested dick and get a rock or two of some heroin! Matter of fact, maybe I'll twist your head off and send it to one of your kids as a souvenir to remember you by. Sort of a 'Momma wasn't never nothing but a neglectful tramp' kinda gift. What say you, Ms. Thang? Would you like that?" Lonnie's smiled was unwarranted and uncalled for. There was nothing to be happy or joyful about in that moment. The devil himself would hide his face in shame at Lonnie's actions. There should have been no celebration of what was taking place; yet, in his mind, it was. The more the panicked ex-drug addict he'd overpowered struggled to break free and hopefully see daybreak, the more pleasure Lonnie evilly derived.

As his victim's needle-tracked arms flung wildly, her legs kicked in another failed attempt to get him off of her smaller body. "Please don't do this! Don't," she huffed out of breath.

Lonnie's adrenaline kicked into total overdrive. He couldn't help himself. The six foot one monster was like a kid in a candy store feeling he'd just won the sugar fix lottery. His mind was gone, focused on one thing: death. Inhaling the musty stench of his own breath bounce back off the frantic female's ear into his face, he smiled once more with satisfaction. "That's right, you dirty-bodied cunt; fight Daddy! Make Daddy work to send you on your way to hell! Make me remember you and this night," he grinned as the once-bright light in her eyes started to grow dim.

"Why you doing this?" barely escaped her now blue-colored lips. "I thought you liked me. I thought we were friends." Frustrated, she was quickly running out of steam to fight off the unexpected brutal attack. With one arm stretched out, she tried to reach a large stick that was near a Dumpster, but couldn't. Plenty more objects and debris filled the alley that could bring harm to her captor, but like the stick, they too were out of her reach.

"Me like you? Seriously? That could never truly happen. See, I'm nothing like you. Never was and never will be," Lonnie snarled coldly, staring into her face. "I'm too good for you; you and all the rest of them conniving homeless whores you run with every day trying to run game. I know y'all true motives."

"No, please," her voice grew faint.

"Stop begging and accept it."

"Please." She had no more energy left to give.

Lonnie shook his head while still choking her. "Naw, sweetheart. Please don't play with my intelligence. I pulled your card, and females just like your ass cards years ago right after my mother died. Y'all go around build up good brothers like me only to tear us down when we not looking; take everything we got and bounce like you worked for it. Like it's yours just because we dicking you down. Well, no more," he hissed in anger. "Just like the other dumb females out here in these streets, the joke is on you! All you women are a bunch of hateful hoes that need to pay! The only woman that was ever worth a damn on this earth was my mother; God rest her soul. The rest of you bitches . . ."

The full moon was semicovered by a few passing clouds. She knew time was not on her side as the brightness of the moon grew darker. Disorientated in a final act of defiance, the wayward mother of three dug her dirty fingernails deeply into the side of Lonnie's face. Dragging them down his jawline, she prayed he'd show her a small bit of mercy or at least momentarily loosen his death grip.

Lonnie immediately felt a breeze blow across the exposed lines of open flesh. Knowing his new "lady friend" drew blood, it was everything the calculating murderer could do not to scream out in ecstasy as she bucked one final time. Knowing the homeless woman he *befriended, then lured, behind the abandoned dwelling was seconds close to meeting her Maker, Lonnie slowed down his near-lethal attack, wanting nothing more than to casually enjoy this; his fourth kill.*

Reminiscing on what he felt was "the good old days" in the streets of Detroit he called home, Lonnie McKay, accused serial killer, was abruptly snapped back to the reality of what was currently taking place: his trial.

"Case MI-1966217-R; the *People of Michigan v. Lonnie Eugene McKay.*" Pudgy in build, the bailiff held in his stomach while still trying to make sure he was being clearly heard. Pretending not to care the case was being recorded by the court TV cameras, he then handed a thick manila folder to the presiding judge. With an expression of arrogance, Officer Martis then passed off a small collection of white and pink documents to the secretary. He was in his element making direct eye contact with the humbled, innocent-eyed defendant. The bailiff slightly pulled up his pants, letting the perpetrator, along with the victims' families, know he was all about his business, and this was *his* house.

"Thank you," the newly elected judge nervously replied while staring out into the shoulder to shoulder packed courtroom. As the bright lights of media cameras shined in her face, small beads of perspiration started to form. "Let me look this over. Everyone, please be patient. And, of course, please remain quiet as I do so. Don't take time to do anything else besides being as still as possible."

"I hope you burn in hell, you fucking monster," an angry voice rang out, followed by another person leaping to his feet.

"Yeah, I swear when you get to jail, my people gonna be waiting for your evil ass! You gonna pay in blood, you bitch!"

The judge wasted no time attempting to regain order in her courtroom. "Officer Martis, can you and the other officers please escort both of them not only out of this room, but the building as well."

"Judge, he strangled my sister in the back of an alley and left her to die behind a garbage can like she was an old stray cat," the man, still on his feet, tried breaking free from his wife's hold. "He needs to die just like that!"

The judge ignored the man's heartfelt statement in regards to his deceased sibling, knowing she had a job to do. "Okay now, I just said I was not going to tolerate any sort of commotion, and I meant it. The next outburst will result in contempt paired with incarceration and fines. Now, if there are any more persons in this courtroom who feel they can't control themselves, please take the time to leave right now." She took the time to scan the room. "I completely understand that five families have been tragically affected by these terrible crimes. And although I completely sympathize with your heightened emotions, I cannot, and will not, allow this system, this courtroom, or these jurors, to be compromised. Justice will be served."

The accused, Lonnie McKay, didn't flinch as his life was threatened. He didn't say a single word while the loved ones of the women whose lives he ended paraded out, one by one, most in tears. It was as if he was oblivious of what was taking place or just had no remorse. As the last person vowed to "see him again," Lonnie finally turned his face toward the court TV camera and disrespectfully grinned.

This high-profile case was one the city of Detroit would never forget. Every "t" had to be crossed and every "i" dotted. There was no room for error; not in any murder trial when a person's freedom was hanging in the balance and the victim's family sought justice. However, this instance was one criminal case that reared its ugly head once every blue moon. The eyes of the entire world were focused on the outcome of the trial of the century; the trial of the "Homeless Shelter Maniac," Lonnie Eugene McKay. The prescription pill-addicted resident was accused of callously kidnapping, torturing, and brutally murdering five people, mostly homeless women and one man, within a year's span. After the Detroit police reluctantly allowed the federal authorities to assist them in the manhunt for Mister McKay, he was quickly apprehended and brought to justice. After tons of witnesses and testimony, today would finally be the killer's day of reckoning. The five families could maybe have some small sort of closure and peace.

"Okay, everything seems to be in order." The judge looked up at both attorneys as well as the accused directly in his eyes. "Let me just say this before reading the verdict. Mister McKay, I've read over your personal history several times. And although this court can indeed commiserate with your unfortunate childhood and early adolescent tragedies, you were overcoming those obstacles and on the fast track to beating those odds. I'm fully aware of your troubled history with drinking and abuse of prescription drugs, yet the court must punish you for violating your probation not to partake in narcotics. In addition to that, whatever took place to cause such a drastic change in your mind-set, the general public will probably never find out, and it's not this court's job to speculate. We live in the here and now and deal in the harsh reality of today. And sadly, for all the families of the people whose lives were cut short, their reality is realer than some." She then signaled for the additional officers from the sheriff's department to stand on point, ready for whatever. "That being said, I don't want, nor will I, tolerate any more outbursts when the verdict is read. Is that understood? Any such action will result in that person or persons being immediately led outside this courtroom and directly to the county jail."

Remaining almost as stone-faced as he'd been since being arrested, Lonnie zoned back out. His demented mind was no longer present with his body. Whatever words the judge was saying no longer mattered. What would be would be. Defiant, the probable to-be-convicted murderer of five closed his eyes. Not muttering a word, Lonnie transported his thoughts back to what ultimately led him to the heavy chain steel shackles that currently bound his feet and arms. He knew he wasn't born the monster the world now labeled him as; his circumstances forced him to become that way.

CHAPTER TWO

The day started just as any other in the crime-infested area of Detroit. Lonnie, a hard sleeper, fought to wake up in the wee morning hours. Allowing his bare feet to touch the splinter-ready floorboards, the teen wiped the sleep out of the corner of his eyes. With each step he took, he wanted nothing more than to jump back in the bed. Splashing semiwarm tap water in his face, Lonnie lifted up from the small white sink staring into the mirror. Checking for any signs of new pimples, he reflected on his reality. He hated the fact his mother had been cursed with cancer, but sadly, she was. So that meant he had no choice whatsoever but to grow up fast, becoming the man of the house.

The only child did the best he could, yet sometimes, came up short. In between the added medications and supplies his mother needed not covered by welfare, Lonnie, most days, went without eating. But to him, his situation didn't matter. His mother being as comfortable as possible was on the top list of his priorities. Faced with the emptiness of the kitchen shelves, the determined youth managed to scrape a small bit of breakfast together to put something on his growling stomach.

Fighting to make it out of his current living situation and make something more out of himself besides a common thug, he remained focused on the positive. Determined in his faith, he left the small one-bedroom apartment he shared with his sickly mother. As always, he made it to school seconds before the second bell rang. Although considered an at-risk student by his teachers and most of his counselors, the living-below-poverty-level Lonnie stayed on the honor roll as well as the dean's list. Despite it all, he was determined to make it out of the hood.

"Yeah, hello! Can you send an ambulance to 5328 Leslie Street, Apartment 417 real quick?" Lonnie's panicked voice trembled shouting through his government-issued cell phone. "I just came home from school and found my mother passed out on the floor! Please send some help, please! Damn, please hurry up!"

"No problem, sir, we will. You just have to try to calm down a small bit so I can understand you. Can you do that for me?" The operator recognized his panicked tone and attempted to get ahold of the traumatic situation so it wouldn't get worse.

"Okay, okay, okay." Lonnie's hand shook as he rubbed the side of his mother's frail face, praying for a miracle. Normally having an even-tempered demeanor and quick on his feet, he was confused on what to do or say to aid his mom. Distraught, he knew his entire world would fall completely apart if she left him. Even though Lonnie knew her cancer was too far gone for any type of recovery, he still prayed every night for God to spare him the awful loss.

"All right now, I just need to type in a small bit of information and help will be on its way."

"Okay, okay; what information you need? I already done told you the address, now send help! You straight wasting time! Come on now; send help! She's dying!"

"Okay, now, like I said, please try to calm down," she reasoned using trained skills, easily discovering he was a nervous and frightened teenager. "A truck is being dispatched as we speak. And the information I'm trying to get will aid the paramedics more efficiently when they arrive."

"All right, operator; but please hurry," Lonnie openly sobbed, watching his mother's lips turn a strange shade of brown.

"Help is on the way, young man. I know it's hard, but just be patient."

"Okay, I'm trying, but it's hard. My mother was diagnosed with stage four cancer the earlier part of this year, and I don't know what to do right now to help her." Lonnie momentarily left his mother's side to get a washcloth, hoping it would cause her to snap out of the unconscious state she was in. While holding the rag under a cold stream of water from the kitchen sink, he remained on the line with 911.

"Okay, I see. Well, did she go to chemotherapy today or have had any other medical treatments in the last twenty-four hours that we need to be aware of?"

Lonnie wasted no time returning to his mother's side. Rubbing her face, he started to cry even more. "No, she hasn't been to the doctors after they made her leave the hospital. Some crazy lady administrator claimed there was nothing more they could do for her and she needed to go to a nursing home or some damn hospice place or something like that!"

"Just hold on a little longer, son. The truck is definitely en route and should arrive shortly."

After following proper procedure in gathering all the required information needed to dispatch a rig, the sympathetic woman, a mother herself, continued to speak with the worried youth. Trying her best to reassure him everything would be fine and that help was on the way, she allowed him to vent as he waited. She knew the young man was at odds and remained as calm as possible as he went all the way through it. The operator understood he was caught in his emotions and bit her tongue as he ran back and forth to the window, looking out for the promised ambulance. After the first five minutes and it had yet to arrive, Lonnie lost the small bit of self-control he did have, calling the innocent 911 operator any and everything, excluding a child of God. He accused her of not truly sending for help to being in cahoots with the devil himself to let his beloved mother die. Over the years, she'd heard folks say many of things and launch various threats, but Lonnie's conviction in tone was strangely different. However, she didn't let that deter her from doing what she was trained to do.

Eleven to twelve long, grueling minutes later, her mentally broken-down verbal attacker heard the paramedics' siren closely approaching their destination. With medical bags in hand containing basic supplies, the bare-minimum medically trained technicians entered the five-story dilapidated building. Opting to use the stairs not the elevator, the pair of white shirt-wearing man and woman team was at Lonnie and his mom's apartment. Flinging the door open wide, Lonnie threw the cordless phone across the room onto the couch. He then wasted no time directing them to his now-barely responsive mother.

The minutes to follow were like a dreadful horror movie playing out in slow motion to Lonnie. The ride in the rear of the ambulance was bumpy and reckless. It was as if the woman driver deliberately ran over every pothole in the city like she wasn't transporting precious cargo; his sickly mother. He overheard her yelling at someone on her cell phone while she was en route to the medical facility instead of concentrating on the road. Only a few minutes after arriving through emergency, Lonnie McKay's cherished birthing vessel and first love of his life, his mother, was pronounced dead at the local hospital. The paramedics claimed they'd done all they could do, but secretly, Lonnie felt differently as they stood around casually drinking coffee, joking with some of the staff on duty. The woman driver in particular showed no remorse or sympathy as she laughed the loudest. It was if no one truly cared what had just happened; the life-altering tragedy that had unfolded in his once-happy existence.

In a trance, speechless from what the doctor had just said, the teen's throat grew increasingly dry. There he stood, pitifully all alone in a room. Staring down at his mother's lifeless body stretched out on a steel, thin-mattress gurney, he trembled. With a winter-white sheet pulled up to her chest area, she appeared to be resting peacefully, but that didn't ease his pain. Lonnie pleaded for her to open her eyes, but she didn't.

"Mom, look at me. Please, please, look at me! Open your eyes, Mom, please!" He begged her to wrap her arms around him as he hugged her tightly. Unfortunately, she couldn't. "Hold me back, Mommy! Please hold me back! I wanna feel you hug me! Please!" Lonnie wanted her to call his name and wake him out of the terrible nightmare he was trapped in, but she didn't. "Please tell me this is a joke. Don't leave me; don't leave me by myself! Please, Mom, please, don't go! Oh my God, please, please, I'm begging you!"

Rubbing the side of his temples, Lonnie faced reality breaking all the way down. As the tears streamed down his cheeks, he became dizzy. His head was pounding. Feeling like there was nothing left for him to live for, he wanted to die too. At this point, anything that he felt could reunite him with his mother was all the devoted son cared about. Lonnie wasn't thinking clearly, and, of course, that was to be expected. His world was turned upside down just like that. Although he and his mother had discussed her losing her battle with the beast named Cancer, Lonnie was still not prepared for her to leave.

Caught in a tangled web of sorrowful what-if's, remorse, and regret, the sad-faced youth was soon interrupted from grieving. Forced to deal with yet another hurdle for the evening, Lonnie wasn't ready physically or mentally to cope with much more. Saddled with the unwanted task of being a strong young man while all he wanted to do was be a weak little boy, Lonnie's heart raced. Now, bombarded with numerous questions pertaining to possible burial arrangements, the only child was spent.

"Hello, are you a relative of the deceased?"

"Huh?" Lonnie shrugged his shoulders as if the woman should've known the answer.

"I'm with the in-house Social Services department here, and it's our job to make sure our patients are cared for even after they have expired. So are you and deceased related? Is she your mother, by chance?"

Lonnie watched the woman closely hold her clipboard to her chest. Trying to appear sympathetic, he could see a cold distant gaze in her eyes; one that said *hurry up and get on with the get on* so she could move on to the next unfortunate family on the list needy of her department's services. Angry at the entire human race, Lonnie wanted to knock her to the ground for repeatedly referring to his mother as "the deceased." Glancing over at his mother's body, his to-be-expected rage depleted some, knowing he had to be brave. "Yes, this is my mother."

Lowering her guard, she reached over on one of the counters retrieving a small box of tissue. "Well, on behalf of the hospital and I, we are extremely sorry for your loss."

"Thank you." He gladly accepted the tissue and wiped each of his beet red eyes.

Feeling she was being extremely fake, he still allowed her to continue. The woman automatically went into what was probably her regular routine about who was next of kin, who would be responsible for any outstanding bills, and what funeral home was going to be called to pick up the body. Not ready for anything other than being grief stricken, he didn't have the answers she was looking for; well, at least not at that time.

The social worker then asked who would be assuming responsibility for him since he was still considered a minor, which caused him to have chills. Looking over at his mother once more to gain some sort of courage, he tossed the used tissue onto the counter, then stepped out into the hallway. He was overwhelmed. The woman's voice sounded like fingernails scraping a chalkboard or an old alley cat getting its tail slowly twisted off. Lonnie couldn't take it. He wanted to yell out that God had just cheated him. His head was spinning. His heart was broken. His soul felt like it had left his body. He wanted to just lash out and go all-out nuts. He was fighting off the urge to tell all the doctors, nurses, social workers, and other people he was coming into contact with at the hospital to kiss his black ass. His reason for living was gone; so, now, was all his rhyme and reason. The honor roll student's mother definitely didn't teach him to disrespect his elders, but at this moment, Lonnie knew she'd understand his inner wrath.

After finding out the visibly distraught youth had no immediate plans of what he or his knowingly terminally ill mother had mapped out in what they knew was the inevitable, Mrs. Bishop had no other recourse but to inform Lonnie he'd be placed in emergency foster care if no responsible relative stepped up to the plate.

"Once again, Lonnie, I'm so very sorry for your loss. I know this is one of the worst days of your young life. My prayers are with you."

"Thank you," he managed to say with his head held down and a continuous flow of tears streaming down the side of his face.

"Your mother seemed to be a very strong woman to battle cancer in such a late stage from home. She should've been hospitalized, so I know she must've loved you very much, young man, to have opted to stay with you until the end."

"Yeah, she did," Lonnie solemnly stared over at the double doors they'd just wheeled his deceased mother through en route to the basement morgue. Using the bottom part of his T-shirt, he wiped his eyes once more. "And you right, she should've been in the hospital, but the old white bitch that runs this motherfucker felt differently! She didn't care about my mother getting better!"

The social worker knew that there had been major budget cuts over the past few years and insurances were paying less and less for patients' extended care. Knowing she was left to face more and more infuriated family members such as Lonnie that felt cheated her heart ached for them. Even so, that didn't mean she didn't have to do what she needed to do or say what she needed to say. Hospital policy was hospital policy. "Once again, young man, I'm very sorry for your loss. But you have to tone your voice down and please refrain from using profanity. I'm quite sure your mother loved you very much and wouldn't want you to behave in a manner that disrespects her teachings in any way. Wouldn't you agree?"

"She did love me, no matter what. She meant everything to me. We was all we had; just me and her. Now she's gone."

Mrs. Bishop had been on staff at the hospital for over eight years. With her Christian faith, she absolutely hated this part of her job; however, this was what she was paid to do to earn her paycheck. Holding the small clipboard in one arm, she leaned over, offering Lonnie a few more pieces of tissue that he readily took. After rubbing the youth's shoulder in an attempt to comfort him, she regretfully got down to the business at hand. "I know you are in terrible pain right now, son. And I have definitely been where you are now, having lost my own mom to an illness not too long ago, but we have to come up with a plan of action for you."

Lifting his head and eyes to meet hers, Lonnie was noticeably confused with her statement. "Huh? Say what?—a plan of action? I already told the nurses I had to figure out how to get money before I called a funeral home. I told them give me some time to get it together. I need to figure some things out."

Mrs. Bishop knew the young man was unknowledge-able of how the legal system worked when dealing with minors in cases such as these. She realized Lonnie had no idea what had to take place next . . . not only as far as his mother's burial but his immediate fate as well. Taking a deep breath, she proceeded to explain to him that since his mother was gone and he was underage, someone would have to assume responsibility for his well-being. "Do you have someone to call; maybe your father or another relative that'd be willing to care for you?"

Lonnie looked at Mrs. Bishop with a blank facial expression. Shaking his head, he ran his hand down the front of his face. "Look, I don't need anybody to take care of me. I've been taking care of me and my mother for the past year and a half after she first got diagnosed. I'm gonna be good on my own. Don't worry."

"Yes, Lonnie. I'm not taking anything away from you, and the hard task you handled, probably better than anyone twice your age. I do understand how independent you had to be and are now, but I'm sorry, dear. It's the law and my job to make sure you are in proper care tonight at least. Then ensure your mother's case gets in the hands of folks that can make sure she gets buried properly, funds available or not. The state can and will help you. We just have to go through the proper channels."

Lonnie lowered his head, thinking what to do next. Praying he had enough available minutes left on his cell to call his always-absent father, and as usual, he received no answer. Lonnie considered himself lucky that the number he had for the deadbeat fool was even still valid. Life was happening at a dreadfully rapid pace since the second he returned from school and walked into the apartment. And as bad as he'd like to slow it down or turn back the hands of time, he knew that wasn't a reality. His mother was dead and gone, and his father wasn't shit; two facts he had to deal with. He was officially an orphan in his eyes. No one truly cared about him in the city of Detroit, the state of Michigan, or the entire United States of America. Lonnie wrung his hands together, knowing from this point on, it would be him against the world.

Not wanting to continue to hear the social worker shower him with dead-end questions and out-of-the-way suggestions, Lonnie got himself together the best he could. He quickly snapped out of his grief, going into full urban street survival mode. Pretending he had to use the bathroom, the calculating young man walked down the hallway. The staff and visitor-congested hospital was bustling with people preoccupied with their own business, not that of a teenage boy who'd just loss his mother. They had their own problems, and he had his. A few sharp turns later and a short sprint down one flight of stairs, Lonnie's still tearstained face was feeling the cool breeze of the night air. Using his T-shirt, he tried his best to get himself together and wipe his bloodshot eyes.

With a few dollars in his pocket, Lonnie soon boarded a bus back to his apartment. The honor student knew that it would only be a matter of time before the social worker had to report his disappearance. However, it was no great secret . . . Detroit was bankrupt. The cash-strapped city had much better things to do with its limited resources besides gathering together a teen task force to try to take him to a foster home to live out the last several months before he turned eighteen. In his mind, she would have to do what she had to do. Going to live with anyone other than his mother was not an option.

In the meantime, Lonnie was going to return home and find a way to get the funds needed to give his mother a proper burial. The drastically overdue bills for rent and utilities would have to wait for now. His mother deserved to have a funeral fit for the queen he always felt she was; plenty of flowers, a beautiful dress, and an all-white casket trimmed in gold. Lonnie wanted nothing more than to make that happen.

CHAPTER THREE

Lonnie returned home. Stepping off the bus, his head hung low. He was still borderline hysterical and didn't want to come to grips with reality. With his eyes close to being swollen shut from crying, he didn't look forward to going inside the low-income building he called home, let alone the empty apartment. Each step felt as if his size ten sneakers were sinking deeply into the ground. Before the distressed youngster could make it up the walkway, Lonnie was met with several of the other tenants. Easily observing the state of the teen, they could tell the fate of their cancer-stricken neighbor, his mother, was not favorable. Surrounded with his peers and elderly alike, Lonnie gladly accepted the overflow of hugs, condolences, and praises of what a great person his mother was. Not once did he hear any of them disrespectfully refer to her as merely "the deceased" as the uppity social worker, the foreign doctor, or the rude female ambulance driver did.

Finally getting himself together, Lonnie found the courage to go inside and face whatever demons he felt were lurking. Deciding to take the stairs instead of the elevator, he started the long climb up to the fourth floor. Arriving at his door, he instantly got pissed. Met with a bright orange note taped to the door, he snatched it off. Immediately he knew what it was. This wasn't the first time he and his mother had a meant-to-be-embarrassing-nonpayment-of-rent-eviction notice displayed for all to see. Since Mrs. McKay's illness had kicked into full swing, they were almost a monthly occurrence at their household. Crumbling the paper up, Lonnie let his anger overtake mourning his mother's demise. It wasn't that he felt they didn't owe the money; it was the fact the entire building knew the ambulance had taken his mother out of the apartment barely alive less than six hours prior. He felt like a note like this could've waited; at least until the following day. But Lonnie knew the source. It wasn't the elderly caretaker's doing to be so callous on a night such as this. He was quiet, for the most part, known to be generous, kind, and easy to get along with. Lonnie knew this bullshit was the work of his longtime live-in girlfriend. She was the complete opposite of her better half. The insecure, middle-aged bitty felt every woman in the building, on every floor, both young and old, wanted her man. Everyone knew the caretaker was nothing more than a first-of-the-month meal ticket to her, but if he liked being used, then so be it.

Unfortunately for the residents of the low-income building, the bitter, overweight female forced his hand to make folk try to live by the letter of their leases; especially the ones she felt her man favored. Which, of course, meant Lonnie's once long-flowing-hair-deep-dimpled beautiful mother and a few others she always boasted were on her list when she got drunk.

Lonnie had bigger fish to fry than to go toe-to-toe with some old broad. She, just like the rent, several months past due, would have to wait. Shutting the front door behind him, he took a deep breath. Opting not to turn on the lights in the apartment, he made his way to the bathroom. After splashing cold water on his face, he tried to gather his thoughts. Coming to the awful realization his mother would never be coming home again, he fell to his knees. With his hands gripping the sides of the toilet, Lonnie violently threw up seemingly every meal he'd consumed over the past week or so. As the terrible smell of the vomit filled the air, he grew even sicker to his stomach. Scared to abandon the porcelain god he was now worshiping, Lonnie curled up on the bathroom floor until he fell asleep.

CHAPTER FOUR

Daybreak came, meaning Lonnie had to man up and try to make some calls. He knew he'd fled the hospital the night before, not informing the staff of what he intended to do. In the light of day, he knew he was probably wrong to do so, but he definitely wasn't trying to hear or accept that crap the social worker was talking. Gathering envelopes of paperwork from his mother's room, Lonnie paused, staring at her bed. They'd had countless talks on what he was going to do when the time came, but Lonnie wasn't trying to hear what his mom was saying, feeling like she'd live forever.

After placing the call, Lonnie was put on hold. A few seconds, later he was greeted by the same social worker he'd run out on the night before. "Yes. Hello. This is Lonnie McKay. I was there last night."

"Yes, Mr. McKay, I know who you are."

"Well, I was calling about my mother. I want to find out about getting that financial assistance you were talking about."

The social worker had worked a double shift and was not in the mood to cater to who seemed like an out-of-control youth. "Listen, son, I tried to help you last night and give you some options. But instead of taking that help, you opted to play games, so I don't know what to tell you."

Lonnie sensed the tension in the conversation and tried to diffuse it. "Look, I didn't call to argue with you.

That's not my intention. I just want to help my mother, that's all."

"Well, you definitely can't accomplish that behaving like some small child. That's all the more reason you need someone to care for you now that's your mother is deceased."

"Stop saying that," his tone deepened.

"Excuse me? What do you mean?"

"Stop saying deceased like my mother is nothing."

"Okay, now, Mr. McKay. I don't know where the major disconnect is with us, but the word *deceased* is proper terminology when speaking of the dead. No harm is meant or intended."

Lonnie was fed up. He'd tried to call his father yet again and received no answer. He wanted to ask one of his mother's supposed friends how burying someone went; however, when she got ill, they all stopped coming around for fear she'd keep trying to borrow money they knew she couldn't repay. So for now, Lonnie tried to hold his composure for his mother's sake. "Look, miss, I just want to bury my mother, and I don't know what to do. Can you help me?"

The social worker had just about enough of his apparent attitude and unloaded. "Listen, young man, I fully understand your dilemma, and as I stated last night, I sympathize, but I'm not going to let anyone, especially a smart-mouthed teenager, disrespect me. Since the beginning of this call you have been nothing but combative, and trust me when I say, I'm over it!"

"What the hell!" Lonnie barked. "I just lost my mother and am trying to get some information about how things go, and you on some crazy power trip! You just like that other lady down there; that head administrator!"

"Oh, you mean the one you referred to as the 'old white bitch' last night?"

Lonnie wasn't in the mood to back down. He'd been through hell over the last twenty-four hours and knew there had to be someone other than Mrs. Bishop that could help him with his plight. "Yeah, well, if the shoe fits, then wear that ugly motherfucker!"

"Okay, sir, I tell you what." She hoped the grieving teen was ready for what was to come next, but if not, so be it. The boy asked for it raw. "Your mother, the deceased! Since no one was here to sign off on any paperwork since you disappeared, as you know, her corpse was taken down to the hospital's basement morgue. And if no one comes forth claiming the deceased from there in the next forty-eight hours, that body will be considered temporarily indigent and sent over to the overcrowded medical examiner's office. So with that being said, you can contact either department for further assistance. Good day, Mr. McKay, and good luck!"

Lonnie was heated. Mrs. Bishop had not only disrespected his wishes by calling his mother "the deceased" yet again, but an "indigent corpse" as well. In his eyes, she was a monster and a true bitch. Wanting nothing more than to march down to that hospital and slap the fire out of her mouth, Lonnie knew he had other business to handle. He did just as she suggested and called the morgue. They informed him that he needed to get in touch with the funeral home of his choice and make some sort of arrangements for them to pick his mother up. They informed him the funeral home could better explain the out-of-pocket costs and what funds, if any, the state would pay. Lonnie did just that.

Upon finding out he was underage and had no available funds to his name, each funeral home sadly turned him away. He created a GoFundMe account on Facebook, but knew that was a long shot in raising money. He'd sold or pawned everything of value they owned to ensure his mother could get her medications so there was nothing left; no television, no PlayStation, or even an old-school VCR. Lonnie had no aunts, uncles, or cousins to turn to. Fighting back the tears, he knew he had to get himself together to go take his midterm exams. Lonnie knew his instructor would probably give him a date to take a makeup test considering, but he had to at least show up at school to explain what he was going through.

Dressed and on his way out the door, Lonnie was met with more declarations of love and respect for his mother as soon as he stepped foot off the elevator. He thought about asking them to help with the burial expenses, but knew most of them were on fixed incomes, living month to month. Concentrating on getting to school to take the test he needed to pass to remain at the top of his class, Lonnie was devastated and his demeanor showed just that. With his head now lowered and his shoulders dropped downward as well, he fought back more tears.

"Excuse me, Lonnie, but did you get the paperwork that was on your door?"

"What?" he paused seeing the caretaker's girlfriend emerge out of the shadow.

"I said, did you get the paperwork; the notice about the rent your mother owed?" She had a smirk on her face as if something was funny.

"Look, lady, I'm not in the mood or right state of mind for this now. You do know my mother died last night, right?"

"Yes, I figured that was going to happen when she left here looking the way she was."

"Hold up. Wait a minute! What in the entire fuck did you just say about my mother?" Lonnie's irate voice could easily be heard echoing throughout the building, and rightly so.

The money-hungry woman could see the teenager was pissed. She was certainly old enough to know she was wrong, yet seemed not to care as she continued to speak. "Hey, I wasn't trying to say nothing bad about your momma. I was just saying she looked real, real bad when they wheeled her out!" The more the woman spoke, the more residents came out of their apartments telling her to shut her crude ass up and keep her outrageous comments to herself.

"Look, I'm warning you, this ain't the time for you to act like you running things around here! Shit is fucked up for me right about now! My mother died last night, bitch! She died and ain't coming back, and your greedy ass taping shit to motherfucker's doors and lurking in the corners dry begging for money that don't even belong to you!"

The woman's intent was to shame Lonnie, but just like that, the tables had turned. Everyone knew what he was saying about her was right as they nodded their heads in total agreement.

"Okay, that's enough," the elderly caretaker finally found his voice and tried to intervene. "Go back to our apartment and leave this young man alone! Don't you realize he just lost his mother?"

"Yeah, you better tell her something before shit gets real up in this place. Me or my mother never caused any trouble around here." Lonnie looked around at the growing crowd of neighbors for affirmation he was telling the truth.

"And y'all never paid y'all rent around here either; at least on time or in full anyways," she hissed back, still trying to go for bad.

"And so what?" Lonnie was at the end of his rope. Female or not; older woman or not—she was itching to get the shit smacked out of her if she didn't fall back.

"Why is you hawking so bad for the white man that owns this raggedy bitch? We all know you fucking the old man here to have a roof over your fat, ugly ass, but is you sucking Mr. Charlie's white dick too?"

"Oh, hell naw," she screamed out as the old man pushed her back down the hallway. "One day soon I'm gonna fix your smart-talking ass! Watch, little boy; you'll see!"

Lonnie was done. Not bothering to say another single word, he just turned and left. *These bitches is out of control with their mouths. First, that damn Ms. Bishop; now, this lady. What the fuck!*

CHAPTER FIVE

The days that followed had to be labeled as bad as the precise moment his mother was pronounced dead. Lonnie's teachers had given him a week to return to school and take all exams that were missed. Like everyone else the teen came in contact with, their hearts broke for his plight, but none offered to donate any money to his cause. After calling back down to the hospital morgue, he found out, just as he was told would take place, his mother's body was turned over to the medical examiner's office. He felt devastated to just think of his mom being handled so disrespectfully, passed from place to place as if she was some old spoiled meat or a stray dog's body scraped off the street. Lonnie grew sick to his stomach every time he thought about it.

Someone advised him to turn to some churches, but since neither he nor his mother were members, the churches claimed they couldn't help. He called the Salvation Army and was told all of their funds were tapped out for the fiscal season . . . whatever that meant. Welfare would pay a small portion as Mrs. Bishop initially said, but only after the family paid the additional amount the funeral home required. Going to the guys on the block that sold drugs and being told he had to "be down" and they'd help him, Lonnie refused, knowing that lifestyle was not for him. The desperate youngster even went to the funeral home asking if he could do odd jobs to pay off the additional funds he needed. The funeral director was willing to maybe work something out, but his daughter, who ran the business aspect of the company, refused, blatantly stating that they were not running a charity.

Lonnie was coming close to losing his mind. He knew he was running out of time before he had to return to school and try to keep his grades up. He'd promised his mother days before she died that no matter what, he'd maintain his grades and be awarded one of the many scholarships he applied for. His father finally returned his call and told him he was sorry for his loss; nothing more, nothing less. He volunteered no financial assistance to bury his son's mother, which was to be expected. And not once did he offer for Lonnie to come and live with him, stating he was not stable and struggling himself. The GoFundMe account he'd set up had only raised twenty-five dollars; so that was that. He wanted to throw up. He felt as if he wasn't a man. He'd let his mother down and maybe he did need someone to "look after him," as Mrs. Bishop taunted that awful night at the hospital before he ran off. Maybe if he'd stayed, she could've helped him bury his mother properly. But at this point, things had gone all the way to the left with her. Lonnie knew there was no turning around trying to cross that bridge. It was burned completely down. Wanting to call his mother's social worker, the teen knew that wouldn't be a good idea if he wanted to keep the food stamp card activated as long as possible.

Lonnie finally gave up on his heartfelt mission for the time being. Consumed with remorse, he called the medical examiner, informing them he couldn't get the money together as soon as he thought; however, please know he'd be there to claim his mother's body before the month's end.

CHAPTER SIX

Lonnie returned to school. Trying to focus on his studies was next to impossible. Knowing his mother was being housed in some huge walk-in refrigerator with a lot of dead strangers that no one gave a damn about or had families and loved ones like him that didn't have the money to do the proper thing was destroying his concentration on the regular. But Lonnie remembered the promise he made to his mother and kept his eye on the prize.

Getting mocked and ridiculed for the clothes he was wearing and the hole in the sole of the sneakers on his feet, Lonnie ignored the other students' cruel, hurtful remarks. For the most part, they hadn't been forced to live the life he had or see the things he'd seen. They were trapped in a world of childhood playing checkers, while Lonnie had to play chess. One teacher in particular knew his best student was catching all-out hell and hooked him up with a part-time job at McDonald's. Getting that news was like Christmas, his birthday, and income tax time in the hood, all rolled into one.

As Lonnie walked home ecstatic about his blessing, he not once thought about buying a new video game with his first paycheck or even some new Jordans to stop the teasing. The devoted son wanted nothing more than to bury his mother. It had been a little short of three weeks since her death, and it was the only thing that constantly stayed on his mind. *Thank you, God, for giving me this job. A brother needed this in the worst type of way. I just wanna finish school and make this money. After I do what I gotta do for my mother, I can start paying some overdue bills and saving for other stuff, just in case I don't get one of them scholarships or grants. Damn, thank you, God!*

Lonnie was in his own world as he bent the corner of the block. Living in the celebration that he would soon be amongst the working class, the teen failed to notice the caretaker's girlfriend standing near the front entryway of the building. Strangely, she had not said much to him since their verbal confrontation the morning after his mother's death. When the two would see each other in passing, she'd just smirk and but not mutter a single solitary word. Well, today was eerily different. As he turned the knob of the huge steel front door of the building, she spoke.

"Well, hello, Mr. Lonnie. I hope you had a good day at school." Her smile was as big as the sun as she looked up from filing her dragon lady fire-engine-red painted fingernails.

Lonnie didn't know what to make of her out-of-the-blue pleasantries. Not wanting an argument with her to rob him of the joy he was feeling, he shrugged his shoulders, ignoring her greeting and statement. As he waited for the elevator, some of the other residents walked by, lowering their heads as if they didn't want to be seen. When the door slid open, Lonnie stepped inside and pushed the number four. As it closed shut, the elated youth thought he heard someone call out his name but wasn't certain. It was too late to see who it was because the elevator was headed upward, so he'd have to catch up with whoever it was on the way out. *Today is a good day. I swear I'm going to go to work every hour they let my name be on the schedule. I'm gonna make all that money!* Lonnie's mind was racing. In between all the tragic events he'd been going through lately, he knew finally he was on the verge of coming up. It was finally his season, as the old folks used to say.

Reaching the fourth floor, Lonnie stepped out into the dimly lit hallway. Staring down at the traffic-worn carpet as he walked, he smelled what was easily recognized as his next-door neighbor's hood-famous spicy seasoned fried chicken. Although he wanted to knock on her door and ask for a couple of pieces, Lonnie, stomach growling, wanted to get home as soon as possible. Lost in the struggle of ghetto-life poverty, he had one can of Spam in the cabinet and a ninety-nine-cent Honey Bun calling his name. But to him, it would taste like a porterhouse steak and baked potato with all the fixings.

After missing school for a week and some days, Lonnie was taking on all the extra credit assignments he could to try to stay at the top of his class as he swore to his mom he would. The grade-A student had more than the usual amount of homework to complete this evening and a conference call with his fellow classmate, also a scholar, so time was not to be wasted. In addition to studying into probably what would become the wee hours of the morning, the anxiously happy new employee of McDonald's had to also try to wash out two of the three halfway decent shirts he owned by hand in the bathroom sink. Although his teacher guaranteed the fast-food job was indeed his, the orphaned youth still had to go in, fill out paperwork, and discuss when he was to come in for training.

CHAPTER SEVEN

"Oh, hell naw! What in the entire fuck? Not now! Of all damn times, not fucking now!" Lonnie stood directly in front of his own door with his eyes bucked. Immediately he grew infuriated. His adrenaline was pumping as his heart raced. With clenched fist, the mild-manned young man was instantly catapulted into total overdrive as he snatched the court order of eviction paperwork down off the door. "This is some low-down rotten bullshit! They know shit been messed up for me! This right here is foul as fuck!" Lonnie's angry-toned voice rang throughout the entire floor of the low-income dwelling, resulting in neighbors peeking out of their doors. The few residents that had been home all day knew what Lonnie's verbal assault beef would consist of and what all the late-afternoon commotion was truly all about. They expected it to be a "y'all got me fucked the fucked up and straight twisted" scene worthy of being cell phone recorded when Lonnie returned from school. It wasn't the first time they'd seen the taped official documents the youngster was seeing; some dramatically experiencing it themselves.

"I'm so sorry, baby," the neighbor to the right that was frying the chicken commented before closing her door, not wanting to be directly involved in what this could transpire into.

Removing his heavy book bag off his back, Lonnie tossed it to the side of the door's paint-chipped frame.

He couldn't believe what he was seeing. The vein in his neck was starting to pulsate. Both temples pounded as he tried massaging them with his fingertips. *This shit right here is so crazy messed up. How they gonna play me after all this time we been living here, giving the white man our money? I can't believe this bullshit! Hell naw!* Not caught up in a fantasy world, Lonnie knew it had been quite some time since his mother had paid anything on the rent so the inevitable was already living on borrowed time. No dummy by far bookwise or when it came to the streets, he knew most folk, if not all, lived by the old adage . . . no pay, no stay. Yet, like so many other emotionally drained people or people who just don't give a damn, they think the rules don't apply to them.

Taking his key out his pocket, Lonnie tried sticking it into the lower cylinder. Even though it went in with ease, it failed to be able to turn to the left or the right. Feeling his fury grow, Lonnie's palms began to sweat as reality set in. Here he was just coming home from school in good spirits feeling like he'd just been personally blessed by an angel and here the fuck the devil shows his ho ass up with some bullshit; straight strong-arm robbing Lonnie of his small bit of joy.

Attempting to twist the knob several times, he used the weight of his body to try to force the door to open. That's when he heard a clunking sound overhead. Not once looking all the way upward, he'd failed to see that there was an industrial-size padlock attached to the door and frame, also stopping him from gaining entry into the place he'd just called home a few hours prior. This couldn't be life, but unfortunately for Lonnie, it was.

His.

Lonnie's having patience was completely over. He felt like he had reached his boiling point. Just like he was hit with dealing with the disappointment of losing his mother and being forced to deal with it, now he'd have to do the same with what this was. Not only was he on his own to navigate through the world, he was now homeless. Homeless with nowhere to go and seemingly no one that cared about his plight. Frustrated, he lifted his worn sneakers and started to repeatedly kick on the door. As he cursed, asking God how much more suffering he had to endure, he failed to hear the elevator open.

"Son, please, wait, will you?" the elderly caretaker urged walking toward an out of sorts Lonnie.

"Wait for what, huh? You tell me! Wait for what!" his emotions were at an all-time high as his voice grew louder.

"I tried to call you before you came up here, but you didn't hear me. I didn't want you to find out like this."

"Okay, you tried to call me. Okay, call me and say what? Say that you locked me out of my own apartment? Say that you don't give a fuck about what I been going through? Is that it? Or was you going to tell me that you changed the locks and is about to give me a new set?"

The caretaker didn't want any problems. Over the years of having to repeat this same lockout process, he always tried to avoid altercations, if at all possible. This time, he could tell things had all the ingredients to go to the left rapidly. He knew the young man was pissed; and rightly so. He'd seen him leave for school every morning for years and always tried his best to encourage him. When he'd have some extra fruit or maybe some spare change, he always made sure to give it to Lonnie. It was those things, along with the fact he was always smiling and being friendly to the boy's mother that had his girlfriend harbor bitter and vindictive feelings toward apartment 417 and both its occupants.

"Listen. I had absolutely no idea this was going to take place today, son; no idea at all."

"Yeah, all right, whatever."

Holding both his hands up, the elderly man pleaded his case to the visibly irate teenager. "Look, son, as long as you and your mother have been living here, I've always been nothing but kind to you and her."

"Yeah, okay, that's true. But how you not know I was gonna be locked out? Correct me if I'm wrong, but ain't you the one that changed the locks and put this damn padlock on the door so I couldn't get in?" Lonnie raised his foot once more, kicking on the door. As the heavy padlock rattled overhead, the wooden frame shook, causing some paint chips to fall from the wall.

"To be honest with you, I was outside picking up garbage on the far side of the building when the owner unexpectedly showed up about ten thirty this morning."

"The owner; the white man that never ever comes around here but once a year maybe just showed up out of the clear blue sky to fuck with me? Come on now. That don't even sound right or make no kind of sense at all."

The caretaker was now standing at the locked door alongside of Lonnie. Looking him dead in his eye, he spoke as directly as possible. "Looka here, Lonnie. I don't have no good reason to lie to you. I mean, what's it gonna gain me one way or another? Now, like I said, I was outside when he pulled right on up out there." He rubbed down on his gray wiry-haired beard. "Shocked the shit outta me too. He don't usually come around here to see what's going on like you said but once a year!"

"Oh, just like that? Really? Are you kidding me or what?" Lonnie's facial expression was full of sheer resentment as he gave the man the serious side eye.

"Yeah, I'm telling you, boy; out of nowhere. No damn warning! He had some Mexican guys trailing behind him in a pickup, and they all parked up front. He showed me a list with three different apartments he wanted me to lock out as soon as I could. I went to my place to get my master keys, and by the time I got back, him and them damn Mexicans had already been up here at your door knocking and snooping around."

Lonnie was heated just listening to the story, "Yo, this is messed up. But whatever; just open the door so I can get my stuff."

"That's the thing, son. He told me to get the other three apartments situated, and he'd handle yours personally. I told him the circumstances about your mother, but you know the white man and his money."

Lonnie was done listening. Just as he was thinking things were looking up, the bottom had just fallen out of his young life once more. Distraught, he just wanted to get as much of his belongings as he could get out of the apartment even though he had nowhere to take anything at the time. He'd figure that much out later. For now, he just wanted to take his stuff and go. "Okay, I'm good on all of the damn blow-by-blow commentary that jumped off while I was at school. I get it. That asshole popped up, singled me out, and now, I'm homeless. I get it! So open the door and let me get my shit and I'm out!"

The caretaker knew what he was going to say next would only cause bigger flames to flare up in an already fiery situation. However, he had no choice but to be the bearer of more bad news. "Lonnie, I'm sorry, son. But the owner had the two guys with him clean out the apartment."

"Say what! What the hell you mean clean out the apartment? Where is my stuff at? I swear to God my stuff better be inside this bitch!" Lonnie started kicking on the door over and over again. The more he kicked and cursed, the more nosey people brazenly stepped out of their own apartments and into the hallway to see what the outcome of the earlier events that jumped off in apartment 417 would be.

"Slow down, son, before you tear something up, I'll let you in." The caretaker eased his hand around his thick leather belt. Unhooking the huge set of master keys, he held them up to his face. Looking over his glasses, the elderly man easily found the one gold and one silver key that looked newer than the rest. Going against the lockout policy, he proceeded to remove the padlock and open the deadbolts. As Lonnie brushed by him entering the apartment, he knew the boy was going to return to the hallway angrier and more disappointed than when he went inside.

Lonnie darted from room to room, sadly finding nothing but emptiness. The once happy place he'd grown up in was nothing now but a hollow shell to him; no home sweet home. *Why you letting this happen to me, God? Why?* No comfortable couch, no chair with the Kool-Aid stain on the left arm, and no six-bulb hanging imitation brass lamp that barely worked. None of his academic trophies were displayed near the window, and Lonnie failed to see the pictures of him and his mother that were framed and on the coffee table. *I swear this is messed up. I swear it is!* Rushing into his room, his twin bed was not there. All his posters he'd collected throughout the years were gone off the wall, leaving nothing but the clean paint surface outline where they were taped. *Not my damn posters too. Damn!* The secondhand desk his mother got him two years prior was not sitting in the corner. And the few decent clothing items he owned were not in sight; just several hangers dangling on the pole in an empty closet.

As Lonnie temporary paused to get his mind right, he exhaled, not believing what had taken place since he'd gone to school and come back. *I don't know why*

God is testing me so much. First, Mommy, now this!
Damn! Shocked, on to the bathroom he ran. The ugly
maroon-colored shower curtain was missing, as well
as his favorite towel and his blue-handled toothbrush.
A toothbrush? Who in the hell so petty they fuck with
toothbrushes and washcloths? This is so messed up! The
agitated youth next discovered the kitchen was just as
bare as the rest of the apartment; vacant in contents. The
refrigerator door was standing wide open, and although
it was indeed empty when he'd left for school this morning, at least, it was plugged in and standing at attention
hoping to be filled.

As he briefly stood in the kitchen, Lonnie couldn't help
but notice that his much-anticipated dinner can of Spam
was gone off the counter, along with the ninety-nine-cent
Honey Bun that would've served as dessert. *Ain't this*
about some shit! That white motherfucker and ho-ass
Mexicans ain't miss a beat. I swear I wish I was here
when they disrespectful asses showed up! Folks always
kicking somebody when they down!

Not wanting to face the facts, Lonnie begrudgingly
made his way to the last but most important room to
him in the entire once-love-filled apartment; his mother's. With his hands firmly clenched on both sides of
the entryway, he stood motionless. He was hurt. There
was no other way to describe the utter pain he was feeling. Since the age of seven, for years on end, he'd run
through the threshold of this room and jumped in his
mother's bed. If he was getting a whopping, he ran in
here to hide. If he had fallen outside or got a splinter
from sliding around the old wooden floor no matter
how many times he was told not to, he'd retreat in here
for Mom to soothe his wounds and make the wrongs
of the world right. As the years went by and Lonnie's
mother grew sicker, the more quality time the two of

them would spend in her bedroom talking about this and that. Lonnie was not just her only child; he was her protector, medical helper, and overall link to the outside world.

Now, tragically, not only was his mother gone from his physical life, the last real attachment he had to her was now no more as well. As strong as he tried to be, he could no longer fight back the tears. The room smelled like his mother's favorite scented candles, but as he scanned the empty four walls area, he knew this was no longer home; no longer a place he felt secure. All his mother's personal belongings were missing, just as he discovered his were. The trio had gone through her dresser drawers; no doubt examined her mail and other important papers. The monsters callously seized his mother's knickknacks and whatnots valuable to only her for sentimental reasons. The bastards gathered all her clothes and removed the small bedside table she kept her medications and nightly glass of ice water on. His mother's blanket he'd been wrapping up in since her death was also gone. It had her scent embedded, and Lonnie felt extremely close to her whenever he touched it.

Tormented deep in his soul, he wanted to run to the other side of the room and jump out the window. Lonnie felt he had reached rock bottom. The building owner and his two henchmen had made sure of that. They had done the work of the devil as far as the defeated teenager was concerned. Without so much as stepping foot inside his mother's bedroom, Lonnie wiped his face with his hands. For the final time in his life, he turned around from what was once his mother's room and headed back through the living room and out the door into the hallway.

"I'm sorry, son. There was nothing I could do to stop them. The owner had a court-ordered eviction."

Lonnie was drained. Shaking his head, then shrugging his shoulders, he had no more desire for confrontations or bullshit as he reached down retrieving his book bag off the floor. "Listen, can you just tell me where they put all our stuff at?"

After telling the young man he'd watch grow up from a small boy what he wanted to know, they both got on the elevator together. The ride down was silent. Neither said a word as the man handed Lonnie some cash he had in his pocket. It was just short of a $184, but to Lonnie, it was everything considering he was flat broke. As they stepped off on the main floor and walked down the hall, the pair was met by the caretaker's always-up-to-no-good girlfriend. Acting as if she was the sun, the moon, and the stars, she started in on the old man.

"Where in the hell you been? I called your damn phone twice. Why you ain't pick up?"

"Don't start with me. I was busy," he barked back, obviously tired of her attitude and mouth.

She devilishly smiled, then snickered at Lonnie as if he was nothing. "Doing what? I know not busy wasting time with *him*. He don't even live here anymore, or did you forget already?"

Lonnie tried his best to ignore the woman he'd had the run-in with a few weeks back and her snide remarks about his misfortune and current situation.

"Go on somewhere now. I done told you a million times to stay outta folk business," the elderly man waved his hand, dismissing her as he and Lonnie kept walking toward the front door. "I'm tired of your mouth and all that constant meddling."

"You funny to me, old man; real funny. If it wasn't for my meddling, no one would make any money around here, and this building would go straight to hell. At least, that's what the owner said when I called him." Her statement stopped Lonnie and the caretaker dead in their tracks. Once she saw she had both their attention, she went all the way in. "Yeah, he said he was going to think about putting me on the payroll since I seem to knowing the comings and goings of this building!" Adding insult to injury, she reached her hand into her cheap handbag. As she pulled it out, she revealed a Honey Bun.

Before the malicious lady had a chance to open the sweet treat, let alone say another word, she was met with Lonnie's fist coming crashing down across the side of her face. The last thing the broken-spirited teenager heard before leaving from his childhood home was the sound of the ruthless biddy crying out for help and the caretaker demanding she get her bullshit and leave before he knocked the shit out of her as well.

CHAPTER EIGHT

Walking around to the rear of the apartment building, Lonnie went into the alley. Lifting the lids one by one of the eight huge metal garbage containers that smelled like dead fish and sewer, he finally found the one the caretaker suggested he should look at. With the top all the way back, Lonnie saw a few garbage bags that contained items he easily recognized as his and his mother's. Luckily, there were several other trash cans that the residents could use and the bags were not yet covered with others' castaways. Snatching out a few of the overstuffed bags, Lonnie tossed them on the side of the Dumpster. Satisfied with the few items the men hadn't probably taken home to their wives or girlfriends, he placed them into one of his old duffle bags that were also discarded in the assortment of debris.

After finding a piece of broken glass in the alley, Lonnie pulled his mother's beloved blanket out and started to cry. Wanting to wrap up in it one last time, he was stopped by the fact one of the residents had dumped what seemed like some old cooking grease on one portion of it. Using the sharpest edge of the glass, Lonnie cut a nice-size area of the wool cloth and stuffed it in the duffle bag already containing the other garbage-can-retrieved items. Ripping a small corner off of that, he then placed that material memory inside his book bag.

Lonnie left the alley feeling nothing but hopelessness. With nowhere in particular to go and no plans, the young man who was forced to grow all the way up overnight started to walk and walk and walk. With a little less than $200 to his name and a small bag containing everything he now owned in the world, his destination was unknown. Lonnie's initial thought was to run down to the funeral home and give them at least something on the amount they wanted; yet, he knew trying to survive in the streets was going to be hard.

After hours of wandering the city in an emotionally charged daze, Lonnie went into Coney Island. He needed to rest not only his body, but his mind as well. Having not bothered to eat since this morning, he was maintaining on fumes. Ordering a cheeseburger deluxe and a Pepsi, he sat down in the booth furthest from the door. Knowing he had absolutely nowhere to go for the night, he took his time eating. Running out of options of what to do next, Lonnie wanted to call his deadbeat sperm donor back and give him a rundown of what happened. He knew the man never really cared about him or was in his life at any time that was deemed important, yet the son prayed that maybe, just maybe, this one time he would show him some mercy or compassion. After a few rings, he finally answered.

"Yeah, Lonnie, what's going on? What's the deal?" he seemed agitated right off the rip.

"Yeah, hey. I know I just spoke to you right after Mom died and . . ."

"Yeah, how did that thing work out for you? Did you get your momma buried?" he unsympathetically asked his teenage son, like he was speaking about a dead bird that had fallen out of a tree, not the mother of his child.

Taking a deep breath, it took everything Lonnie had not to curse his father smooth out for being so black hearted.

Instead, he closed his fist as tightly as he possible could and asked God to please give him strength. After a few brief seconds of being silent and opening his book bag to touch the small remnant of his mother's blanket, he finally replied. "No, not yet. Like I told you, the funeral home needs a certain amount of money, and then the state will kick in their portion."

"Oh, wow; damn," Lonnie's dad responded in between choking off what he told his son was some good-ass Kush. "That's real fucked up. Your momma was a good girl; even back in the day. Yup; sorry for her luck."

Lonnie knew that was about as good as it was gonna get in the way of his dad showing any sort of sympathy. With that much being said, the youngster felt this was the opportune time to not only update him with his present living predicament but also cut into him once more about housing with him. "Yeah, me too, but listen, Dad. Earlier today, they threw me and momma stuff in the garbage and—"

"You mean you got evicted from the damn apartment?" He choked a few more times before waiting for Lonnie's response.

"Yes, Dad. And now I don't have anywhere to go. I'm out here in the streets bold; homeless," he wanted to cry as he noticed how many minutes he'd used on his government-issued cell.

The older of the two knew exactly where this conversation was going and cut right to the chase. "Listen, Lonnie, like I told you the other week, your pops doing bad right about now. So if you called me looking for me to put a roof over your head, I can't do it. I'm out here bold my damn self. I'm chilling with this female at her house."

"Yeah, but, Dad, at least you not homeless like me," Lonnie pleaded his case as the cashier started to give him the evil eye as to why he was still camped out in the restaurant.

"Yeah, little nigga, I'm not shit like you. And I'm damn sure not trying to be. Now, you and your momma used to think y'all was all that and the hell with me; cool. Now she dead and gone you can keep the tradition going."

"It's like that, Dad, seriously?"

"I guess so."

Lonnie hung up, knowing that was the last time he'd ever speak to his father again in life. If it was fuck him, then the feeling would be more than mutual.

Just as the anguished adolescent was about to order another large cup of soda, this time no ice so it would last longer and he'd be able to stay put without judgment, his cell phone rang. Praying it was his father having a sudden change of heart, Lonnie swiftly answered. "Hello."

"Hey, Lonnie, this is Karisma; from school Karisma. I told you I was going to call this evening so we could discuss the project."

"Oh, hey. What's going on?" Lonnie's voice was weak, which his classmate immediately picked up on.

"Dang, Lonnie, what's wrong with you? Are you okay? You sound like something is strange with you."

Karisma was not only Lonnie's classmate, she and he were going head-up, neck and neck for who would be the class valedictorian. A friendly rivalry at best, the two would sometimes study together or bounce ideas off each other. He used to comfort her when her foster mother was being mean or the other kids at school would judge and bully her for not only being homosexual, but for being different, period. That was the extent of their always-during-school-hours relationship. However, like most of the students at their school, she too knew Lonnie's moms had just died of cancer. The once-blessed Lonnie had his mother's love and a roof over his head;

now that was gone, she felt for him having to go it alone out in the world. Karisma wanted to be there for Lonnie the best she could but didn't know what to say. The young truly orphaned girl didn't have much of anything to really offer. Truth be told, the homeless Lonnie had more cash to his name than she did. But whatever she had, Karisma made sure Lonnie knew he was good for it.

Karisma not only offered to give him some words of wisdom seeing how she'd been without parents for years. Her foster mother was all right for the most part when it came down to basic needs; however, anything else of any type of real affection was out of the question. Lonnie had rejected Mrs. Bishop's idea because of the way Karisma was being treated by the system.

Hearing her classmate's plight, Karisma took it upon herself to come up with a plan. Giving him her address, she told him to come around to the side door of the house she lived in and she would sneak him in the basement to spend the night. She had been having special visitors for the last six months or so creep and never once got caught. The huge difference was Lonnie was a male and most of Karisma's other company was females. Without hesitation, he eagerly told her he was on the way.

CHAPTER NINE

It was well past midnight and Lonnie had cried on Karisma's shoulder just about from the moment he'd arrived. Maybe it was because she liked girls and dressed like a dude that made her seem to understand his dilemma and not judge like most of the other females he'd encountered over the past month or so. The white administrator who denied his mother a bed in the hospital when she needed it the most; Mrs. Bishop who tried to throw him in foster care and vindictively wouldn't give him some basic information; the money hungry heffa at the funeral home that refused to let her father work for free; that side eye giving thot cashier mad because he was sitting in the booth too long; and, of course, that old casket-ready, makeup-wearing skank that caused him to be homeless. All five of them were nothing more than some dick-thirsty whores that seemed like their lives' ambition was to make men miserable.

Thankfully, Karisma was different. She was willing to help a brother when he was down and out. Like his teacher and the caretaker and funeral director, they all got it. As for his father, Lonnie had counted him out as a man and knew he was nothing more than an honorary female.

Stretched out on an old pullout couch near the furnace room, Lonnie slept like a baby. It seemed like this was the first good night's rest he'd gotten since his mother's death. It was as if he was free from whatever hold, good or bad, that apartment he once called home had on him. Blessed with a small portion of Karisma's breakfast and dinner for three days straight, Lonnie was in halfway good spirits. Having had the opportunity to make it to his interview at McDonald's, he was ecstatic to be starting work by week's end.

Getting out of school an hour or so later than Karisma, Lonnie called his friend's cell phone twice and received no answer. After waiting a short while and she still hadn't returned his call, he sent her a text. Lonnie knew, like most kids their age, they kept their cell phones basically glued to their hands. Ready to meet Karisma back at the house, Lonnie texted her again. This time leaving several question marks asking what time, he waited while checking his book bag for his homework assignments. After a few seconds, his chime notification went off. Much to his relief, then disappointment, he got an immediate reply.

This is no longer Karisma's cell. Please don't text/ call this number again.

"What the heck?" Lonnie mumbled out loud after reading the message two or three times. Of course, the teen immediately hit her number back asking just who was texting. And most importantly, where in the hell was his friend Karisma.

"This is her foster mother."

Lonnie was thrown off. He didn't know what to say or what to think. Clearing his throat, he finally spoke. "Hello. I was looking for Karisma."

"Oh, really?" she sarcastically replied with attitude.

Lonnie could easily sense the tension in the woman's voice but remained as respectful as possible. "I'm sorry. I don't mean to bother you, but—"

"But what?" she barked, not letting up.

"I'm just trying to get in touch with Karisma, that's all."

"That's all?" she questioned, raising her voice as if he'd stolen something.

Lonnie was confused. All he wanted to do was speak to his friend and find out what the 411 was. "Miss, I don't mean to go against what you texted me, but I really need to talk to her."

"About what?" she fumed obviously pissed off. "About you and her taking over my house; breaking my rules, and doing what you both damn well please? Is *that* what you two low-life-scheming throwaways need to plot on?"

At that point in the one-sided heated conversation, Lonnie knew his friend's foster mother had somehow found out their secret. As if matters could get any worse for the troubled situation teen, now he and Karisma were straight busted for what they'd been up to. Although Lonnie felt bad for her having to suffer directly from the fallout of their basement living deception, he quickly realized he was the one that was gonna catch the short end of the stick. Karisma was in the system, so the worse that was going to happen to her was she's probably get sent to another foster home. Lonnie, well, he was back where he started from a few days ago; homeless. "Look, I don't know what you're talking about. I just wanted to speak to your foster daughter." He tried to keep his fronts up, in hopes he might be wrong about what the woman was insinuating, but deep down inside, he knew the gig was up.

"Okay, you wanna be a smart-ass, I see, huh? So, okay, I'll play your little game. Is your name Lonnie Eugene McKay? Is it?"

"Huh?" He was thrown off. She'd said his entire government name.

"You heard what in the heck I said, boy! Is that your name?" she demanded to know with authority.

"Well . . ."

"Well, what?"

Lonnie had no other recourse but to answer truthfully, so reluctantly, he did just that. "Yes, that is my name."

"Of course, it is. And do you want to know just how I know that?"

"Well, umm . . ." he puzzled out loud.

"Because I have a duffle bag with some of your stuff in it; a damn bag that you and that sneaky Karisma had hid behind the old couch in the basement."

"Miss, I can explain. It's definitely not what you think. If you can just listen and hear me out."

"Naw. It's no need to hear any of your sure-to-be lies. You see, one of that Karisma's little supposed girlfriends she was apparently having sex with in my house felt the need to knock on my front door and ruin my day. All of you are going right to hell. God's Word doesn't condone none of that sinful crap those girls were doing! And right under my roof, no less!"

Lonnie's eyes grew as he listened to her reveal how she'd found out. He was shocked but knew what he had to do and say. "I'm sorry about all of that. I truly am. But I swear to you I never touched Karisma in that type of way. I promise; we are just good friends, that's all. I didn't have anywhere to go so she—"

"So she took it upon herself to let you come here; to *my* home where she herself was a temporary visitor?"

"Well . . ."

"Well, I guess I should be glad you two devils at least didn't fornicate in my house like she did with those other confused-minded she devils."

Lonnie listened to her go on and on about this, that, and the third for at least five minutes or so. She not once mentioned where Karisma was at and he not once found the courage to ask. The only part of her angry rant he focused in on was that she was throwing his bag of possessions, along with Karisma's personal property, into the Dumpster in the rear of her home where all the "sinful devil-worshiping garbage" belonged.

Saddened that he'd have to find somewhere else to lay his head at that night, he was even more distraught that Karisma's foster mother saw fit to make the judgment to toss his beloved belongings back into the trash as the apartment owner's workers had callously done only days before. She was just like every other ho in the world as far as he was concerned. With each step he took on the way to what was apparently his friend's ex-home, Lonnie had tears streaming down his face. The teen was down to his last money since treating himself and Karisma to fast-food lunch and dinner for the past few days, thinking he had a secure roof over his head. Now that was over. Lonnie couldn't win for losing. Once again out of options, he had to man up, and quick.

CHAPTER TEN

Thank God Lonnie made it. Checking the time every few seconds, he panted out of breath. He was minutes from being turned away for the night. However, as luck would have it, the director of the homeless shelter had forgotten some cases of can goods in his trunk and enlisted the youth, a sometimes regular visitor, to assist him. Since getting evicted from the apartment he'd called home, Lonnie slept where he could, when he could. Initially, in Karisma's basement; sometimes, in abandoned houses; and sometimes, here, when he was fortunate enough to meet the deadline.

In between working a part-time gig at McDonald's for a month and monkey hustling, he'd made enough money begging at gas stations, throwing handbills, and cutting grass to finally lay his poor mother to rest. However, that meant neglecting the other necessities he required. Fighting to stay in school and graduate on time, the library was where Lonnie spent most his free time studying when he wasn't performing petty hustles for small amounts of cash. Sometimes he'd post up in the broom closet and focus on his books.

After eating two stale ham and cheese sandwiches, an apple, and drinking a small carton of milk that was provided from the nonprofit facility, Lonnie's stomach was happy off scraps. Worn out, he'd just settled into the small foldaway cot when the unspeakable, but sadly common, occurrence jumped off. "Hey, get your damn hands off me, fool! I'm not down with all that funny shit you and the rest of these busters around here be on. I'm a man! A *real* man! So raise the hell up before it be a true misunderstanding before daybreak." The echo of certain resentment bounced off the paint-chipped walls and filled the ears of everyone around.

"Okay, chill out, young blood. It's all good my way. Don't be all up in your feelings. I was just trying to make sure you was warm; see if you needed a little company or something like that!"

"Warm? Company?" Lonnie's voice grew louder, drawing more attention to the dark area of the huge room they were in. Fist balled, he leaped to his feet. His inner rage could be felt as the tension grew. With his worn-out blue jeans slightly sagging and once winter-white T-shirt torn on the sleeve, it was evident the young annoyed warrior was ready to put in work if need be. "Dawg, I'm warning you. You better get the fuck on with all that dumb shit. Ain't nothing soft or sweet this way."

"Oh, yeah, is that right?" The man placed his hand on his chest and smirked. Defiantly winking at his intended victim only seemed to make matters worse.

"Okay, old nigga, I swear to God you don't want them type of problems with me. I might be a little messed up right now, guy, but I ain't that damn desperate to be dealing with you or yours!"

"Look around you, boy. You in the same place we in, so stop tripping. It ain't no big thang," the elder of the two put both hands in the air, letting the teenager know he didn't want any problems.

"Well, make sure it ain't! For real, for real; you and the rest of these bums got me messed up. I don't wanna catch a case tonight, but I will. Whatever ill intentions you got in mind, you better reconsider that bullshit!" Lonnie had blood in his weary eyes. He was beyond fed up. This

couldn't be life. Not the one he'd dreamed of since he was
a kid. The barely seventeen-year-old had been through
enough chaos over the past few months to fill three life-
times. Now, here he was, forced to sleep on a thin, filthy
mattress. One that smelled of garbage and musk, being
sexual harassed by a man twice his age and size. Clear
out of any options on where he could rest his head at for
the night, Lonnie was at the last place he ever wanted to
end up at: Emergency Relief Services, also known as the
men's homeless shelter.

"Like I said," the man, although scared of getting
socked in the mouth, continued to speak out of turn. "It
ain't no big thang with me, young blood. But never say
what you won't do out here in these coldhearted Detroit
streets. When you homeless, trust me, life gets real!"

Refusing to give the troublemaker any more energy,
the youth bit his tongue. Ensuring the medium-size duffle bag containing all he owned in the world was within
arm's reach, he felt somewhat reassured. Not wanting to
get kicked out of the strict policy-run facility into the ele-
ments of night, he fought to calm his nerves. Like a hawk
focused on his prey, Lonnie watched the toothless creep
roam over toward the far side of the building in hopes of
pushing up on someone else. Letting the man's corrupt
words of wisdom fester inside his already-tormented
mind, the miserable teen tried to block them out.

Lonnie Eugene McKay was ready to collapse. Exhausted
physically as well as mentally, the man-child wanted
nothing more than to forget what the seasoned shelter
predator had said and go to sleep. However, deep down
inside, he knew the asshole was right. *When you homeless,
life gets real.* Unfortunately, Lonnie, totally alone in the
world thanks to his mother's death and no assistance from
his father, was tragically learning that lesson firsthand. He
had become one of Detroit's faceless throwaway residents,

and his crazy life was as real as shit gets. As Lonnie drifted off to sleep, he started to have the same reoccurring dream; that his beloved mother was still very much alive. Tossing and turning, some of his restless nights were just as long as his tedious days.

CHAPTER ELEVEN

"Yes, Mister Lonnie Eugene McKay, will you please stand?" The judge held a huge stack of papers tightly with one hand and a ballpoint pen with the other. As she waited, the other occupants in the crowded courtroom grew eerily quiet. Receiving no immediate answer, she once again asked the seemingly preoccupied defendant to show some respect and stand. "Hello, Mister McKay. Excuse this court for trying to conduct its business, but can you follow proper procedure and rise for the reading of the verdict?"

Staring off into space, Lonnie had to be physically shaken by his lawyer to come out of the trance he was obviously in. Snapped back into reality, the arrested criminal was seconds away from hearing the outcome of his life from twelve of his peers charged with determining his future. Trying not to be defiant, he stopped reminiscing about his past and did as he was asked. Seeing that the defendant had obliged, the judge proceeded to read from one of the many documents she had in her hand.

"All right, Mister McKay. Back in March of this year, you were arrested after a series of investigations by not only the city of Detroit police detectives, but state and federal officials as well. Those allegations were, and still stand, as five counts of first-degree murder. Those five criminal counts were unaugmented and unchallenged, thus, being consolidated into one trial." The judge never wavered from her even-toned voice as she spoke directly to the defendant labeled an utter menace in the media. Despite the annoying glare of one of the court TV small-size cameras recording live, she remained cool as a cucumber.

"When you were originally apprehended and arrested, you were read your rights. Upon your arraignment, your attorney advised this court, without objection from you, that it was your desire to enter a plea of not guilty by reason of insanity. That plea was accepted by this court pending medical examinations. Those examinations took place, and after consideration of the results, your original plea was thus rejected as you were deemed competent to stand trial. Within your rights, you asked for a jury trial, and it was so ordered. You were advised by your counsel as well as this court that each one of the five felony murder charges you are facing are punishable by life imprisonment with no possibility of parole if found guilty. If convicted today, you will immediately be returned to the county jail where you have been held at for the duration of these legal proceedings, and then remanded to the State of Michigan Correctional Department and be under their jurisdiction throughout the extent of your sentence. Are those facts clear to you, Mister McKay?"

Once again, getting no type of response from the dangerous offender awaiting his fate, she posed the question to him in another manner. "Mister Lonnie Eugene McKay, have you heard what was just stated to you? Are you comprehending what this court is relaying to you, or are you deliberately choosing to be defiant? Be advised, either way, these proceedings will continue in a timely fashion. I hope you understand that much to be true."

As the occupants of the courtroom and all of the tele-vised viewing audience waited for the would-be serial killer to blink, cough, sneeze, smile, or at best, slightly nod his head to acknowledge the judge, he did none. In the midst of what Lonnie felt was the mumblings of yet another "callous bitch with a slit attempting to fuck him over," he zoned back out of his current reality thinking about the unconventional life he'd been forced to live.

Sadly it had been the roughest year of his young life. Struggling to keep food in his stomach, wash the clothes he copped from the donated box, and just simply stay alive was more than a notion in the city of Detroit. Times were hard in the Motor City, but the people living in it were even harder. The mental abuse Lonnie withstood was more than any man, woman, or child should have to face—alone or otherwise—but somehow, he managed. Not only had he been mocked, teased, dogged, and slandered at school, Lonnie was ignored, slighted, and made to feel second best at most of the shelters he'd slept at.

Yet now, he felt the tide was about to turn. Things were looking up. He finally could see the sun rising from the darkness. There would be no more of some of the gatekeepers at the various facilities making the rules up as they go along. No more would Lonnie have to wake up early in the morning to ensure eating a free breakfast or rushing to make it back before curfew. The woman living in the shelter across the road wouldn't be able to stand in front of the building and tease him about being less than a man because he was in the same predicament as they were. Much like all the other women he'd been unfortunate enough to come in contact with since his mother's death, they were evil, spiteful, out for self bitches as well. The fact they, like him, didn't have a pot to piss in or a window to throw it out made no difference. However, there was about to be a serious changing of the guard. The tide was about to turn. The silver lining every-one spoke about was finally coming into view. Lonnie had beaten all the terrible odds stacked against him. The still grief-stricken teen was a wonderful miracle in progress. He was finally graduating from high school. Homeless, parentless, and penniless . . . He'd made it.

Not attending the prom or participating in any of the other senior activities, the long-suffering teenager could care less. The only thing the social recluse young man focused on was getting that diploma and starting the next phase of his life. If he could excel in the scholarship-sponsored advanced computer design program, Lonnie was guaranteed paid housing and a small cash stipend once a month. That would be all the youth from the wrong side of the tracks needed to be on his way to some sort of normalcy.

CHAPTER TWELVE

Settling in to his very own tiny studio apartment, Lonnie was relieved. Nestled in the middle of the university's diverse student population, he felt like a fish out of water, but strangely linked to his neighbors. This was the first place Lonnie could actually call or even consider home since his mother's death. Still carrying around the same duffle bag full of his meager possessions, he felt secure in finally unpacking them. Blessed with a full-size bed, a desk, and a small-size couch from the scholarship board, Lonnie took the time to thank God for keeping him safe and sound throughout his time lost out in the streets. No matter how much mayhem and chaos he went through, the now-eighteen-year-old young man knew it could've been way over a hundred times worse.

Sitting down on the arm of the couch, the poor but content teen removed a new benefit card issued from the Department of Social Services out of a manila-colored envelope. Dialing the telephone number located on the rear of the card, the near destitute Lonnie smiled upon hearing it had not only close to $400 in food stamps loaded, but $100 in cash as well. That, along with the school program's initial payout of $356, Lonnie felt as if he'd hit the lottery. Knowing he'd have to continue to study hard and hit the books if he wanted his blessings to stay flowing, he started to plan out the next year of his life, week by week. By evening's end, he'd walked to the closest grocery market and the Dollar Store to get provisions for the days to follow. Elated at how far he'd come on his own, Lonnie walked over to the window and gazed up at the many bright shining stars. With great hope for his future, he tightly closed his eyes, praying for his mother to give him strength.

The nightmares the teen had went on almost nightly. His mind was unsettled, and he was starting to have severe headaches that wouldn't go away. Consuming every brand of aspirin on the market, nothing seemed to help. Still tormented by his mother's death, Lonnie was content being off on his own. He missed her more than anyone could ever know and was having a hard time adjusting to her not being around. Feeling like he'd been basically shitted on by everyone that'd come into his life since that day she left the earth, especially females, he trusted himself and only himself. When he was in class and it came time to form study groups, Lonnie tried his best to complete most projects on his own in order not to form any sort of relationships. He needed to be alone to concentrate and not be distracted by others' seemingly wonderful lives. When doing something as simple as getting his mail out of the box, the youthful teen that should be out having a good time was doing the opposite, avoiding all contact with his peers. The carefree college experience didn't apply to him. Even though he was starting to be rumored as being weird, strange, and standoffish, Lonnie was still invited to party after party. Although he declined, the offers still came in.

"Hey, guy, you live in apartment 7C, don't you?"

Lonnie had just stepped on the elevator. With his book bag tossed over his shoulder and a tuna fish sandwich from Subway in one hand, he pushed his floor number. Assuming the white guy couldn't be asking him, he ignored the question. After the dude repeated himself, Lonnie realized he was indeed speaking to him. "Yeah, I do. Who's asking?"

"Whoa, man, slow down. I don't want any trouble." He immediately sensed his standoffish neighbor was becoming defensive. "I live down the hall from you in seven-H; the unit on the corner by the stairs."

Lonnie thought he'd seen the guy and some of his friends come and go at different times, but wasn't sure. Not wanting to be any ruder than he'd already been, he eased up on attitude. "Oh, yeah. Sorry, guy. I ain't mean to come off so rough. It's just the neighborhood and—"

The white man smiled, understanding exactly where Lonnie was coming from. "Come on now," he teased while holding onto a six-pack of beer. "Try being half as white as I am in this neighborhood, and then talk shit!"

They both shared a brief laugh as the elevator doors opened on their floor. Lonnie was content on being on his way to study and eat his sandwich. However, the guy who had introduced himself as Kevin when they passed the third floor wasn't quite done.

"All right, then. Stay up," Lonnie tried to brush him off.

Trying his best to be as cool as he automatically assumed Lonnie was, Kevin closed his fist to give his black neighbor a pound. "Hey, just FYI, we're having a little get-together later this evening."

"Oh, yeah?" Lonnie was disinterested but felt he had to at least act like he was halfway paying attention.

"Yeah, dawg. Nothing special, just some of the homies getting together to throw back a few and watch the game. You know, smoke a little weed; a few pills or whatnot. Maybe get a few bitches drunk and high and mess around."

Lonnie couldn't believe the nerve of this fool. He was really talking about smoking trees, running hoes, and taking pills to him, not knowing if he was the police. *Damn, white motherfuckers these days don't give a shit no more; they reckless as hell.* "Trees, females, and pills, huh?"

Kevin was proud of what illegal activities his night was going to hold and continued to boast. "Yeah, buddy. You know how it is. We been hitting the books all week for finals and need a little something to take the edge off."

"Yeah, finals is a motherfucker," Lonnie acknowledged gripping up on his book bag. "I got two more this week my damn self."

Kevin nodded in total agreement. "Well, I see this you," he motioned toward Lonnie's apartment with a huge letter C on it. "So I'll let you get to your food and them books. But if you feel like taking a break, my friend, you know where to find us. And in the meantime, here, take this to get you started." Kevin reached down, grabbing Lonnie a beer out his pack and laughed, turning beet red. "Remember, weed, pills, beer, and hoes! It's the all-American dream; well, the white dream anyways!"

The evening seemed to drag on. And the night was doubly worse than that. It was like the more Lonnie tried to concentrate on his studies, the more commotion he heard in the hallway of people coming and going down the way. He could easily tell they were some of Kevin's friends by the way they came passing his door sober, then would leave an hour or so later fighting to stand up and talking loud cash shit all the way to the elevator. Part of him wanted to try to stop being so antisocial and go check Kevin out; at least for another cold beer or two since his was warm. While the other part of him knew trying to link up with some wild-style white boys that liked to get high was nothing but trouble waiting to jump off.

Searching through the Pandora app on his cell, Lonnie tried to focus on some music and get back to the books. With the tunes on random play, he was suddenly frozen. Feeling a chill come over him and a harsh dryness in his mouth, the teen closed his eyes. Allowing the sounds of one of Al Green's songs take over his soul, Lonnie was lost thinking about his deceased mother. This was one of her favorite songs in the world; or so she used to claim. His first thought was to turn it off, but his inner self kept saying no. Lonnie was no dummy. He knew himself better than anyone else in the world. The still very much grief-stricken youth knew if he kept listening to old Al, he was subject to get caught up in his emotions. And as if on cue, a few seconds later, Lonnie was close to tears taking a trip back down memory lane.

Taking both index fingers, he started to slowly rub them on his temples in a circular motion. Quickly realizing he couldn't stop the onset of a rapidly approaching headache, Lonnie snatched the half-drunken warm bottle of beer off his desk. Jumping to his feet, he ran to get a few extra-strength aspirins to help him chill out and relax. Twisting the cap off, he shook three or four pills out and washed them down with the remaining beer. *I gotta stop tripping like this. I got to! I swear I got to!* Lonnie, like a fool, kept turning the volume up on his cell as loud as it could possibly go. And Pandora, being Pandora, played several more songs that equally reminded him of the woman who gave birth to him and loved him until the day she died. He felt like he was going stir-crazy. Lonnie kept hearing the voices of the women he felt had mistreated him or done him wrong over the previous year. He couldn't seem to drown them out. Finally, he not only turned the volume of the music down, but shut his cell all the way off.

Feeling out of control, Lonnie finally broke his self-imposed code of not generating any bonds, friendships, or relationships with any of the party animals at his school. He wanted to do as he'd been doing all semester; keep his head in the books and his mind focused on something other than the streets. He'd sworn off any bullshit, including partying and ratchet-ass females that he knew ultimately meant him no good. Yet, here he was walking down the hallway of his building heading toward Kevin's. He had to get out of his dreary existence apartment. Less than three yards before he reached his destination, as fate would have it, the intoxicated off of God-knows-what Kevin opened his apartment door to let someone out.

"Heyyyyyyyy," Kevin slurred, bringing his hand down on Lonnie's shoulder as a female staggered away looking zoned and stoned out of her mind. "My brother, you made it! Come on in; we just getting started on round three, or is it round four? Whatever it is—come on in!"

Not muttering a single word, Lonnie eagerly stepped through the threshold of Kevin's domain and into a dark world he knew nothing about—but would one day regret.

CHAPTER THIRTEEN

It's been often said that drugs were the devil. Well, if that statement rings true, then alcohol is his sister, and pills definitely a first cousin. For Lonnie, the past six months he'd been friends with good ole Kevin from down the hall proved to be a constant family reunion of the substances. Not used to being under the influence of anything stronger than a gigantic dose of sugar from his Halloween candy or a cherry-flavored Arctic Blast from 7-Eleven, Lonnie stayed lifted. Thankfully, the teen was blessed to be one of the ten percent of the population that could actually hold their liquor, be high as a kite, and still function from day to day. With Lonnie born and raised in the hood, Kevin and his other close-knit circle of fellow students found it amazing that Lonnie had never once even experimented with weed or pills. They couldn't believe he'd never so much as tasted a bottle of Boone's Farm or Wild Irish Rose. They joked with him often, that he was whiter than they and had missed out on real life growing up in the ghetto; as if they really knew.

Lonnie not only maintained his grades, in some of his classes, they even improved. It was as if the pills especially proved to be an aid to his overall creativity. Easily fulfilling all his obligations to keep his scholarship intact, the teen felt like he was living in an entirely different world than his deceased mother had raised him. Elated to be sometimes delivered from the severe headaches he was used to having and nightly dreams about his moms still being alive, Lonnie welcomed getting high.

Still harboring a deep-rooted hatred for most women he'd come in contact with, Lonnie played the game with Kevin and the other dudes when they wanted to throw wild parties. They invited females with loose morals that wanted to get buzzed and do just about anything with anyone for kicks; Lonnie's outwardly weird ass included. In most instances, he'd avoid contact with the women as much as possible; yet, this would soon prove to not be one of those instances.

"Hey, Megan, why don't you and my guy Lonnie go in the bedroom and see if any more beer's left? I mean, we need some more out here if we wanna stay feeling good."

Megan, just like her other two friends, giggled, knowing what the real deal was. "Yeah, right, Kevin. You so damn bogus. Stop messing around so much. You know there isn't any beer in the bedroom."

"There just could be," Kevin, drunk and in a good mood, stood to his feet pointing to Lonnie. "Why don't you two go and look just the same. I think I may have left a case stashed underneath my bed."

Megan wasn't the prettiest of the three, but she had by far the biggest breasts. Watching Lonnie's eyes grow twice their size while focusing on them made her feel even sluttier than normal. Always wanting to see what all the hype was about venturing on the "dark side," Megan licked her lips and grabbed Lonnie's hand. Leading him into the room, she took charge, closing the door behind them. Using her palms, she seductively placed them on Lonnie's chest, then pushed his body backward onto the bed. Empowered, Megan untied the string on his track pants. Practically snatching them down to his knees, she exposed his manhood.

"Oh my freaking God! Lonnie, it's so big, and it's not even hard yet! I've never been with a black guy before, but my friends all said yous all had big dicks."

Lonnie was at a loss for words. He'd messed around here and there back in the old neighborhood with a few random girls, but this female was much different. Besides the fact she was white, Megan was a grown-ass woman; one that seemed like she'd been around the block on more than one occasion. Fighting his demons, Lonnie was a nervous wreck. He'd been drinking whiskey and popping pill after pill since early noon. Sadly, no matter what tricks of the trade Megan tried, his dick wasn't in the mood to stand at full attention. He wanted it to get hard, or so he thought. However, banging Megan or getting some head just wasn't in the cards for him.

After ten minutes of being in the bedroom, Lonnie and Megan emerged. With several more people gathered in Kevin's small apartment, another one of his infamous get-high parties was in full swing. Ashamed, Lonnie ducked out without saying a word. No sooner than the door shut, he heard Megan and her friends laughing, saying he was no more than a broken dick slave. Wanting to storm back inside and slap the fire out of all three of their prejudiced mouths, he opted to just go home where he belonged in the first place.

A week had flown by since Lonnie had inconspicuously left Kevin's crib. Trying his best to avoid his friend, the mentally drained teen added Megan and her homegirls to the list of females that were no more than pieces of shit. Sneaking up the back staircase, Lonnie's luck ran out when he swung the door to his floor wide open without checking to see if the coast was clear. Unfortunately, Kevin was standing at Lonnie's door knocking.

"Hey, dude, where you been?"

"Oh, yeah, hey, Kevin. What up, doe?"

"Man, I been calling you; texting you, and down here damn near beating your door down."

Lonnie was ashamed he couldn't sexually perform that evening with Megan and was still not in the mood to get dogged out behind the fact. "Look, guy, I just been trying to stay straight and focus on the books, ya know what I mean?"

Kevin had been drinking and popping pills before puberty and already knew the side effects that could and would occur. In reality, the same thing had happened to him on more than several occasions as well as the guys who ran in his druggie crew. Not wanting to lose a friend behind Megan and her band of pill groupie freaks, he spoke out. "Look, man, we better than that; at least I thought we were. Fuck them skanks; especially Megan. She ain't shit but a crack whore anyhow. It's always gonna be bros before hoes!" Kevin grabbed his manhood and yanked it slightly downward. "Shiiiiiddd, my hookup wouldn't wanna holler at her ugly ass neither. The bitch just got some huge-ass tits, that's all!"

Lonnie was relieved his boy had said what he had, but it still didn't make him feel any better as a man whose dick wouldn't get hard. "Yeah, dawg, I feel you, but—"

Kevin cut him off midsentence with some news that would take Megan and any other chick off Lonnie's mind. "Man, forget all that from the other night. I got a proposition for you. One that's gonna get us more pussy and ass and props from motherfuckers than you can ever imagine. That's why I been looking for you."

Lonnie was intrigued and couldn't pretend he wasn't. Sticking his key in the door, he unlocked it and stepped inside. After Kevin entered the apartment, he informed him of what was the opportunity of a lifetime. His father's business partner was being temporary transferred overseas for the next year and wanted Kevin to housesit. After explaining that he had to pay absolutely no rent, no utilities, and the upscale neighborhood home had an inside heated pool and a high-tech game room, Lonnie was all in. After the year he'd been having, he felt like it might be like having a small vacation from the cruelness of the city.

Kevin informed Lonnie his dad's business partner had already given him the green light to have one of his college classmates stay there with him as well. So, in Kevin's mind, it was a no-brainer. He knew the rest of his buddies were knuckleheads and didn't deserve any breaks or come ups. For the most part, they, or their parents, were like him and his family; financially stable. However, Lonnie was different in his eyes. Not because he was less fortunate. And not because he was often the voice of reason when they were getting too high and needed to slow up, but the brutal honest fact, Lonnie was black. Crazy as it seemed, their other get-high counterparts were intimidated by Lonnie's mere presence. Kevin wasn't prejudiced by a long shot, but wasn't a fool either. He understood Lonnie's being there could make others not get so wild and out of hand when they were partying.

After a few more minutes of Kevin laying out the details of the arrangement, the two friends celebrated with popping a few pills and downing a few shots of rotgut cheap gin as chasers. Lonnie may have been avoiding contact with Kevin and didn't miss him, but his urges for the pills his boy always was holding was something else. He'd become almost dependent on them to stop the reoccurring dreams and nightmares of his mother's death.

CHAPTER FOURTEEN

It had been less than four months since Lonnie left his low-income apartment and temporarily located to the suburbs. Smart enough to keep his grades up and the small sum of thirty dollars a month paid up for his rent, Lonnie took the time he was granted right outside the city as a privilege. The house he and Kevin were chilling in was exactly everything Kevin said it would be, and more. And just like Kevin claimed when he first gave Lonnie the good news of their change of address, the parties they had grew and grew. It seemed as if they had more and more classmates, friends, bitches, hoes, and just random motherfuckers somehow finding themselves stopping by.

Growing up in the hood, Lonnie was exposed to just about a little of everything. In the ghetto, there was no-holds-barred. The gloves were off in just about every aspect of life you could imagine; good, bad, and ugly—but for the most part, bad. He'd seen no-morals heroin addicts standing on the corner in their gravity-defying lean, delusional crackheads floor surfing, searching the carpet for a small sliver of rock that wasn't even there, and young girls barely out of junior high pregnant by old men that promised them the world if they could just get some pussy.

However, this life Lonnie was caught up in living in the white world of privilege was something else altogether. He'd never experienced folk who openly lived like this with no shame. These people he was hanging with had no off buttons or pause. They felt the world owed them something; a sense of entitlement. The drinking, the drugs, the pills, and all the promiscuous sex was like it was nothing. In Kevin's world, this bullshit was apparently second nature. Yet, as much as Lonnie had grown to love popping pills and drinking, he not once had an urge to venture over to the stairway to the next level: hardcore drugs. He knew how he was living was next to foul, and his mother would be disappointed, but he reasoned with himself that she was gone and he was still here on earth to fight the good fight; even if that meant he had to pop a few Xanax or Norcos to help him wage the battle.

Late for class, Lonnie waited for the bus as he did every morning. Not blessed enough to have a car like Kevin, the now semiaddicted-to-prescription-pills teen did what he had to do when need be. If Kevin had class and was going to the city, then he would catch a ride with him. If not, the iron pimp was Lonnie's only recourse. Putting up with the unwanted attention from suburban residents who felt like a young black teenager out in their neighborhood could only mean one thing, many days he had to swallow his pride. Part of the functioning pillhead wanted to just move back to his apartment near campus and save him not only the hassle of the travel time, but the sheer hatred he was forced to endure. Most of the women he'd come in contact with there would hold their purses extra tight, advise their kids to walk on the other side of the street, or just plain ignore him, like he didn't exist. Lonnie knew if it wasn't for the pills he was taking that kept him pretty much numb when it came to emotions, he would've snapped. Instead, he focused on his books, going to class, and getting back to the party house so he could get even higher.

It'd been over an hour, and the bus had yet to come. Lonnie was slightly buzzed but not out his mind enough to want to miss class. He had been staying up studying for his business management test all night. Having missed a few days during the semester and getting an incomplete on his project, Lonnie knew he had to make at least a strong B on the test if he wanted to keep his scholarship intact. He'd already been placed on academic probation from the "once a month used to be bleeding cunt" dean of students, as he nicknamed her. So, Lonnie getting to school was crucial. He'd already lost a part-time job he'd gotten at a law firm through the work study program by being suspected of possibly being "high" off of some substance. In his emotions, Lonnie refused a drug test; so, of course, that was that.

Starting to feel panicked, the always cash-strapped youth checked his pockets for cash thinking maybe he could catch a cab. Coming up with nothing but a few coins and a crumbled up dollar or two, Lonnie knew that option was straight out the window. *Shit. I gotta get back to the city. I gotta get to class and take that test before they kick my black ass out of school. I can't let my mother down! Fuck!*

Lonnie got back to the house he was staying at. Letting himself in, he found Kevin still knocked out with two naked females in the bed with him. All three reeking of alcohol, Lonnie picked up a bottle of Grey Goose that had a small amount left inside. Turning the bottle up, he killed it, along with an ice-cold beer he'd gotten from the refrigerator. Snatching Kevin's car keys off the table, Lonnie figured he'd drive to the city, take his test, and be back home before his homeboy even woke up to take an early-morning piss.

With not much practice when it came to driving, Lonnie was like any other dude from the hood. Where there was a will, there was a way. He knew after a few quick right and left turns to get out of the upscale community, it'd be a straight shot on the freeway. Backing out of the driveway, he popped in a piece of gum in hopes of masking the smell of his beer and Grey Goose mixture breath. Still spinning off the Percocet he'd taken when he got up this morning, Lonnie turned on the radio to try to refocus on what was really important: making his mother proud.

Changing the station from Kevin's annoying rock station, Lonnie found some music to his liking. With both hands on the wheel, he drove toward the freeway. As if he wasn't mentally drained enough and worried about getting to school on time, the unthinkable happened. Tears started to pour out of Lonnie's weary eyes as Al Green's voice sang through the speakers. Lost in thoughts of his mother, the distraught, unlicensed driver blew by a stop sign in a crowded intersection. Before Lonnie knew what was happening next, flashing red and blue lights were flying up behind him. Roughly snatched from the car by two white cops, he was thrown to the ground, then handcuffed, accused of everything one could imagine, including shooting Martin Luther King and J. F. Kennedy.

"Please give us a reason to shoot your black ass," one of the cops, a female, tried to get tough with her hand firmly gripping up on the handle of her pistol.

"Yeah, why are you out here in our jurisdiction this early in the morning? Don't you think you're out of place?" the male officer joined in on the unwarranted verbal assault but was nowhere as near as mean-spirited and gung ho as his female counterpart.

Lonnie had been spaced out, but his high was totally blown by the quick chain of events that were jumping off. Losing the feeling in his hands because the cuffs were so tight, he yelled out in pain. "Hold up, Officers. Hold up.

Why y'all going on me like this? What I do? Hold up! This bullshit wrong as hell!"

Using more force than necessary, the female officer smashed Lonnie's face down onto the filthy concrete street with her department-issued boots. Making sure no one was looking, she then bent down, shoving her knee in his lower spine. "Okay, look, we don't need any of your ghetto hood mouth talk. You smell like you been drinking, and your eyes look like you on that stuff. You done fucked up this morning, for sure."

"Naw, wait," Lonnie pleaded, knowing he was indeed buzzing when he got behind the wheel, but was trying to drive as carefully as possible. "Y'all got it all wrong."

The female cop was amused and laughed in response to his statement. "Nah, I think we got it right! Now is this your car or what? One answer; yes, or damn no?"

Lonnie struggled to speak as she gorilla-style inter-rogated him as if he was resisting. "It's my friend's car; Kevin O'Brian."

"You hear this?" she glanced back over her shoulder talking to her partner. "This guy claims he has a friend named . . . get this . . . Kevin O'Brian. Yeah, come on now, Lonnie McKay," she arrogantly read the name off his state-issued ID. "You gotta come a lot better than that with your lie. What's a guy with a Detroit address in the heart of the war zone doing with a friend named Kevin O'Brian? Just tell us the truth and things will go much smoother for you. My partner is running the plates now."

Of course, when the plates came back registered to Kevin, the dominate female officer was even more pissed than the initial moment she'd assisted with snatching Lonnie from the vehicle. With the car not being reported stolen, they still arrested him on other charges that were easy to see and prove. Driving without a license, driving while under the influence of alcohol and drugs, disorderly conduct, refusing arrest, and a few other choice items the white spiteful female officer decided to throw in for good measure. For Lonnie, his run of good luck had just played itself out.

CHAPTER FIFTEEN

"I can't believe that menopausal-in-full-swing judge went so hard on me. It wasn't fair. I didn't even have a chance to really speak," Lonnie whined as Kevin and a handful of their so-called friends left the courthouse. "And that welfare lawyer I had didn't make matters any better telling me to just plead guilty and get it over with. She acted like she was working hand in hand with the damn prosecutor's office."

Kevin shook his head while shrugging his shoulders. An expert at drinking and driving and getting caught, he'd been down this road before, truth be told, on more than one occasion. He knew that because Lonnie had never had any contact with the law whatsoever, including as a juvenile, the judge had no choice within the guidelines to sentence him the way she had. "Come on, Lonnie, shut that shit up and quit your bitching. It's only probation and community service."

"Only," Lonnie barked as if the world was ending.

"Yeah, only. Man, it ain't like you have to go to jail and do some real time or something."

"Kev's right, Lonnie. That same bitch gave me forty-five days in the county last year this time. She don't play."

Lonnie didn't want to hear any of the crap his home-boys were talking. That day he'd got pulled over and treated less than human was terrible; locked up in the county for six days until Kevin bailed him out. In his eyes, they could say what they wanted; the court system ain't no joke, especially when a young black male is caught up in it. Not only had the dirty-ass female cop taken it upon herself to report his arrest to the dean of students, Lonnie felt the two of them conspired to make him lose his scholarship. Now expelled from school, he had to wait for the next semester to roll around so that he could apply for financial aid and hopefully get accepted in another top-notch program.

"It's easy for all of y'all to talk that 'she went easy on me' bullshit because all y'all peoples got money. I'm out in this world by my damn self. Now I'm all the way fucked up. I swear my mother must be looking down like, 'Damn fool, what in the hell you done become?'" Lonnie was irate and disappointed thinking of all he'd messed up just like that.

With the cancellation of his scholarship, that meant he'd have to move out of his apartment for good in sixty days or less. Even though he'd been camping out with Kevin at the party house, he knew that was a temporary thing. Bottom line once again, Lonnie Eugene McKay would be homeless, which was ironic since the judge had ordered him to do community service at some homeless shelters of his choosing as long as they were inside the county boundaries.

Deciding to go back to the city and spend his last few weeks in his own apartment, Lonnie lay back on his bed. Yearning for some pills, the wayward young man fought the urge, knowing from this point on, he had to drop once every two weeks. And if he dropped dirty, even once, the asshole judge promised to throw him back in the county; which was the last place he wanted to be. Interlocking his fingers behind his head, Lonnie closed his eyes, trying to figure out what his next move would be.

CHAPTER SIXTEEN

With all of America seemingly awaiting the verdict to be read, the judge was quickly losing patience with the entire showboat proceedings. First, with all of the unexpected but understandable outbursts from the family members of the five various victims of Mr. McKay; then Mr. McKay himself, acting as if this day would not go on if he wasn't an active participant. She'd put up with outlandish requests from the media and added pressure from city officials, including the mayor, governor, and even a few calls from a couple of senators. Everyone seemed to have a horse in the race, so to speak, in wanting Lonnie Eugene McKay thrown in jail without so much as passing go. She promised them and the residents of Detroit that the defendant would receive his due process and have his day legally in court as stated in the Bill of Rights. She was sworn in to do her duty, and her duty was just what she was going to do.

"Okay, Counselor, I've had just about all I'm willing to, or am going to, take from Mr. McKay. Now, he can respond when spoken to, or I will find him in contempt of this court and escorted back into the holding cell, and he can choose to watch the verdict read on the monitor. The choice is entirely up to him, and you and your client have all of thirty seconds to make up your minds what it's going to be. And the clock starts now!"

With less than thirty days left to stay in his student housing apartment, shit was getting real. Lonnie woke up with a headache. He didn't know if it was because he'd gone cold turkey on taking the pills and was suffering from a side effect, or if the anxiety of dreading this day was in full control. This was the day the judge had ordered him to start his community service. With the threat of his freedom hanging in the balance, the weary-minded teen dragged himself out of bed. Weak and having little energy, he'd slept only a few hours last night, and even those weren't sound. Lonnie kept waking up in sweats from the nightmares he could no longer treat with pills. After washing his face with cold water to help him wake up and brushing his teeth with the last corner of toothpaste in the tube, he made his way into the kitchen.

Having a burning desire to have a shot of gin instead of a glass of milk, he opted for the childish drink. He didn't want to waste an alcohol buzz confined within a homeless shelter. Plus, he didn't know if they'd make him take a breathalyzer before entering for service. What he did want to do was pop some pills.

Having had dropped yesterday, he wanted to test his luck and take an X-pill today, wanting to treat himself to getting high one more good time before being forced to stay in the one place he hated more than life itself: the homeless shelter.

Expected to follow the schedule of several different shelters that'd agreed for him to volunteer at, Lonnie looked at the digital clock that sat on the far corner of his desk. Realizing it was almost time to leave, he had a strange grin on his face as he decided to take the X-pill with him in his pocket; just in case some of the same no-good, demanding, coldhearted women were still in charge of the facilities, and he needed a tension reliever.

The disgraced college student hoped like hell they'd gotten fired for their bad dispositions toward the misfortunate clients they were supposed to be helping, or at least moved on to pursue other endeavors. Whatever the case was to be, Lonnie had to face it head-on; especially if he wanted to remain in good standing with the judge and probation officer.

The bus dropped him off two blocks away from Oakdale Combined Family Services. The first of eight shelters on his list to have to show up to and do as he was told. Lonnie grew agitated at the fact he felt like he was now nothing more than a modern-day slave nonpaid laborer. For all intents and purposes, he was the court system's bitch. Regretting the crazy decisions he'd made in his life since hooking up with Kevin, Lonnie looked up at the clouds and apologized to his late mother for turning his back, deliberate or not, on everything she'd taught him. He wasn't raised to be labeled a drunk as well as a pillhead, but so be it. Here he was looked upon as just that. Wanting to ease his "emergency get-right pill" out of his front pocket and swallow it before bending the next corner, Lonnie fought off the urge.

Shit, I hate this place. I swear I wish it could have been anywhere but this dump. This the worse one outta all the ones I had to lay my damn head at. Mad at the world and himself for having to be here standing at the front door of what he remembered to be hell, Lonnie rubbed his hands together, then cracked his knuckles. After ringing the buzzer a few good times, someone finally came to let him in. As the huge brown-painted metal door swung open, the anxious teen was relieved. The woman in her early thirties holding a semiwet mop in her hand was not a face Lonnie recognized from the many agonizing nights he slept there when not making curfew at his regular spot. Thank God she must have been one of the countless temporary residents of the shelters that were blessed enough to stay around during the day. Whereas most of Detroit's faceless throwaways without housing of their own had to vacate the premises immediately after breakfast is served, a few handpicked favorites that did odd jobs and tasks at the paid staff's leisure could remain on the premises.

"Yes, can I help you?" the woman asked, trying to sound as professional as possible.

"Yeah, I need to speak to the daytime supervisor. I'm supposed to be doing some volunteer work this week."

The woman held the mop handle in one hand while looking Lonnie up and down. Not used to seeing a young man dressed as nicely as he was in or around the shelter, she hated she was looking a hot mess. Ignoring the fact he was years her junior, the woman made sure to put an extra swing in her hips as she let him in and led him to the office. Upon getting to the door she tried touching him on the shoulder telling him good luck, but Lonnie wasn't having any of that. He wasn't in the mood for anyone in this hellhole to have any sort of physical contact with him, pleasant or otherwise.

"Yeah, just come in and have a seat over there," one of the secretaries rudely motioned to a set of chairs on the far side of the room.

Dismissing him as if he was one of the faceless homeless individuals that paraded in and out nightly, Lonnie had a burning desire to run across the room and slap the cow shit out of her. She was no better than anyone else, although the way she was dressed, Lonnie knew she couldn't be told that. And if she was, she'd never believe it. Doing as he was asked—or ordered—he took a seat and waited. After being forced to hear about two different guys she was dating, the fact she needed brakes on her car, and she'd braggingly just purchased several packs of expensive human hair from overseas, she was ready to deal with him. "Yeah, my name is Lonnie; Lonnie McKay."

"Okay and . . . Soooo . . ." she kinda sucked her teeth as her stank attitude increased.

Thrown off by her unprofessional manner, Lonnie had to catch himself from dishing out what he was receiving. He'd been dealing with all sorts of women since hanging with Kevin, so nothing that came out of a female's mouth surprised him at this time. It didn't matter if they were a doctor, a lawyer, a factory worker, ballerina, drunk, or pillhead. To Lonnie, all bitches were the same; headaches waiting to happen. Containing himself, he simply responded by handing her a set of court-ordered documents that someone in charge of the shelter had to sign off on at the end of the day. "Here you go. I'm supposed to have these signed."

Her attitude seemed to get worse as she read over the lower portion of the form. It was apparent she'd come to the part where he was to do whatever work, within reason, the shelter needed him to do. It was as if she got on a power trip and was ready to ride high. "Oh, I see. You just didn't come here to 'volunteer'; you here to us by force. I should've known a young man your age wasn't into helping others; just because."

Not wanting to cause trouble, Lonnie tried to keep his mouth shut, but couldn't resist knocking the uppity woman down a few pegs. "Look, I'm sorry you're having a bad day; I truly am. However, for a person that has the charge and responsibility to help others that are less fortunate, I find it outrageous that you look down at me for being young and for having made a mistake. I had a choice to do other forms of community service," he decided to lie and add it on extra thick, "yet I chose to be here and at other shelters and do what I can. Now here I stand, hat in hand, and you make me feel less than human. I'm sorry I can't fix your brakes or afford that hair, but I can carry boxes or move furniture."

The woman felt like shit on a stick after Lonnie finished reading her. Before she could even try to cop a plea for her over-the-top judgments, the man who was in charge came in. Relieved he wouldn't have to take orders from such a bitch, Lonnie went with Mr. Reynolds into his office.

"So, yeah, Mr. McKay, or can I call you Lonnie? Will that be all right?"

"Lonnie is cool with me. I'm good with that."

"Well, great. Let me just say that even though you are here to perform volunteer hours with us, we still try to slip our people a li'l something something under the table when we can." He went in the top drawer of his desk and took out an envelope. "Now, this type of thing isn't a regular thing you can count on, but when I can bless the next person, why not. I've been homeless before as well as in trouble as a youth, so trust me when I tell you, Lonnie, I know how it is to be a young black man out here trying to navigate through these streets."

Not knowing what to make out of Mr. Reynolds's out-of-the-blue openhanded generosity, Lonnie happily accepted the envelope. Not knowing its contents, he put it in his back pocket. Living practically hand to mouth, the youngster knew at this point in his life he needed all the assistance he could get, free or otherwise. "Thanks."

"No need to thank me, son, just lend us a strong helping hand while you're here and do the best job you possibly can, even if there is no full-scale paycheck involved. Now, I might not be around every time you leave, so my secretary can sign off on the amount of hours you put in. The night shift staff comes in after six, but you and I both will be long gone by then for the day."

Lonnie was happy that he wouldn't have to come in contact with any of the persons that worked at night. He wanted to confide in his elder that not only was he in trouble with the court system, he had also been homeless for some time and had actually slept in this facility on more than several occasions. Lonnie wanted to tell him all the sneaky deviant behavior that went on in the coed common area after dark as well as the drug usage. But he wasn't one to be labeled a snitch; especially since he was on the verge of possibly having to house back under this roof in the very near future. Instead, he dummied up and let shit be.

The alone-in-the-world teen felt at ease as the older man schooled him on the way he wanted things done around the shelter. Not wanting him to think he was a slacker or unappreciative of whatever blessing was in the envelope, Lonnie picked up quickly. When he took a break, the exhausted teen opened the envelope, finding a few weeks' worth of bus tickets and a fifty-dollar bill. Thinking this experience might not be so bad, he smiled, not even giving a second thought to the Ecstasy pill still in his pocket or buying anymore with his small, but much-needed windfall.

When it was finally time to leave, he looked for Mr. Reynolds but was informed by the woman that'd let him into the building earlier that he'd left the premises.

"Baby, he's gone for the day. He usually leaves about three or so. Sometimes five on Fridays." She tried flirting as if she wasn't down and out on her luck and should have other things more important on her mind besides trying to push up on some young dude that was clearly paying her no attention whatsoever.

"Oh, all right, then, thanks, Miss."

"Oh, no problem; no problem at all. Anytime, baby, or anything you want to know just ask. I gotcha!"

Lonnie nodded at the woman, hoping she'd just stop pretending to clean that same damn multicolored framed mirror so she could be in the hallway right outside the

office door. *This bitch done lost her mind or something.*
With no recourse but to have the uppity-mouthed secretary sign off on his paperwork, Lonnie braced himself to
do verbal battle. No sooner than he turned the doorknob
and stepped inside, he was met with a much different
attitude. The originally crude creature informed him
her first name was Brenda and asked him to forgive her,
she was having a bad day. Lonnie was not in the mood
to hear or except any fake apologies. As far as he was
concerned, she could keep her little con game and run
it on one of those naïve fools she was talking about like
dogs on the phone earlier. After she signed his paper, he
was out the door praying he'd beat any of the night staff
arriving early.

CHAPTER SEVENTEEN

"You done whining for having to do some time for ya' crime?" Kevin told a bad joke at Lonnie's expense. Slurring and giggling like a girl, it was easy to tell the privileged white boy was high as a kite, as usual. His friend's misfortune hadn't slowed down his habit or his partying in the slightest bit.

"Yeah, I guess," Lonnie responded after his first day of volunteer work, not really in the mood for his white friend's personality. "It wasn't as bad as I thought it would be, real talk," he said honestly, but not really wanting to talk about his unfortunate circumstances.

Loner Lonnie was more consumed and interested in the beer can he was trying to find the bottom of. He was growing nauseated, but was trying to fight against it. Lonnie wasn't sick with the stomach bug, just going through withdrawals. His body had gotten used to the daily regimen of pills, so not having them made him ill. The unsettled adolescent wished he had the means to run away or at least money to make all his problems vanish.

"Good, that shit'll be over and you can be back over here partyin' and bullshittin' with the crew in no time." His words managed to lift Lonnie's spirits. "But I don't know about moving in. My homeboy needed somewhere to crash and you were gone so—"

"What the fuck, man? I know you ain't call me to run me in the ground even more," Lonnie snapped, hearing another person was getting off scraps just as he was heading toward getting back on them.

"Aw, man, before you get back on that whining shit, let me hip you to what a bitch I stuck my dick in put me onto today. It'll help you with your troubles."

Kevin could never be of any assistance with homework, studying, or any positive stuff like that. His specialty was pills, booze, partying, and bitches. Lonnie wondered what Kevin could help him with that he could indulge in without getting in trouble with the judge.

"I got these pills that make them Zannys seem like Flintstone vitamins," Kevin slurred, speaking the truth because he was as high as a kite. "These motherfuckers be having me not caring 'bout shit. They so strong that you only need to pop half, but you know I like to get wild."

"Kev, man, damn. You forget I gotta drop or something?" Irritated, Lonnie wanted to get off the phone and find some solace. Because today hadn't been so bad, he wanted to get some rest and prepare for day two of fulfilling his sentence. Lonnie was dog-tired but fighting sleep, not wanting a repeat of last night to see his mother in another nightmare.

"Naw, I ain't forgot. Shorty, who I'm sticking my dick in, works at a clinic, be selling scripts, and charging a few extra bucks if you need her to make you up a file." Kevin was extra excited since his favorite pastime and all-the-time activity was to pop pills. What he was telling Lonnie was that he'd found a semilegal way to do drugs. He'd also told Lonnie he had a pharmacy in his backpack.

"Say, word? That shit sound too fuckin' good to be true. I been over here spazzing out trying to see if I should tiptoe on the tightrope and pop this X-pill for one last high, and yo' ass over their plugging up the plug." Lonnie was live, right along with Kevin. So much so that he agreed to take a few of them off his hands—just to try.

He didn't have the money to pay the girl for the pills or the file he'd need, but he could try the testers Kevin was offering him. Instead of taking the X-pill, he'd experiment with the Chill Pill, the name Kevin told him he'd nicknamed it. He couldn't, however, remember the actual name for the comparable but better drug than Xanax.

Kevin had a female in the passenger's seat when he brought Lonnie the tester pills, although it wasn't the same woman from the clinic. Lonnie hoped his friend didn't mess up a good thing with ole' girl at the clinic before it got started. Walking up the stairwell back to his apartment, Lonnie swallowed the capsule dry mouthed before reaching his door.

CHAPTER EIGHTEEN

Unlike the first day Lonnie woke up having to do community service, he woke up the second day without a headache and feeling like the day wouldn't be so bad. Matter of fact, his musty-smelling pillow was covered in slob. Well rested, Lonnie had slept uninterrupted and without nightmares. He didn't even remember getting naked in bed or falling asleep. Scratching his head, yawning out a foul odor of morning breath, he remembered the Chill Pill he'd taken the night before and the fact he still had one more.

It was different than Xanax and gave him an even more relaxed feeling. That's why he and Kevin nicknamed it as such. Before even getting out of the bed, he sent a text asking him how much for a full prescription. Since Kevin had gotten the scripts from a chick he was banging that interned at a medical clinic, Lonnie felt it was all good and safe to get it back on and popping with his pill habit. He needed them to cope, especially after seeing how it felt to go through withdrawals.

Just like yesterday, he could put in his hours without running into anyone he'd had dealings with; then get home and get high. All he intended on doing was his job and staying out of trouble and dealing with Mr. Reynolds. He hoped he was there today so he'd get a chance to thank him for the gift. Lonnie didn't want the man to think he was unappreciative and not bless him again.

Lonnie got out of bed, shook the wrinkles and any dirt crumbs from off his clothes, and slid them on like they hadn't been worn for the last few days back to back without being washed. The accustomed-to-struggle teen didn't frown today, however. He was happy that at least he had the fresh fifty he'd been gifted with in his pocket, along with the bus passes. Lonnie hadn't spent a dollar of the bill. He knew what his future could hold. What he didn't know was when Mr. Reynolds was going to gift him with some more money. As always, Lonnie had to play it smart, unlike many of his peers. It sometimes depressed him that he couldn't be careless like Kevin.

Lonnie went through his same routine of getting ready and was out the door headed to the bus stop within fifteen minutes from first getting up. Despite all the negative circumstances around him, he was trying to look on the bright side of things. He'd be able to eat meals at the soup kitchen, take a few toiletries for himself, and even get a few dollars whenever Mr. Reynolds felt like blessing him. He knew it wasn't much, but it could be counted on.

It even crossed his mind that maybe he could work at the shelter for a few dollars during the morning shift after his community hours had been fulfilled. That way, he could have money to pay room and board somewhere at least. Lonnie knew it was a long shot to think with some hope, but nothing else so far had worked.

Many of the people waiting on the same city bus that ran by the schedule of the driver, not what the route truly said, made Lonnie their early-morning topic. They thought they knew him well, despite them not knowing his story at all. The two women who were always late to work behind Lonnie paying his fare in all pennies or begging the driver for a free ride or transfer rolled their eyes. Because of him, they'd been put on probation.

"Don't even stand here waiting on the bus if you ain't got enough money or what little you do maybe have in order," one of the women rudely addressed Lonnie.

"Yeah, matter of fact, start counting that shit out now. That way, you won't be up there stumbling and mumbling when the time comes," the other woman joined in clowning the teen.

Lonnie bit his bottom lip. He knew he'd seen these women before, and he knew he'd also held the bus up before. Yet and still, he didn't deserve to be belittled. He was growing tired of people treating him inhumane and acting like his feelings didn't matter.

"What? You can't hear either? Hello!" The woman who'd started the verbal attack against Lonnie yelled and waved her hand in his face.

Something in Lonnie snapped. Here he was trying to find the rainbow in a hurricane that was his tumultuous life and yet another random woman has pissed in his cornflakes. He felt his chest rise and fall three strong times as his blood surged though his veins. Grabbing her wrist, he twisted it, then pushed her back. Not enough for her to fall to the ground, but enough to shake her out of his face. Lonnie didn't want any problems, just to be left alone. "Keep your hands up outta my face, lady. I don't know you, and I swear fo' God you don't wanna know me."

The lady, in disbelief that she'd just been checked by a man so dirty and disheveled, ran her hand across her bunched clothes, then balled up her fist. She wanted to bark at Lonnie, attack him back even, but knew he'd probably beat her to a pulp. And she also knew she was wrong for being in his space in the first place. And it was too early with no one else around. If things went left and the police needed to be called, she knew they weren't coming for petty shit, especially in the hood. They barely responded to burglaries of businesses and homicides. She took her friend's advice as well as the little voice in her head telling her to back down and did.

The bus arrived, and Lonnie was everything but a gentleman. He was tired of being nice and having women be disrespectful for no reason. He hadn't been taught to put his hands on girls, even told he'd be less than a man for doing so; yet, he'd just learned that's the only way to put them in their place. For the first time since his mother's death, he didn't wonder how she felt looking down on him. Lonnie was tired of taking the cards he's been dealt. Especially when everyone else cheats.

With his bus pass in hand, he stepped up and handed it to the driver.

The smart-mouthed woman, who Lonnie thought had learned her lesson, spoke up. "Slide it in the machine where the dollars go. I know you don't know that since it seems you never have none." She felt bold with the bus driver there.

Lonnie's face turned red. After sliding the bus pass into the slot, he hung his head and walked toward the back of the bus. Back there, he could hide his shoes with worn out soles, dirty clothes, and maybe perhaps if he was lucky—the bad luck that always followed him.

Lonnie managed to ride the entire route without having another verbal or physical altercation with the lady, or anyone else, for that matter. The driver had announced he didn't want any shenanigans from anyone and would gladly put those that couldn't adhere to his rules off. Not one person complained. Even the school-aged kids who normally clowned him and took pictures of Lonnie for their social site pages kept their space and their snickers to themselves.

***

Getting off an exit too soon, Lonnie wanted to stop at the nearby liquor store first. He knew he needed to hold onto the fifty dollars, but it was more important for him to relieve his frustration and tension before going into the shelter for community service. The last thing Lonnie needed was for Mr. Reynolds or anyone else that had some sort of ranking to send a bad report back to the judge.

Walking with his hands stuffed into his pockets, one of them holding the money tightly, his footsteps shook the ground. Lonnie remembered his mother telling him to keep the devil underneath his feet and to stomp on his neck when the devil seems to have a hold on him; so he was trying to follow her advice now. He would've done just about anything to catch some peace. Overstressed, Lonnie couldn't wait to take another Chill Pill.

Walking into the store, he grabbed a big bottle of water from the cooler, then headed straight for the counter. He'd woke up early and had gotten a good start, but was now close to running late because of this detour.

"Let me get a couple packs of Tylenol, one pack of Motrin, and a Snapback," he spoke loud enough so the attendant could hear him through the thick Plexiglas. Strategically waiting for the attendant to get the over-the-counter pills, Lonnie then asked for the two-dollar shot of liquor he wanted. The low-dose pills wouldn't give him the strong high he was chasing without the alcohol. Mixing them all together, Lonnie had learned from Kevin how to intensify the side effects of any pill.

"Ten for the pills, my man; and I'ma need to see ya' ID for the liquor," the store worker told a slick Lonnie, then exchanged the packs of pills for the money.

Working in the hood, although he didn't indulge in getting high himself, he was, however, familiar with all the street drugs and concoctions the kids were making.

They'd get high off anything. Not caring how they mistreated and poisoned their body, he would've sold Lonnie
the liquor without making him show identification to
prove he was twenty-one and legal to drink; yet, he had
just caught a helluva fine. The store owner was lucky
to still have his liquor license and wasn't getting
ready to risk fucking up how he fed his family for the
poor Negroes he took money from daily. He tapped
his foot, waiting on Lonnie to tell him a lie.

"I forgot my shit rushing outta the house," Lonnie
lied, desperate, but proving the store owner right. "You
can take an extra dollar if you look out for me this time."
Trying to bribe the store owner with a measly buck,
Lonnie was desperate, and it showed.

"You can take those pills and get the fuck on up outta
here, dude. I ain't even 'bout to entertain what you just
said to me, embarrassing yourself and trying to play me
like a sucka." The store owner spoke like he was from the
hood, not an Arab traveling up the highway daily from
suburbia to the hood.

Waving Lonnie out of his store with his hand, he
frowned at the teen, feeling sorry for yet another black
man. Day in and out he saw their kind trickling in his
store to buy bottles of poison, tobacco that's labeled it'll
kill you with cancer, and snacks with so much sodium
in them they'd kill you with high blood pressure; yet
their ignorance was the money he lived by. He didn't tell
Lonnie not to return to his store, because he'd take his
money for what he could legally purchase. And when the
heat died down from the state trying to enforce rules and
regulations, he'd probably sell Lonnie a pint an hour just
to speed up the young black man's destruction.

Being turned away for trying to buy liquor being
underage, Lonnie asked for change and took one of the
five-dollar bills out to the bum he'd seen sitting on

the side of the building. He knew the man would do him the favor of buying him a shot of gin. With the change, he offered to get the bum one as well. Lonnie might've not had the money to spare, but he knew nobody in the street was scratching backs without getting theirs scratched. The bum grabbed the green bill, ran inside the store, and Lonnie licked his lips, already tasting the liquor.

Standing right by the door to make sure the bum didn't get the bright idea to run off with his money, Lonnie watched traffic passing him by. The prostitutes were walking as close as they could to the streets with their skirts hiked high up advertising their overused and fishy-smelling twats; the alcoholics were lingering a few feet from him begging for change from even the kids that were running errands to the store for their parents, and the hardworking homeless man was scouring the earth for trash and pop bottles to return for a deposit. He scratched his head and took a deep a breath, wishing the bum would hurry up.

The bum, laughing to himself because the attendant of the store told him he knew he was buying liquor for a kid, came out with Lonnie's change and two shots of gin. He hoped the desperate boy didn't notice he'd spent an extra dollar on a bag of chips and a cheap juice for later. The bum didn't care about pressing his luck, since he didn't have nothing to lose. Lonnie, desperate to make the over-the-counter pills react, was completely oblivious to how much change he'd stuffed into his pocket. He was too caught up in ripping the packages open of his over-the-counter pills and washing them down his throat with his shot of dark liquor.

It wasn't out of the norm for a boy to have grown men problems when he lived in the hood. Like Lonnie, the majority of them are born into poor families that work hella hard and still don't have a pot to piss in or a window to throw it out of. The bum was used to seeing li'l niggas do grown thangs like smoke weed, drink, steal, sell dope, and even shoot up; but Lonnie looked like a different type of youngin' to him. His eyes told a story of pain instead of a story of just having it hard.

"Damn, young blood. You ain't even old enough to have no real problems," the bum said, seeing Lonnie pop all the 200 mg pills into his mouth, followed by drinking the shot like it was a cold glass of water on a scorching hot summer day.

"Age ain't nothing but a number, O. G., on the real. I wish I didn't have a story to tell."

"Buy me another two-dolla' shot and I'll point you into the direction of the dope man around here. He ain't but a block away and got every pill known to man. You ain't gonna catch the high you chasing with them weak-ass capsules," the bum joked but was very serious.

He sat outside this liquor store day in and out, not begging for handouts, but watching all the crime that unfolded in the neighborhood. Although it was a foreign hood to Lonnie, it wasn't to the bum. He knew how every drug dealer, prostitute, and Arab business owner was making money in the run-down area. Never a part of any of it, he was the go-to guy if you needed some information on someone. He'd blab for any amount of money or drug. The bum didn't care about Lonnie or what he had to say. He was just hopeful that the young buck spared him a few more dollars to feed his alcohol addiction.

Lonnie didn't have to think about how he'd answer. "That's a good look, old man. Grab us two more each. Then I'll be looking forward to hearing where ya' connect is at. You better not be selling me no shit so you can get another drink," a slightly suspicious Lonnie warned, without having a plan of revenge if the man didn't have a pill seller connect. Even if the bum didn't know a man, he was still a help because Lonnie wouldn't have been able to get the liquor had it not been for him.

The first shot hadn't done Lonnie any justice. It went down warm but settled like soda pop. He was happy that the bum offered to go in the store and buy more, even if it was going to cost him more money. The plans of holding onto the fifty spot was completely gone out the window by now. The only thing on Lonnie's mind was liquor.

The same rotation occurred of Lonnie sitting by the door and the bum coming out with their bottles. Separated by at least forty years, the two were bonded together by their desperation for the alcohol. Scurrying like field mice back to the side of the corner store, just like a few minutes ago, they guzzled down the shots and tossed the bottles on the ground.

"Yup, that oughta set me straight to work these hours down," Lonnie spoke out loud to himself, stretching his arms out and cracking his neck. He could feel the liquor working through his bloodstream.

"All right, young man. I'm a man of my words, and I appreciate the booze. Come on over to my office and let's talk."

The bum welcomed conversation from any and everybody when he wasn't in a liquor-induced coma. Having two broken-up lawn chairs at the very end of the store, he sat down in one and propped his feet up on a crate, then motioned his hand for Lonnie to sit down as well. Misery loves company. The senior citizen bum wanted some.

"Naw, I'm good, but I appreciate you looking out. I'm actually about to be late for my second day of work over at the shelter."

"Oh, okay, young fella. Don't let an old man like me stop you from whatcha' gotta do. I'll be around. Don't forget what hookup I've got." He waved good-bye to Lonnie, hoping to see the young man again. If he didn't or until then, the bum would be watching and plotting on his next minor come up.

Lonnie walked the few blocks it took for him to get to the shelter. He was grateful for the air and exercise to get the liquor settled and pills working and settled. He wasn't trying to get caught drunk while doing community service, or even buzzed. He'd just wanted to calm his nerves from the bullshit that occurred at the bus stop, then go on about his day. Lonnie never wanted any trouble, although it always seemed to find him.

CHAPTER NINETEEN

The mixture of the shots, the Motrins, Tylenols, and Snapbacks had Lonnie feeling just right. His mood was mellow, he was focused and alert, and his feelings were somewhat numbed. One of the reasons he liked getting high is because not only did it make him less anxious over his problems, but able to deal with bullshit life threw at him.

He hadn't noticed the woman who'd been flirting with him yesterday lingering around the office again today, his second day at work, because he was trying hard to ignore Brenda's constant but sly staring. A paranoid Lonnie didn't know if she was trying to be frisky or picked up on the fact that he was high. Lonnie's second day of volunteering started off much different than the first. The moment he stepped off the bus and walked through the front door, Brenda was strangely on him. It was as if she'd done a complete 360 in her attitude. Making sure he had everything he needed to complete some of his tasks, along with items he didn't, Lonnie was unmoved by her change in demeanor. Developing a thick skin, he gave everyone, females especially, one chance, and one chance only, to fuck him over. Brenda had her one chance and shot her load; unfortunately, she fell short. Mr. Reynolds walked in right when Lonnie was about to walk out.

"Good morning, Brenda—and Lonnie, let me see you in my office," Mr. Reynolds spoke and commanded, never breaking his stride. With a cup of coffee in one hand, a bag from McDonald's in the other, he seemed to be in a rush. Lonnie wondered if he was hungry, because he sure as hell was. The bag of food hit Lonnie's stomach, making it even more hollow and hungry for nourishment.

"Good morning, Mr. Reynolds," Lonnie greeted him back. "Is everything okay?" Always having to deal with unfortunate circumstances, he wouldn't have been surprised if something was wrong. Regardless of him liking it or not, he knew the world was working against him in every way imaginable.

"Oh, yes. Everything is fine. Close the door," he told Lonnie. With the door closed, Mr. Reynolds slid the food across his desk and in front of a chair. "Have a seat and some breakfast."

Lonnie wanted to ask the man why he was feeding him, but he didn't. He summed it up to the same reason why the same man just gave him money yesterday. Mr. Reynolds was a stand-up guy. As the hot food made its way into Lonnie's mouth, he felt more than grateful for being at the shelter despite his initial feeling when getting the assignment.

Lonnie scurried to the chair and started tearing into the meal. That was enough of a clue to prove he was bad off in the food department. He didn't care what his behavior displayed.

Mr. Reynolds watched a starving Lonnie stuff the two hash browns and sausage McMuffin patty down his throat, barely chewing the pieces. He knew the vacant feeling within Lonnie's belly was filling up, thankful for the quick less-than-five-buck meal. He remembered back to his homeless days, scouring the street for a few coins to put together for a McDonald's breakfast meal. Frowning at the thought, he smiled at the young man before him, feeling a sense of gratification for helping him.

Lonnie stuffed the last piece of grease-covered hash brown into his mouth, and then licked the crumbs off the wrapper. Eating beans, drinking milk, and having his much-needed beer each day had him forgetful about what semireal food tasted like. He wasn't the least bit embarrassed in front of the shelter worker, knowing Mr. Reynolds has probably seen it all. All types of sins went on behind the closed doors of this shelter, since everyone who desired help was fighting some sort of demon.

"I don't know why you felt the need to bless me, but thank you," Lonnie finally spoke, consuming his last bite of food. He felt warm and tingly all over and wasn't the least bit caring that he hadn't had a drink to wash any of it down. Mr. Reynolds sat drinking the coffee.

"You're welcome, son," Mr. Reynolds said and nodded. "And I did it because I wished someone would've noticed I wasn't a tough kid, just one that couldn't catch a break, and helped me out every now and then. It's hard building yourself up when ya ain't got a brick to stand on."

Lonnie didn't know what to say, having the man be so kind to him. He'd already grown to like Mr. Reynolds because he'd given him the money and the bus passes; but now he felt even more of a connection. He wasn't sitting across from someone who pitied him, someone who wanted him to live in turmoil, or someone who was too caught up in their own life to see that he needed help with his. Lonnie was in the presence of someone who seemed to be genuine about helping.

"You're right, Mr. Reynolds. It has been hard for me to get things right. But I'ma keep trying," Lonnie partly lied in an effort to make the man more sympathetic to what he was going through. Some days, because his battles always seemed to win when he fought his hardest against them, Lonnie gave up and gave into the pills and liquor he'd grown to love. It wasn't the type of unconditional love one has for their child or partner, but the type of love that only an addicted person knows. Whenever popping a pill, he always hoped it would be strong enough to cure his ailment forever; when, in fact, the potent capsules only made his life much worse.

"Well, if you ever need to talk or some assistance, stop in and let me know. I might not be able to work miracles, but I can help you with a few things here and there."

Lonnie thought about asking the man for some more money since he'd broken the fifty buying over-the-counter pills and liquor for him and the bum, but opted not to. He knew the man would put two and two together, knowing that per his record, Lonnie was up to what he shouldn't have been indulging in. He chose to simply thank Mr. Reynolds, acknowledge his offer, and let him know that he'd reach out to him if he needed further help. He just wanted to get to know the man a little bit more.

In all the time since his mom died and he's been on the streets, the only person that gave him a shoulder to cry on had been Karisma. He'd been thinking of her often, wondering what her evil stepmother did to her, because he hadn't heard or crossed paths with her since that night she allowed him a place to crash. Not having nobody, it was hard for Lonnie to trust anybody.

Out of the office and starting on his first task, Lonnie was opening up boxes of food a company had donated to the shelter so smaller boxes could be assembled to help more people. He knew the chore would take him a few hours, if not all day, because the company had dropped the donation off in a small U-Haul truck. They'd blessed the shelter with fruit, vegetables, bread, cereal, chicken, canned goods, potatoes, and more. Some of the stuff looked like it was donated to the company and some looked to come straight from grocery stores because of how those boxes were labeled. He wondered if the shelter always got this food, but gave it to the workers and their families. Because he'd never gotten a hot meal in the soup kitchen comparable to the food he was opening today.

Appreciative of the box cutter Mr. Reynolds loaned him, he lined all the boxes up and slit them open one by one. There were about thirty, and he'd burned his nubs trying to peel the tape off the first ten before Mr. Reynolds handed the tool to him from his pocket. He was also happy that Mr. Reynolds told him he could take a box home as well. He wasn't treated this humanely when he was actually seeking shelter at the facility.

"Lonnie, darling, please be a dear and make sure all the boxes get broken down and tossed into the Dumpster after you're all done. I forgot to write that part on the task list," Brenda said, peeking into the room and interrupting Lonnie's work flow.

Not liking the woman referring to him as "dear" and "darling," Lonnie took a deep breath before responding. He didn't want to snap on the secretary, but she was treading on thin ice. Already having an underlining dislike for women, the cards of dislike were stacked against her even more. Lonnie answered smartly. "I figured as much. I might be considered a deviant, but my momma taught me some manners before she passed away."

Not knowing how to respond, and instead of the woman giving Lonnie her condolences and saying 'sorry for your loss,' Brenda nodded and disappeared out of the doorway just as quickly as she'd peeked in. That made Lonnie resent females even more. To him, they were always quick to run their mouths but not as quick to be supportive. He hoped Brenda would stay clear of his path for the remainder of the day.

Breaking down and repackaging a few more boxes, Lonnie then carried the unsalvageable ones to the trash.

"Oh, shit! Please don't call the cops. I swear I wasn't doing nothing but looking for something to eat." Standing before Lonnie was a girl around his age, with long locks and a pretty face. Although she had smudge marks of dirt and fresh purple bags underneath her eyes from not sleeping, Lonnie still thought she was attractive. Much easier on the eye than Megan.

"Naw, you good. I ain't nobody to be calling the cops," Lonnie nonchalantly replied, then tossed the boxes into the trash.

"Good. Well, not good that you ain't nobody but good that you ain't calling the cops. Well, not that I'm agreeing that you're nobody—" the homeless girl was all caught up on her words. "Damn, nothing I say seems to be coming out right."

Lonnie laughed. Not offended at all, he actually found the girl a little amusing. He hadn't a reason to laugh in a long time. "Again, you're all right. I know what you mean."

The girl, seeming relieved, took a big bite of the donut she was holding. "Great. I'm starving like a motherfucker, so you've gotta excuse me for not showing any manners." Chomping down on the donut like a savage, she gobbled the entire tasty snack down within three bites and maybe ten chews. "I would offer you one, but I don't know if you eat from the trash. They were still closed up in the box . . . that's if you're interested."

Lonnie threw his hands up. "Naw, I'm good; but I ain't judging you tho'. I know how it is to have hunger pains," he related to her, making her doe eyes soften. "Matter of fact, I'm doing some work at this shelter, and they've got a big donation of food today. I can sneak you a box real quick if you want it," Lonnie offered. He didn't know why he was being so nice to the girl and willing to risk getting in trouble for sneaking her a box. It might've been because he wished someone would've just given him a hand instead of a cold shoulder when he was on his knuckles.

"Hell yeah, I'll take a box of food. Me and my dad been living off scraps for a little over a month. We've caught a bed at this shelter a few nights, but shit's been rough."

"I know all about rough. Say no more. I'll be right back," Lonnie assured her, then disappeared back into the shelter. Barely having help himself, he wanted to help the girl. Grabbing a food box, he made sure the hallway was clear before darting to the back door. He hadn't thought of an excuse to give if Brenda or Mr. Reynolds saw him, so it was a good thing neither of them popped up.

"Wow, I don't know what made you be so nice to me, but I'm glad that you did," the girl showed her gratitude, then bent down to inspect the box. She was truly appreciative of Lonnie and what he'd done for her. Even though she didn't have a refrigerator to store the items or a stove to cook it on, she planned on feasting on all the perishables as soon as possible and sharing them with her dad. Opening the loaf of bread, she whipped a slice out and stuffed it in her mouth whole. Looking up from her unexpected treasure, she addressed him with a grin. "You don't know how much this means to me. Thanks again."

"It ain't no thang. If I see you around again and they've got something I can sneak out, I will."

The girl leaped up. "This box of food don't come with no strings, does it?" Having doubts about taking the sudden token, the homeless girl wasn't trying to be compromised or caught between a rock and a hard place when she and her dad sought shelter here.

"Look, like I told you earlier, I know what it's like to be down on luck. Plus, you're wearing the color pink, and my mom died of cancer. Ain't no strings attached. You can trust that." Lonnie didn't feel offended. With all the crazies of the night and men looking to prey on women, he understood the look of *should I trust this nigga* written on her face.

She breathed a sigh of relief, then opened up a bit. "Cancer, huh? That's fucked up. I wish they'd come up with a cure, or at least quit playing like the shit ain't scientifically made." She seemed like she was getting ready to stir up a philosophical rant Lonnie heard many times during his mom's support group sessions. "My bad, I just get emotional over the topic. My aunt died of cancer a few years back, and I guess I'm not over it. So I get it, and I'm very sorry for your loss. You, mom . . . I know that had to be a tough pill to swallow." Her words didn't seem like pity but empathy. "Sorry, I'm Trina, by the way." She said a mouthful, and that meant a lot.

Lonnie felt good on the inside. "No apology needed; and thanks for your condolences. You're right about it being a tough pill. I think it's still caught in my throat," he responded to Trina about how he felt. "Anyhow, nice meeting you, Trina. I'm Lonnie Eugene McKay. See how much you can trust me? I told you my whole government name," he smiled, to break up the seriousness of their conversation. Lonnie actually liked the girl. Not in a creepy way that meant he'd be stalking her or no shit like that, but her personality and how down-to-earth she seemed to be. A man like him could appreciate her chill temperament.

They stood silent sharing an awkward silence. Trina finally spoke the first word. "I don't want to seem like I'm grabbing the box and running, but I'm dying to get some of this food back to my dad," she honestly admitted.

Lonnie, not upset at all, thought it was admirable of her to want to feed her father. Just like he and his mom had been a team, it seemed like Trina and her pops were on the same level. "I ain't taking it like that. Here, take my number and call me when you come back this way. I'll try to look out again."

She took his number without hesitation. "I'll be sure to use it. Nice meeting you, Lonnie."

"Same to you, Trina. Be safe out there."

Lonnie watched Trina clear the alleyway before going back inside the shelter. Not because he wanted to make sure no one got to her, but because her cute little booty had just the right amount of jiggle as she walked. Hormonal, as any teenage boy is, Lonnie had felt a little stiffness in his boxers.

For the remainder of his second day, Lonnie stayed to himself. He was able to finish all of the tasks on his list without a weird interaction with the secretary or being weirded out by the other woman. He wasn't trying to be bothered by either of them, especially since he had happy thoughts of Trina on his mind.

By the time he was done, Mr. Reynolds was again gone for the day, and his office was locked up. It was Friday, and he remembered Brenda telling him he left early. Lonnie wasn't able to return the borrowed box cutter and didn't want to wait on the secretary to return from her cigarette break to give it to her. He made plans on returning it to Mr. Reynolds on the next day. He signed out, grabbed his box of food, and walked out so he could catch the bus. Lonnie knew there was a chance the same women from earlier would be on the bus heading home from their shift at work, but he dared the brazen one to try him again.

Sliding his bus pass into the machine, Lonnie took a deep breath to prepare himself for the potential passengers on the bus but didn't see either of the women sitting. He didn't know if it was lucky for him or them. He sat down in the first empty seat, and successfully stayed to himself. Thankfully, unlike this morning, Lonnie was able to get all the way to his stop nearest home and off the bus without having a problem. If the rest of the night went off without a hitch, only then would Lonnie consider himself winning.

CHAPTER TWENTY

Lonnie climbed the stairwell with his box of food, happy to have it and to be home after his second day of work. He heard several of the people within his building partying and enjoying their lives, and although he was a little depressed by his constant misfortune, he continued each step to his apartment with a grin on his face. He knew what was waiting on his nightstand, and to accompany it, he was about to put together a helluva meal from the care box of food.

A worked-over Lonnie stripped down, then climbed into the shower. Then he proceeded to wash away all the sweat and musk he'd built up from the day, plus carried around on him from the days before because his clothes hadn't been washed in days. He planned on starting and finishing his one load of laundry before Sunday.

The thought of how he was all alone having to take care of all his needs crossed his mind, making him somber. He wished there was a way he could permanently numb the pain instead of always having temporary fixes. Knowing he should've been probably seeing a psychiatrist who could help him talk out his problems, especially with women, but Lonnie didn't have insurance. That meant he had to self-medicate with street drugs or higher-priced prescription pills sold on the streets. Suffering from anxiety, pain, and depression, Lonnie needed help. However, he didn't want any additional government officials or even doctors in his business. To Lonnie, they all worked

together and ultimately against him. Too many coincidences don't equate into a conspiracy theory. Real talk,
when Lonnie thought about it, not even the medication
his mother was taking was effective and saved her life.
Sliding on a pair of dirty drawers, he found the Chill Pill
and self-medicated.

Lonnie put together a meal that left his stomach swollen
and satisfied. He'd fried potatoes in butter, ate a whole
can of green beans, and one can of yams, then baked the
chicken on top of some aluminum foil he'd cleverly put
on the racks to serve as a pan. Using all of the things from
the box he'd gotten from the shelter, Lonnie felt lucky
not to have spent a penny. Thinking about Trina several
times while preparing his meal, he fixed her a plate just
in case she hadn't come up on one.

He wanted to feel settled, and could've had he not
caught the DUI charge. As soon as he started feeling
content, gloom overcame him even quicker. He wished
there was a way he could stay in his apartment and have
his scholarship back.

He remembered back to the first day he got the keys
to his place and set it up as his own and how proud
of himself he felt. Comparing it to today, he knew his
mother had to be ashamed of the son she'd treasured
and worked hard to raise. Even if it meant serving more
community service days, he had to present something to
the judge and dean in addition to graveling for a chance
to start over.

With the offer of help on the table from Mr. Reynolds,
Lonnie thought that maybe he could get him to write a
letter in advance of the community service hours being
completed that would change the dean's mind of punish-
ing him so harshly. Lonnie even planned on asking for
probation on his scholarship instead of a blatant termina-
tion. His mother had told him several times before dying

she was a fighter and to learn from her to never give up. Lonnie never stopped wanting to make his mother proud. Dozing off to sleep high, he felt like he was in a good place.

"Good night, Lonnie," he heard his mother loud and clear.

"Good night, Ma. I love you," he said, starting to drool on his pillow.

"I love you too. Sweet dreams."

Lonnie woke himself up when he responded to the voice of his mother again. His eyes popped open; he jumped up from the bed and looked around with a racing heartbeat.

"Lonnie, are you okay? What's wrong, son?" He heard his mother's voice questioning him.

"I'm not crazy. I don't hear her for real," he spoke out loud, refusing to answer the voice again.

Going into the bathroom, he washed his face with cold water and relieved himself. Dangling the last few drops of piss from his penis, he flushed the toilet, then turned to leave the bathroom.

"I taught you better than that, Lonnie. Put that toilet seat down and wash your hands," he heard his mother's voice again.

This time he hollered. Jumping back into the wall, his eyes fell out of his head looking at a ghost. Lonnie had popped several pills with Kevin and the crew when they were and weren't partying, and he'd never seen his mother while high. Lonnie didn't know if his mind was playing tricks on him. First, he'd heard her voice; now, he was seeing an image of her. His mother was standing before him with her arms folded. She looked so real to him, so in the flesh, that he reached out trying to touch her.

"Wash your hands first, son."

Lonnie hurriedly moved to follow his mother's direction. Lathering his hands as best he could with the tiny bar of soap, he washed them just as he'd been taught, all the while, he saw his mother in the mirror standing over his shoulder watching. Rinsing and drying his hands, Lonnie spun around to hug is mother since he didn't get a chance to before she died—and she was gone.

"Ma! Mommy! Ma," he called out for her, running through the tiny apartment, looking everywhere for where she could've been hiding. She looked too real to him to have been a hallucination. However, after not finding her underneath the bed, in the cabinets, or the closets, Lonnie chalked it up to his mind having, indeed, played tricks on him, and the side effect of those Chill Pills might've been too drastic for him to keep popping.

Finding his cell phone, with no missed calls as usual, Lonnie called Kevin's phone to see if he had some other type of pills or could get some from ole' girl at the clinic in the morning. Irritated when he heard the click on the line before hearing Kevin's voice mail greeting play out, Lonnie still left a message, then followed up with a text. He figured Kevin was either partying or with a girl, seeing as if it was the same late hours he used to be lifted and twisted with the crew.

Turning off all the lights in his apartment and turning the ringer up on his phone so he wouldn't miss Kevin's return call, Lonnie retreated back to his bedroom and got even more comfortable than he was the first time his mother came to visit him. He was trying to create the same moment again. Dozing off to sleep, this time, he didn't hear his mother telling him good night.

CHAPTER TWENTY-ONE

Lonnie woke up Saturday, shivering and in a bed of sweat. He was hot but trembling cold. The last thing he remembered was seeing and talking to his mother last night, but not having a nightmare. He didn't know exactly why his body was having the unusual reaction, but it was, and it was scaring him. Getting up from the bed, he rushed to the kitchen sink and drank straight from the faucet until his stomach felt close to exploding.

Lonnie wanted to blame this reaction on the Chill Pill as the hallucination from last night, but wasn't sure because it didn't have the same effect the morning or night before. Seeing that Kevin hadn't called or texted, he tried again, but was sent to voice mail once more. Just as the first time, Lonnie sent a follow-up text, then texted himself to make sure his phone's messaging service was working.

Lonnie was lost as to why his friend hadn't reached out. Kevin had hollered at him to bring in another condom while in the middle of stroking a broad, so a part of him didn't think it was because Kevin was partying. With his own set of problems before him, Lonnie shook the thought of Kevin completely out of his head. He had a long day of nothing to do ahead of him.

It took Lonnie the whole morning to get himself together. Not able to prolong washing any longer, he'd walked to the Dollar Store for some dishwashing liquid and some body soap. In the tub, he squirted some dishwashing gel in it, then filled it up with hot water. Then he stripped his bed of the sweaty sheets and gathered his clothes. Everything went in the tub and sat for an hour or two soaking except for a shirt and a pair of jogging pants, just in case he had to leave.

This was his way of washing the clothes while saving money on the laundry soap and change he'd need if he'd used the washing machines downstairs. Lonnie had learned how to survive without having a lot of means, and that was cool with him. It was luck, a blessing, and help that he needed a lot of.

Once the clothes were done soaking, he rinsed everything out and laid them all around the apartment on the floor and across the little furniture he did have. That way, he'd save money on the dryer too.

The day had passed, and Lonnie hadn't done much of anything. He'd spent it washing, looking over all his books and notes from the classes he had, and even doing homework with the wishful thought on his mind he'd be given a second chance and the expulsion reversed. His intention was to work hard for at least two solid weeks before graveling and asking for pity.

Kevin still hadn't called him back. Not knowing how to take it, Lonnie chose not to call or text him again and to hear from him only if Kevin reached out. He didn't even know if he'd speak to Kevin first if he saw him on campus. Lonnie had gone from feeling confused, to concerned, to angry.

Not feeling the side effect, good or bad, of the Chill Pill, Lonnie started feeling even more anxious that it was wearing off, and he didn't have one on standby. Pacing back and forth, looking out of the window wishfully, wanting Kevin to pull up and say his phone was broken or some shit, Lonnie watched the sun start to set. That's when he really started to panic.

They say a true fiend always finds a way to feed their body its addiction. Lonnie was a living example of that. Kevin didn't have to call him back. He remembered the bum from yesterday. Lonnie snatched up the money he had left. With a couple of bus passes in hand and a few Tylenol, Motrin, and Snapback pills stuffed in his pocket he was saving for his Monday medicine, Lonnie walked out the door in search of a needed fix.

"Ahh, if it ain't my li'l buddy from the other day," the drunk bum slurred when Lonnie approached him.

"Yeah, what up, O. G.? You looking to make good on ya' word and do me another favor?"

Seeing Lonnie approaching, the bum felt like it was his lucky day. His reddened eyes would've widened to the size of saucers had they not been strained from watching the hood and out for an opportunity to scam someone out of a few dollars for hours. Assuming the teen was coming for his services again, the scheming bum planned on working Lonnie out of a fifth of alcohol, if possible, and a burger from the woman who sold dinners out of her house a few blocks down. He figured the odds of him getting his needs met were high since Lonnie seemed not to have any other person to go to. The liquor shots, potato chips, and juice from the other day pumped his addiction, fed his hunger, and quenched his thirst; but also made him want to try his hand at getting more. The bum didn't know where Lonnie came from, nor did he care. As always, he was out for himself.

***

After running down what he wanted from Lonnie in exchange for the ninety-nine cent can of beer he could legally purchase, the bum happily shuffled into the store leaving Lonnie wishing he didn't have to come up off so much money for such a small favor. Especially since it was taking away from what he could spend on pills. Lonnie was tired of always finding himself in situations where he had no control or options. Feeling cheated, had he had it his way, Lonnie would've only sprung for the fifth of liquor to be pointed in the direction of the trap house.

The bum told Lonnie what he wanted, and Lonnie agreed to the terms, though he really didn't want to. He wanted the bum to only buy the fifth from the liquor store, not want the food, but couldn't set the terms since he was the one in need. Sending the bum in with a ten-dollar bill, Lonnie now only had fifteen dollars for his pills before he'd only have lint in his pocket. The store run wouldn't cost the whole ten since he only asked the bum for a tall can of Milwaukee's Best beer. The can would only be ninety-nine cents of the ten. The bum had nine dollars to spend on whatever he liked. Lonnie felt that was more than enough for the bum only pointing him the right way.

Lonnie carried his beer along with them as they walked to the woman's house who sold food. He tried to talk and responded shortly when the bum said something to him. Lonnie wasn't looking for a person to help keep him up with conversation; all he wanted to do was get his pills and push on.

Walking down a couple of blocks, then around the corner, Lonnie sat on the porch while the bum ordered his food. He didn't get any because he needed his money for pills, plus he still had tons of food from the box he'd gotten from the shelter. He did, however, take the condiments that the bum didn't want. Lonnie laughed to himself, never having met a privileged poor person before, who had the nerve to be picky when it came to food.

Lonnie's mother always told him that if he didn't eat the veggies she'd cooked or the canned meat that was left at the end of the month before food stamps disbursed on the first, that he wasn't hungry enough and would starve. Knowing his mom wasn't the type of woman who'd lie on her back, spread her legs, and let a man bust it wide open for her to afford some groceries or him some name-brand clothes, Lonnie learned to work with what he had at all times.

As he took the onion and tomato from the bum, he ate them without a second thought. The seasoning that was on them from the burger and the sauce tasted good, so much so that he planned on going back to the house for a burger whenever he touched a large enough piece of money. Even a few scraps were considered a delicacy to Lonnie. He wondered what made the bum act privileged like Kevin when his knuckles were bruised just like his were from barely surviving day to day.

The bum was like a savage eating the burger. The house in the hood always sold food, no matter what time of the day it was. The grandmother cooked a lot of food all day while she was awake, stored it, or served it fresh, then her daughters and all their children served the folks of the neighborhood. Even if the whole house of people were asleep, which was rare, someone would rise and answer the bell. Pooling together three sets of food stamps, the house-run business was how they maintained with so many family members. It was the grandmother, her two daughters, and each of their three kids who made nine of them in a three-bedroom house.

The bum would've made number ten in the house had he been a good husband to the grandmother. The two dollars he'd spent on the burger was for him to cure the hunger pains in his stomach. The other three was his contribution to the household as a husband, father, and grandfather. He'd filled up the old juice container he'd gotten off Lonnie's buck with water from the hose on the side of the house he'd built for his family back in the day. That's before he experienced a hardship he never bounced back from.

No longer wanting Lonnie's company, he settled into his own pit of depression. Knowing he'd just kicked a crack habit, the bum made the decision not to go close to a spot with his feelings on his back. From experience, he knew a monkey could replace those feelings and wear him down even further than he was already wallowing. The bum pointed Lonnie in the right direction, described the house, and then hurried back to the store for some more liquor. He was using one vice to stay clean from the other.

Against his better judgment but thankfully getting his pills and leaving without a problem, Lonnie was back on the bus headed back to his apartment with a pocket of three different pills. They were five dollars each, set his pockets on zero, but was told to test each one to see which high he'd like. The blue one was for mental stimulation. The white oval one was for sleep. The third star-shaped purple pill freaked him out and was supposed to make Lonnie think he was Superman. He planned on welcoming the out-of-body experience if it was true. Lonnie wanted the hero's powers in real life.

Back home, Lonnie chewed up a few slices of bread and drank a glass of water to fill his stomach up. Since he'd cooked and eaten a decent meal earlier, there weren't any hunger pains forcing him into the kitchen.

The impromptu adventure had drained Lonnie. Finally cracking the beer open, he sat on the couch and turned the TV on. He didn't plan on watching it. He planned on it watching him. Popping the white oval-shaped pill, he drank the beer within a matter of five minutes, then got caught up in the lineup of old sitcoms that played late at night.

In the middle of an episode of *Sanford and Son*, Lonnie jumped, startled by his ringing phone vibrating across the table. Hurrying to pick it up before it stopped ringing, he thought it was Kevin returning his many calls and texts, but it wasn't. It was Trina calling.

"Hey, hello," he answered, slurring, and then wiped some drool from off the side of his mouth. He hadn't even realized he was slobbering.

"Hi, is this Lonnie?" she questioned, with a tiny voice he could barely hear.

Scrambling to find the remote, he turned the television down, then answered her question. "Yeah, this is me. Are you good?" Not like he could play captain and save a ho. He couldn't believe she was calling his phone so late. Remembering her saying she'd use the number, he hadn't expected her to do so at this time of night.

"Yeah, everything is as good as it's gonna get. I just wanted to thank you again for looking out with that food box. It really helped both me and my dad out of a cramped spot," she expressed her gratitude once again.

"Trina, please stop thanking me. It's getting kinda weird. I didn't do the shit for you to be forever in debt to me, but because I wish someone would've done that for me. I've caught a bed at that same shelter, although I'm putting in some free hours of work nowadays," he opened up with the truth to her. It wasn't that Lonnie was necessarily hiding it from her; he just hadn't given her his autobiography.

"For real? Say word," she sounded surprised. "You sho'll clean up well."

Lonnie took her words as a compliment, especially since it sounded like she was smiling on the other side of the phone. "Thanks. It ain't hard to clean up when you've got a little somethin' somethin' to work with." He remixed Mr. Reynolds's li'l speech to him. "I ain't got much, but it's ten times more than what I had." The more Lonnie divulged, the more he realized he'd fucked up royally by not saying no to drugs. He wished he had a beer to drown his reality in.

"I can't wait until I can get up on my feet. When I get a nudge on the back, I ain't never gonna look back." Trina sounded like she was wishing upon a star. The homeless girl, although without a place to call home, never stopped having a positive spirit. She truly believed she and her father's misfortunate circumstances would be temporary, and they'd be relieved from their ultimate stress any day.

Lonnie was lost in Trina's words. He'd gotten a chance, one similar to the one he was about to ask for again, and lost it all. Whereas Trina reminded him of his mom before; she was reminding him of his faults at the present moment. Listening to Trina talk about her unfortunate conditions and her personal story, he tried not to feel some sort of way.

"Hello, Lonnie, are you still there?" Noticing he hadn't responded to anything she'd said, she called out to him, thinking he'd hung up or fallen asleep.

"Uh, yeah, I'm here. My bad. I'm listening. I've just had a long day," Lonnie half-lied, knowing the pills and beer had him feeling a little loopy.

She giggled. "It's okay. I guess it's really my bad because I shouldn't have called this late without knowing if you had a girl or side chick." Trina was bold with her attempt to phish for information on Lonnie. She'd thought he was cute when he walked up on her digging for food in the trash, but was blown away by how nice he was. Trina wasn't looking to get wifed, play the side chick, or even be the girlfriend. All she wanted was a friend, someone with a few connections that could help her stop struggling at the level she was at, or upgrade. She wasn't necessarily using Lonnie because she thought he was cool and wanted to chill; yet her moves were somewhat strategic.

Lonnie laughed out loud. "Ain't nobody on my end to be worried about. You can use this number whenever you feel like it."

"Good, then I'll call you tomorrow afternoon." She spit her words out real fast, then the phone hung up. Trina knew she was on a free government phone that was only allotted 500 talk-time minutes per month. Out of every single one, she couldn't wait for the next twenty-four hours to pass when they were scheduled to reload. She had every intention on hanging around the shelter in the morning after they threw her and all the homeless people out. Trina wanted another chance to kick it with Lonnie, plus see what other shit she could get.

Lonnie, across town and holding his phone in his hand, felt like Trina had been bossy and hung up on him. He flicked the flip phone closed and found his bag of pills. He needed a melatonin pill to tap him all the way outta the game for the night.

CHAPTER TWENTY-TWO

Sunday morning, Lonnie woke up violently throwing up all the food he'd eaten yesterday. Bent over the couch, he didn't have enough energy to get up and run to the bathroom because of the sleeping pill, so he allowed his stomach to be emptied until he began dry heaving and overheating. That's when he fought against the sudden sickness, and slid off the couch to crawl to the bathroom. He was too light-headed to walk.

Lonnie stayed in the bathroom for about an hour trying to get himself together. With a cold towel on his neck, trying to bring down his spiked temperature, the young pill-addicted teen was trying not to pass out and die in the bathroom. It wouldn't have been any better even if someone, like maybe the friend he once considered Kevin to be before he strangely disappeared, was here to help him. Or maybe even Trina. An absolute stranger would've been better than having no one at all, even under the circumstances. The oval-shaped pill he got off the street last night had him going through some wicked side effects. His body was whopping its own. Lonnie was gonna have to live that struggle all on its own until the pill worked its way out of his system. It hadn't helped that he'd downed a cheap beer at the exact time of consuming the pill. All Lonnie could think about though, was getting his hands on another pill to help with the hell he was going through on that particular one.

Grabbing the toilet, he threw up all the water he'd been drinking from the bathroom sink faucet. In science class, he'd learned that if you are sick and to the point of throwing up stomach lining, that drinking water will give your body the fluid it needs to wash the stomach out, so to speak. He remembered the professor's lesson as he repeated the process until his stomach finally settled.

Out of the bathroom and feeble, Lonnie couldn't rest before cleaning up his vomit. He did so, found his couch cushions, and then grabbed a granola bar that was stuffed into the food box from the shelter to put something healthy in his stomach. Lying flat on his back on the dirty mattress, Lonnie didn't have the energy, nor did he care about, putting the sheets back onto the bed. All he could think about was feeling better so he could hit the streets to ask a few old women coming from church for some spare change.

Not able to doze off because he was busy running back and forth to the bathroom, Lonnie finally was able to drag himself to get dressed. He was determined not to miss the after church rush. Rushing out of his apartment, he almost slipped down the stairs to the first floor, but caught himself and was out the door only breaking a bead of sweat.

Lonnie couldn't believe the person he'd become. Although he wasn't addicted to hard-core drugs, he was still addicted to pills. He knew it was a sickness, but at one time, he'd been able to cope and was an A-student while taking them. If only he could get the right mixture going, the right amount of peace in his life, and some stability, he'd be able to handle his addiction better. Until then, he was only trying to cope. These are all things he kept telling himself, making his way to the megachurch a few blocks from where he lived.

The preacher was still deep in his sermon when Lonnie arrived. Feeling dehydrated but not having any money, he remembered the bum from last night getting water out of a hose on the side of a house, and did so himself. Filling up his palms about five times, Lonnie hydrated himself, then found a spot near the far side of the church parking lot. He needed to go in the church to get the Word, but Lonnie wasn't ready to face his sins, nor clean himself from them. The only thing he was prepared to do was beg for change; he'd lie to feed himself.

The first couple that came out had kids that seemed to be their grands, and they looked at Lonnie like he better zip his lips and not speak. Lonnie hung his head until they drove off, wishing he'd done better with managing the gifted fifty.

"Lonnie McKay?"

Hearing his government name, Lonnie looked up and lost the breath he needed to respond in his chest. His mom used to say God worked in strange ways. He laughed to himself wondering if this was an act of God or his mother sending a helper his way. Only a second after thinking about Mr. Reynolds's generosity, the shelter manager was standing before him with a Bible in his hand and a woman's purse in the other. Behind him was an elder lady standing with a cane, whom the purse belonged to. Lonnie managed to stop stuttering and finally speak.

"Hi, Mr. Reynolds. Ma'am," he acknowledged the woman who was frowning at him like he was no more than filth.

"I didn't know you went to this church, Lonnie. It's nice seeing you. This is my mother, Mrs. Reynolds." Lonnie took note that the woman wasn't introduced along with her first name.

Just like she'd nodded when he spoke, he nodded and smiled at the introduction in the same fake manner. In response to Mr. Reynolds's statement, Lonnie didn't know what to say. He couldn't say he was a member of the church or that he was even waiting on a family member because Mr. Reynolds might've asked who. Biting his lip and fidgeting, he didn't know his uncomfortable behavior told the tale Mr. Reynolds was all too familiar with. Except for in Mr. Reynolds's case, he used to beg for spare change from old folks while his mother sat in the congregation embarrassed.

That's the reason why Mr. Reynolds, now clean and a positive member of the community, takes his mother to church while carrying her purse each Sunday. Despite the weather or his mood, they'd be mother and son in the first pew. Not only does it refill Mr. Reynolds's cup of hope to keep fighting his addictions and demons, but allows his mom to be proud of her son in front of the worshipers he once lied to and begged from.

Mr. Reynolds, although off the clock as the shelter manager, jumped right into his helper role. "Stay right here for a second while I get my mother settled into the car," he told Lonnie, then grabbed his mother's arm to help walk her to the car.

The mother, who'd been evil eying Lonnie, didn't want to budge and leave her son and him alone to converse. You couldn't tell she was a Christian by the judgment she was passing off on Lonnie without knowing his story. All the woman wanted was to live the remainder of her golden years in peace and maybe find her son a nice churchgoing wife to make some grandbabies with. Tucked comfortably in the passenger,s seat of the Cadillac that was once hers but now handed down to Mr. Reynolds, she asked her Lord not to let her son forsake her for drugs again.

Lonnie knew what Mr. Reynolds's mother was think-ing without her speaking a word. He'd been looked at like scum by enough women to know she didn't think much of him or his worth. Not discriminating against the old woman, just like all the others, it was fuck her too.

"Look, Mr. Reynolds, I know you've got more import-ant things than looking after me on your day off. I'll see you on Thursday," Lonnie said, turning to walk away.

"Naw, it's cool, Lonnie. Hold up," Mr. Reynolds called out for him, then reached out to stop Lonnie by grabbing his shoulder. "Are you good? Do you need anything? A ride home or a few dollars?"

"Well, I hate to ask, but I do need a few dollars, as a matter of fact. Just enough to get me some stomach medicine. I think I got that bug that's been going around, but ain't got no insurance to go to Urgent Care. You think you could help me fill out the forms when I come in Thursday? It's all online." Lonnie thought he'd throw the last part in as a deflection from him asking for money. He'd also lied about having a stomach bug. Lonnie knew damn well he was trying to buy some more pills.

Mr. Reynolds knew Lonnie was playing him. He'd read his record from the court and knew the teen wasn't supposed to be doing drugs but looked to be high on them. Staring at the youngster, he saw droopy red eyes, a sunken-in face, and ashy skin. He having a bug could've been believable to Mr. Reynolds—if he didn't know the signs of a pillhead.

Not wanting to enable Lonnie, he offered his help another way. "I don't have any cash but can do you one better. Come on, I'll run you up to the pharmacy for some medicine, and then the store for some juice and crackers. You'll be like new in the morning."

Lonnie wanted to tell him no but knew he couldn't. He wasn't a fool and knew his story would've fallen apart in an instant if he turned down what was offered to him. Mr. Reynolds might've been off the clock, but he could surely report Lonnie's behavior when he was back on the clock. Lonnie made sure to play it safe. In the car ride to the both the pharmacy and the store, he stayed still as a statue. He even closed his eyes so he wouldn't get locked into a stare down with Mr. Reynolds's mother. She didn't hide her utter disgust and discomfort with the troubled teen riding in her backseat.

"How do you know my son?" The woman was rude as soon as Mr. Reynolds got out of the car to pump the gas.

Lonnie wasn't caught off guard or surprised. Mr. Reynolds's mother was just like all the women he's been meeting lately: rude, obnoxious, and bitchy. Lonnie wanted to wish himself out of the backseat and back to the far side of the parking lot, begging, where they'd found him at. Instead, he had to answer.

"I'm working over at the shelter he manages, ma'am," Lonnie tried being polite, as his mom taught him to be.

The woman grunted. "Are you one of them? Or like my boy?"

One of them? The woman sounded racist. Even more so than the most loyal Klan member. In this case, however, she'd drawn a fine line between homeless people who lived at the shelter, and those who worked to help those misfortunate souls.

"Um, I'm not sure, ma'am. I think you'll have to ask your son," Lonnie answered, trying not to say the wrong thing.

The woman grunted again. She was mighty mouthy when her son was out of the car, but quiet as a church mouse once Mr. Reynolds got back in. Lonnie noticed the change in her behavior and knew she wouldn't have a chance to interrogate him again because they'd never be alone again. He even made a mental note to never beg at that church again.

***

Missing all the church traffic getting caught up with Mr. Reynolds, Lonnie hadn't been able to beg from the worshipers. Climbing the stairs up to his apartment, he decided on being content with what he did have. All the queasiness and nausea he'd been experiencing earlier seemed to be over. He was thankful for that since he was starving. Choosing to keep it simple, he heated the skillet up with some butter and two pieces of bread. All he planned on eating was some toast.

While that was grilling, Lonnie began unpacking his bags. Mr. Reynolds paid for him to get a gallon of orange juice, two different types of stomach medicine, some Tylenol, and a box of saltine crackers. Putting everything away but the capsules of Tylenol, Lonnie took five of them to equal a 1,000 mg dosage, along with a chocolate-flavored Melatonin sleeping pill; then ate his toast, showered, and dozed off. He didn't have anything else to do.

CHAPTER TWENTY-THREE

That Sunday night, snoring loudly, Lonnie had been fast asleep ever since returning from being in the streets. Waking up early ill, then going out on a quest to beg, had Lonnie completely drained. It was his body's way of shutting down on its own to prevent him from killing himself with all the narcotics he was pumping into it. The Tylenol and Melatonin pills he'd taken only sedated him even more. Hours had passed, and he hadn't budged off the couch.

Not stirred by a sound, not even his ringing cell phone, he finally heard his name being yelled to the beat of someone pounding on the door. At first thinking it was in his dream, maybe even his mother again, Lonnie's finally eyes popped open to reality. It wasn't his mind playing tricks on him. It was Kevin.

"Where have you been and what rock have you been hiding under?" Lonnie bitterly questioned, sounding salty like a girl when he opened the door for Kevin to enter.

"Dude, that's my bad. I got into some shit last night similar to the madness yo' ass is into," Kevin called himself relating to Lonnie. "My dad's partner came in from out of town earlier than expected and busted my ass having a party. There was prescription pills, coke, and pussy everywhere." Kevin was dramatic as he told the story, but he was telling the truth. "Remember that scene in *What's Love Got to Do with It?* when Tina Turner comes home from the hospital after Ike beats her ass, and he's having a party in the house . . .? Yeah, imagine that scene, but with me having a lot more hoes and a lot more drugs. My dad's partner went psycho crazy, then called my dad. When my dad arrived, he called the cops and had the whole house of high motherfuckers carted off to jail. Me, I'ma be sent to some rehabilitation center up in the sticks when the semester is over."

After saying a mouthful, Kevin plopped down on Lonnie's couch and cracked the seal open to the bottle of 1800 he'd brought over to bid his friend a farewell. Although Lonnie wasn't living with him anymore, he still considered them friends. He also heard the voice mails and read the texts Lonnie sent once he was released from his dad's daylong berating session. Kevin had come with gifts: alcohol and a bag of various prescription pills. He hoped the gifts would keep him in the good graces of his pal, especially since he couldn't guarantee him ole' girl at the clinic would give him a file now that she had a record behind Kevin's wild party that got broken up.

Lonnie might've felt elated to have Kevin in his apartment with both his favorite vices yesterday; but today, the sentiment was bittersweet. No longer was Lonnie upset over Kevin disappearing. He was upset that Kevin was about to get a chance to get a clean slate and would be able to start over. Wasn't nothing similar to their situations, as Kevin stated when their conversation first started.

Kevin was getting to finish his semester, then start fresh the next one. Lonnie was expelled; no gray area about that. Kevin was getting a chance to detox in a rehab, whereas Lonnie would be left a pill junky. The more Lonnie compared him and Kevin in his mind, the more depressed and angrier he got. He found a reason to drink the liquor and pop the pills Kevin was presenting him with.

"To my last night partying." Kevin lifted his shot glass for a toast.

Lonnie didn't say anything. He wasn't toasting to no shit like that. Kevin had gotten him addicted to drugs, only to run off to get clean. Throwing his pill, then his shot, down his throat, it was clear to Kevin that Lonnie was on some hating shit, but he didn't give a fuck. It wasn't his fault he was born white and into a family that had enough money to fix their broken kid. Leaving the bottle and his stash, which was the sandwich bag of assorted pills, Kevin told Lonnie he'd see him around, then walked out door. He never mentioned they'd lose the pill hookup with ole' girl. He knew Lonnie would find that out when it was too late, but that wasn't his problem as a privileged kid with a daddy to bail him out.

Jealous, bitter, tired of always getting the short end of the stick in life, Lonnie watched out his window for Kevin to exit the building and drive off in his overpriced luxury car. As soon as he was gone, Lonnie picked another pill from out of the bag Kevin left and washed it down with another shot of 1800. It must've been an X-pill because he started to feel horny. Not having a girlfriend but still being a man with needs, Lonnie reached for his cell phone and clicked on a free porno site.

Clicking the link, he pleasured himself until climaxing. Then he stroked it back up and jacked himself until he came again. It was then Lonnie really wished he had a warm body to cuddle up with, that could probably be his partner in life.

With so much continuous drama and turmoil, Lonnie hadn't had a connection with a woman since Karisma. And even with her, it wasn't sexual. He was eager to get his jollies off with a chick tonight but settled for watching the porn over and over again. Lonnie wasn't gay; he just hated women who were bitches. Trina had been the only female not to turn his stomach into knots as of lately. The thought of her pretty face, cute curves, and delectable smell made Lonnie even hornier than he already was. Between the porno and being lost within his own drugged-up mind of dirty thoughts, Lonnie pleasured himself time and time again. He even called her a few times, but was disappointed to get the generic playback message that the caller couldn't be reached.

CHAPTER TWENTY-FOUR

Sunday night had been a long one. Now that it was Monday morning and the sun was shining, Lonnie was ready to climb into the bed, but he had things to do. Time had become of no matter to him. His days and nights were mixed up. Lonnie popped damn near one of every pill in the sandwich bag Kevin left. The stash and the 1800 were both faithful companions to him all night long. He spent the night pacing his apartment, jacking his dick until it was sore, and comparing Trina to his mom. As odd as it sounds, he was more attracted to the girl because she reminded him of the one woman who'd ever been unconditionally loving, kind, and compassionate to him. Lonnie hadn't said it, but that's why he was so compelled to help her. He'd helped his mother till her dying day as well. Since they hadn't spoken but for a minute over the weekend, he was hoping to run into her at the shelter. Just in case, he'd planned on taking the plate of food he'd set aside for her the other night.

Washing his face with cold water, he dressed, and then picked an Adderall pill out of the sandwich bag to help wake him up even more. The master pill, popular for helping even the laziest person rise and shine, would keep him up and give him the extra boost he needed to get his day going the right way. With the pill in his system, Lonnie didn't need a cup of coffee or even a Mountain Dew for caffeine.

***

Mr. Reynolds gave Lonnie an old disconnected cell phone with a wide variety of music already loaded on it, along with a pair headphones when he arrived for his second day of community service. He had gotten the 411 on the boy's record and recognized the pain in Lonnie's eyes as the same that once beamed through his own. He was also impressed with Lonnie's drive, being that the young boy was smart and enrolled in college even while dealing with the brutally harsh reality that is his life. Mr. Reynolds genuinely wanted to help Lonnie, and at least make his days working at his shelter as pleasant as possible.

Lonnie was in the zone listening to music and completing his list of tasks. Unlike the first two days where he had to move furniture and do a lot of muscular jobs that made him sweat, his third day was more tedious and involved less hard labor. He appreciated the simple tasks of cleaning the men's bathrooms, mopping the stairwells, and repainting the wall he'd repatched holes in from a fight between two men over a rock that wasn't supposed to be in the building anyhow. Brenda was gossiping on the phone about the event when he walked in.

Off an Adderall pill that he and Kevin nicknamed A-Pluses because they kept them on their A-Game, Lonnie bounced around the room needing a Ritalin to calm down. Every move he made and thing he did was quick and sudden. He found himself going beyond the call of duty while cleaning because he had so much energy.

He wondered what it would be like to pop A-Plus and an Abilify at the same time. Two seconds later, he answered himself by saying he wouldn't have the problem he had with Megan for sure. He'd been having strange thoughts about her lately and didn't know why. The only thing he paid attention to was how hard his dick got when he did think of her. Which was another strange thing to him. If only it would've done that the night they were alone and it mattered.

The worst thing ever was for Kevin to get a connect that worked at the clinic. Initially, Lonnie had been able to fight the side effects and not succumb to his pill-popping addiction. Yet, as he couldn't stop thinking about his mother, having anxiety about what he was going to do once he was kicked out of his apartment, and nausea spells brought about from not taking the pills, he'd called Kevin up with the last of his gifted fifty.

On that particular dreary day, he decided to no longer care about dropping a dirty piss test. Lonnie was tired of trying to live by the rules, only to be punished for doing so. Basing his future on his past and the current state of his present days, the troubled eighteen-year-old Lonnie didn't have hope that he'd be cleared by the judge even if he did stay clean. Bullshit always followed him. The day he called Kevin was the day he got tired of wondering why karma was kicking his ass so viciously.

With rap blasting in his ear, Lonnie had mopped three whole flights of stairs twice and was still pumping with energy. He couldn't wait to finish up with his list of work so he could run out of there to grab a beer. The mixture of the pill and liquor was Lonnie's trick to mellow out. Since he wasn't partying with Kevin, there wasn't any reason he needed to be bouncing off the walls drunk.

Lonnie bopped his head to the beats coming through the headphones all the way up the hallway to the janitor's room. So happy and content with the gift from Mr. Reynolds, he wasn't paying attention to anything else. He dumped the dirty water, cleaned out the mop, and then put everything in its place. Although he wanted to get out of the building and find some beer, he couldn't stop himself from overworking. He decided to clean the janitor's room up and arrange everything so he'd be able to access it quickly.

At the speed the pillhead was moving at, he'd gathered an entire bag of trash filled with empty cleaning solution bottles, organized the remaining bottles of solution by what they were or were needed for, and even swept and mopped the room's floor. He was sweating like he needed a break, but the A-Plus pill was his strength. He couldn't calm his adrenaline down if he wanted to.

Lonnie wasn't having a bad day until that damn Al Green song came on. It sent him into a pit of depression almost instantly. Needing to hit the next button so the song would skip to the subsequent one, Lonnie tortured himself by listening to each word Al Green sang. The thought of his mother always made him sad. She'd gone from the woman he'd loved and looked up to, to a symbol for the day his life went straight to hell. The melancholy teen wished his mother wasn't tied to such ugliness, and that tore him apart even more.

Feeling like he was rushing into a sinkhole of pity, Lonnie dug into his pocket fishing for the lonely pill he'd snatched from his stash this morning. Pulling it out like it was a rare gold coin, he reveled in its beauty like a true addict, then finally put it in his mouth. Washing it down with a handful of water from the workman's sink, he then leaned down on the sink in an effort to regain his composure. Popping pills had become his method of coping.

Lonnie didn't want to finish the few things he had left to do around the shelter extra sweaty. Deciding to wipe himself down, he took his shirt off, then shook it out, laying it flat on the floor. He wasn't worried about it getting dirty since it was already dirty, plus he'd just cleaned the floor. The only thing Lonnie was concerned about was freshening up the best way he could. Using some paper towels, he wet it and put a few dabs of the industrial soap the shelter had stocked on it. He figured a little bit wouldn't hurt or burn his skin, especially since he wasn't about to wash his pee hole with it.

After running the paper towel over his chest and underarms, he then used a fresh piece of paper towel he'd drenched with water to wipe his face, neck, his torso, and arms. The still-high Lonnie felt better and even a little calmer. He also got the bright idea to use the janitor's closet to wash up instead of the common showers if he had to move back into the shelter. At least in here he could be alone.

Right when he was getting ready to put his shirt back on, the doorknob jiggled, then the door opened. In walked the woman who'd let him into the shelter the other day. No matter where he was at, she kept seeming to pop up. For a slight second, he thought she was watching him per the request of Mr. Reynolds or the secretary; but then he recognized the flirtatious look in her eye like the slutty hood rat Megan had back when his dick couldn't get up. In comparison to Megan, there was absolutely nothing about the rag-wearing homeless woman that was sexy or eye catching to Lonnie except the humongous titties attached to her chest.

"Oh, I didn't know you were in here," the woman lied to Lonnie.

Standing in the doorway with her eyes fixated on his young chiseled chest, the woman had been watching him and knew he'd come in here. She just didn't want Lonnie to know about her stalkerlike ways. She knew she was older and had fallen from the graces of beauty she once ranked high in; yet, her body still craved attention. Her woman parts in particular.

Unbeknownst to Lonnie, because he was too consumed with his chores and the pills flowing through his bloodstream, he hadn't realized or felt the homeless woman's eyes watching him from the time he entered the shelter for work. Lonnie was too caught up in trying not to tell on himself by appearing out to space high.

After watching him through the small window of the doors on each floor level, the homeless woman saw him come from the stairwell and enter the janitor's closet alone. She even put her ear to the door to listen, and was pleased not to find out a destitute peer of hers had gotten to him first. The homeless woman didn't consider herself a stalker or mentally crazy, just fixated on getting the young man to notice her.

"Yeah, I was just about to leave from cleaning up in here," a caught off guard Lonnie responded, hurrying to slide his moist-from-sweat shirt over his head.

"Oh, wow." The woman looked around, marveling at how clean and organized the once junky room was. She'd been in here getting supplies to clean several times a day and knew what a mess things were. "You did a helluva job in here."

"Thanks." Lonnie kept it short and sweet, not interested in having small talk. Unlike several of the women he's come in contact with, this homeless lady wasn't getting smart with him or attacking his character. Yet and still, he wasn't trying to be around her. In his mind, befriending people from a homeless shelter meant he was accepting homelessness as his fate.

Digging the folded up sheet of paper from out of his pocket, he wanted to see what the next task was for him to complete so he could push on. Lonnie saw the flirtatious look in the woman's eyes as well as her attempt to fix her low-grade appearance. Nevertheless, just like he wasn't interested in the swish in her wide hips yesterday, he wasn't taking a second glance at her today.

"All right, stay up, and I'll see ya around," Lonnie told her, then got ready to dismiss himself.

The desperate-for-attention woman, not wanting the conversation to end, quickly moved into Lonnie's path so he couldn't walk out of the tiny closet. "Um, so, do you work here, volunteer here, or what?" She'd ask him anything to get him talking.

The furthest thought from the homeless woman's mind was the old adage "be careful what you wish for." She never thought she was barking up a slightly deranged boy's tree. From the outside, Lonnie looked like a normal young man who'd suffered a hardship, yet still was easy on the eye. The homeless woman was even more attracted because while on the streets, she hadn't seen a man on her level worth approaching. That's why a few days after seeing Lonnie, she'd gone out and stolen some clothes from the Salvation Army; and today, finger combed her hair into a Vaseline-slick ponytail. A smile spread across her face when she got young Lonnie to freeze in his tracks. That was the last time the homeless woman smiled.

A pill-infested Lonnie's eyes bucked wide, his breathing deepened, and his mind started playing tricks on him. The homeless woman continued to smile, thinking she'd locked him in with some interest, but was completely and utterly wrong. The perfume she'd managed to borrow off a paid shelter employee's desk and spray over her subtle funk might've been more of a risk than she'd anticipated. When she'd jumped in Lonnie's pathway, he'd managed to catch a whiff of how she smelled, suddenly taking his mind into a dark place of anger.

Had he not swallowed a handful of pills with a swig of beer when the sun rose this morning, or maybe if destiny would've lined his cards up differently and not crossed paths with Kevin in the first place, he wouldn't have snapped on the seemingly innocent woman.

Caught up in the silence instead of the devilish look in wannabe lover's eyes, the woman started to tingle with Lonnie being so close to her. Stepping in two steps closer, she felt his body heat radiating from him and mistook it for horniness building up . . . when it was really pure rage. She couldn't stop making moves when she was so close to getting what she wanted. The woman thought Lonnie wasn't moving because he was open and accepting her gestures. Never once did she think he was listening to the voices in his head.

"Don't be scared," the woman said her final words.

"I ain't fucking scared of you, bitch," Lonnie whispered coldly in a raspy voice at the woman.

Had Lonnie not been doped up on pills and experiencing side effects that required him to be locked away in a psychiatric ward, he would've separated the two women. He would've been checked into reality realizing the ruined woman before him wasn't like the women he'd hated and grew a passion of resentment for; but instead, was someone that was interested in him.

With his rough hands wrapped around her tiny neck, he could feel the dirt sliding off as he gripped it tighter and tighter. Slinging her arms in an effort to break free, the homeless woman began losing momentum each split second she was being choked.

"Why in the fuck did you bring your nasty-looking ass in here fucking with me? Huh? Is *this* what you wanted?"

Trying to shake her head no, the woman couldn't move because Lonnie's grip was too tight. She felt her face flushing, about to explode. She tried getting the words "let go" and "please stop" out of her mouth, but she couldn't. In spite of her landing punches to Lonnie's back, head, and even face, she was no competitor to his strength. The womanly parts she was looking to get nurtured were indeed wet, but with warm urine from her pissing on herself. The pungent smell began filling up their small space, but Lonnie's senses were honed in on the fragrance that reminded him of Megan.

The woman's dirty yellow skin began turning blue from lack of oxygen. The less she fought, the more Lonnie attacked. There was a small voice he could hear in his mind telling him to stop that sounded like his mother's. He squinted, trying to listen closely, but started shaking violently when he heard several voices at one time telling him to kill. The dangerous mixture of pills he'd carelessly swallowed when he woke up had Lonnie far out of his mind.

Foam erupted from the woman's mouth, a sign that she'd been strangled to death. Her body was limp although Lonnie's was still weighted on top of it. First thrown into a rage by the scent, he was now turned on by it because he was in control. Strangely, he leaned into the dead woman's neck and inhaled as deeply as he could, in his mind, cuddling up to Megan.

"You're so much prettier when you're not talking," he said to the dead woman. Unlike the night when they'd been in Kevin's bedroom and his dick failed to stay up, Lonnie felt strong and at a point of power with her limp and speechless body beneath him.

Megan had made him feel less of man, spread rumors about him, and like many of the women who crossed his path since his mother died—was a mean bitch. A mind-altered Lonnie didn't feel like a murderer; he felt satisfied for finally being able to have the last word.

Finally moving his hands from around her neck, he grabbed at his hardening dick, then ran a fingertip across the woman's mouth. Shaking his head trying to get the voices he heard to slow down and speak one by one, Lonnie was experiencing his first sadistic episode. He reached into his pocket and pulled out the box cutter Mr. Reynolds gave him to cut all the plastic from the new mattresses, and held it like a scalpel as his professor taught him in anatomy class. The first voice he'd heard was one telling him to cut her tongue out.

Before carrying out the first voice's order, he put his headphones back onto his ears and started bobbing his head to the music. He grinned psychotically, then proceeded to mutilate his first dead body.

Uncaring of the foamlike saliva, he pried her mouth open and pulled her tongue out. Then deranged Lonnie used his box cutter to slice the vessel straight from her mouth. Following the last order of the first voice, he stuffed her tongue back into her mouth and closed it up. The final gruesome thing he did was slice her lips from left to right with the sharp blade. Lonnie's manhood was as hard as steel. He didn't want to mutilate the woman's body he saw as Megan with sex; he wanted her to be silenced permanently.

The second voice Lonnie heard told him to get rid of the woman's body. That voice sent him into a panic. Still hyper off the A-Plus pill, he quickly moved around the room, trying to figure out how he was going to do just that. When he spotted the box of trash bags he'd just set on the top shelf, Lonnie knew he'd be able to fit the woman inside of one because they were industrial-sized. Detached and unstable, a now-cutthroat Lonnie quickly snatched them off the shelf, grabbed a few from the box, and then prepped her body for disposal.

Quickly checking her pockets first, Lonnie pulled out four crumbled-up dollars and a Lifestyle condom. Knowing he could use the few bills for something, he stuffed them in his pocket but tossed the free-from-the-clinic condom to the side.

Bending the woman over, he tied her neck around her legs by wrapping and taping a few trash bags around them until they were secure. Then he doubled up two bags, then two bags more, totaling four, and put the woman inside. Only five minutes into death, the woman's bones hadn't stiffened from rigor mortis. All Lonnie did was snap her bones out of the sockets to make the woman more flexible than she'd been created to be.

Dragging the bag to the door, Lonnie took his shirt back off and started cleaning the area where the woman's body had been with the cleaning solution within the closet. He was just as hyper off the pills as he was when he first walked in after cleaning the stairs. Bouncing his head and dancing, Lonnie was completely dismissive of the dead body waiting to be carried out. Once everything was back in order, he took a quick wash-up again and was able to slide his shirt back on in peace. No one disturbed him or caught him at the scene of the heinous crime.

Flicking the light switch off, he dragged the bag out of the janitor's closet and down the hallway. Twelve paces later, he saw Mr. Reynolds coming off the elevator with an envelope similar to the one he was handed before. Fresh out of the fifty, Lonnie hoped the envelope was for him.

"Hey, Mr. Reynolds, thanks again for the phone. The music surely helps my day go faster," Lonnie weirdly spoke—like he wasn't dragging a dead body up the hallway toward the exit.

"Yo, Lonnie, it looks like you're feeling better. You've been doing a fine job around here today. Matter of fact, go on home after you dump that trash and rest up. I'll see you around." In a rush, he disappeared. Mr. Reynolds gave praise where it definitely wasn't due. He wasn't wise to the crime that had just gone down on his watch. Had he been, he would've killed and tossed Lonnie into the trash too. Lonnie wasn't the only one with a dark past and a secret . . . or who could lose his mind.

CHAPTER TWENTY-FIVE

Lonnie felt his heart pounding as he walked away from the shelter toward the bus stop after stashing the dead woman's body behind the Dumpster. His first kill. He was relieved to have not seen Trina while doing his dirty work. Every few moments it was like he had an out-of-body experience and could see himself but wasn't in his body to control himself.

Getting blood on his hands for the first time hadn't traumatized Lonnie; instead, it satisfied his need to shut women up. As sick as it may have seemed to the normal person who's never lived through one traumatic event after the next with no help, to a troubled youth like Lonnie, the pain he inflicted on the woman helped him release the pain he'd been holding in. Walking toward the bus stop to go home as if nothing happened, Lonnie wiped his brow from the sweat that had built up from dragging the woman outside. He wasn't the least bit tired, just worked up. Not feeling remorse, only satisfaction, Lonnie knew without a shadow of a doubt that he could kill again.

"Hey, you." Trina walked up seemingly out of nowhere.

Lonnie damn near jumped out of his skin. Pushing the thoughts of the murder to the back of his mind quickly, or at least trying to, he didn't want Trina to pick up on his edginess. "Hi," he responded shyly, a little jittery and nervous since he knew what he'd done. "You just crossed my mind a few seconds ago."

"Oh?" Wrapping her finger around a strand of hair making a spiral curl, she mistook Lonnie's words as flirtatious ones. "Care to share the details of those thoughts?"

"Um . . ." Lonnie hesitated, trying to come up with a quick, yet believable lie on the spot. "Nothing major, just if you were okay or if I had missed you stopping by." He wasn't telling an absolute lie. Those weren't his thoughts a few moments ago; however, Trina had crossed his mind once or twice.

"Aww, Lonnie, you sure do know how to make a girl feel special."

He gagged. "That's not a phrase I've ever heard my name with." Lonnie was amused by Trina's read of him. So much so that he wanted to keep the charade going. As she stood before him doing some funny thing with her lips to make sure he saw the pink gloss on them, his mind flashed back to him jacking his meat to the porno. At that moment, he no longer had to wonder how his manhood would respond with all the mixtures floating in his bloodstream. Even Trina saw the rise in his pants.

"Okay . . . That's weird," Trina didn't waste a second calling Lonnie out. He followed her eyes straight to his erection, then back up straight so they were looking back face-to-face.

"Shit, that ain't nothing." He laughed uncomfortably, taking a cop. "I gotta take a leak but didn't want to interrupt our conversation. Especially since you claim I make you feel special," Lonnie lied, trying to divert her attention from the hard-on.

She giggled. "Although I'm flattered, don't let me stop nature. I'll be here when you get back."

Lonnie walked off with his head low and sort of feeling like he did when things went terribly wrong in Kevin's bedroom. A loser. Going on the side of what once was a laundromat, he turned his back to a watching Trina and jacked himself quickly and erratically till he came. From the experience he had last night, Lonnie knew there wasn't another way to relieve the stiffness. Shooting his load off like he was pissing, he locked his legs and fought against the urge to quiver. During the euphoric moment, a blurred image of the girl he'd killed popped into his head.

He shook his head from left to right like he was clearing the image from his mental Rolodex, then looked over his shoulder at Trina. She was looking the other way, but tapping her foot like she was growing impatient. Lonnie started to yell that he'd be one second, but was glad he didn't when he saw a squad car roll up and slow down in front of Trina. Quickly stuffing his now-squishy penis back into his pants, he darted up the alleyway while making sure to stay close up to whatever garages were left standing. Not looking over his shoulder again until popping out at the end of the block, he saw Trina looking around for him, dumbfounded. Lonnie didn't stay around to see what happened next.

Trina felt like a fool when the cops pulled up on her asking why she was holding the corner down. Knowing what they were insinuating, she dismantled their assumption and told them she was waiting on someone. The foolish part came in when she tried finding where Lonnie was so she could point him out. Of course, he was gone, and she seemed like a liar. Trina was lucky they only told her to push on.

Walking away, wondering where Lonnie had disappeared to, she was bummed for two reasons: she hadn't gotten a box of food or a small treasure to open up like a kid on Christmas Day; and two, she thought he'd be shading her from here on out. Deciding not to let the thought consume her, she opened her purse and pulled out an apple that came from the food box he'd given her.

She snacked on that all the way back to the hospital. Her dad was faking having pains in his body so they'd have somewhere warm to sleep with some nibbles of food. This scam got played by them every so often and in emergencies. Every homeless person has a clever way of surviving.

CHAPTER TWENTY-SIX

Opening his eyes when his alarm clock went off on Tuesday morning, Lonnie wasn't asleep, just resting his eyes. He'd been popping pills and drinking Red Bulls all night. Although during some of that time he'd thought of Trina, he'd thought more of the murder he'd committed and what the cops wanted when they pulled up on Trina. He continuously flipped through the channels to see if a trash man, innocent bystander, or another homeless person, or even those two cops he'd laid eyes on himself, found the body he'd stashed and jumped at every noise. He kept thinking he heard knocks at his door or taps at his window, although he was three floors up. Paranoia had set in, not regret.

Climbing out of bed with his clothes still on, Lonnie was prepared because he'd gotten dressed in the middle of the night. Between pacing back and forth looking out the window, watching for a breaking news story, and washing the box cutter over and over with soap and water, he'd showered and prepared for his community service day at another shelter. This one was a women's shelter for those who had kids.

Lonnie wondered why the judge had him working all over the city for free when he'd told her he was penniless and struggling himself. He knew it was her job to punish him because he was indeed driving under the influence; yet, he felt no justice was served because he was now on the fast track to being a complete failure. Not having time to throw himself a pity party, he shoved a few pills in his pocket to help him cope throughout the day—just in case he needed them. Not only did he hear the voices he heard yesterday, but now one that sounded like the woman he'd killed as well. Lonnie's personality was splitting. He was losing his mind.

Almost out the door without the box cutter, he doubled back and slipped it into his pocket.

The women and kids' shelter was much different than the other shelter Lonnie had been working at. Whereas the homeless population of the other shelter was gone during the daytime hours, at this one, they got to stay all day. That meant Lonnie had to stay on his p's and q's, and not submit to his pill addiction for the whole community service shift. He was worried because of his track record with women. He and they seemed not to ever get along. That was evident to him since he'd now murdered one. Trying to push yesterday from his mind, the teen walked to the door of the shelter to face his woes . . . as always, not having a choice.

A woman with a little boy on her hip let Lonnie in, then a girl that appeared to be around Lonnie's age instructed him to sign in and have a seat while she called the director. This shelter seemed to have a rigid set of rules, unlike the other; so he told the young girl he needed to excuse himself for a breath of fresh air because he was nervous about his first day and would be right back.

Telling a lie because he wasn't fearful of his first day, Lonnie had really thought quickly on his toes and wanted to hide his stash of pills. He'd only brought along an extra Adderall in case the one he took wore off and a few of the Tylenols Mr. Reynolds mindlessly purchased for him. Using his finger to dig up some dirt in the flowerpot by the door, he looked around to see if anyone was watching, then put the pills in the hole, making sure they were covered. Lonnie made a mental note that his fix was directly underneath the wilting red flower, then found his way back into the shelter.

Miss Humphrey, large in stature, was standing by the table he'd signed in a few moments ago with her arms crossed and her eyes looking over the rim of her glasses. Lonnie felt the woman ripping him apart as he approached her with his hand extended to shake hers.

"You're late," she spat, cold and unwelcoming.

Instead of backing down and apologizing, Lonnie chose to stand up to the woman. With one murder already under his belt, Lonnie felt powerful and like he'd put this woman in a permanent place if she needed him to. "No, I was here and just stepped out for a breath of fresh air. I was on time, actually," he set the woman straight. Quickly digging in his pocket, he pulled out the assignment sheet and handed it over after looking for her name. "Miss Humphrey, I'm Lonnie McKay."

She looked like she wanted to say so much more than "right this way." Putting her eyes back where they needed to be, she escorted Lonnie through the shelter and told him to pay attention because this tour wasn't going to happen again. Lonnie made sure his ears were open. It wasn't that he was listening to her because of her ranking, he simply didn't want to be bothered with the woman in the future. He hoped, like the other shelter, he only had to get his task list daily and push on.

Bumping into kids and interrupting group therapy sessions, Lonnie learned his way around the shelter. He thought it was pretty neat how the place was set up like a big apartment building for homeless women. They even got daily donations from people dropping off their kids' old clothes and toys.

"Amanda, this is Lonnie McKay. He'll be helping us around here for a while." Miss Humphrey introduced Lonnie to the woman who'd been sitting at the desk by the door. Amanda was like the manager and would oversee him.

Unlike Brenda, she wouldn't give Lonnie a list but give him his tasks and check the last one as he finished. Off rip, Lonnie could tell he wasn't going to like the controlling woman. She reminded him of someone he hated, yet he couldn't figure out exactly who. He didn't have time to with Amanda breathing down his back like a dragon.

"Let's go, Lonnie. Let me take you out back to the shed so you can get started mowing the field the kids play in. From there, you'll be going around front." Putting on a sunhat and grabbing a book, she marched toward the door, then waited on him to catch up.

"I swear I hate a power hungry bitch," he mumbled.

"Huh? Did you say something?" Amanda smartly questioned, knowing she couldn't have heard him curse, let alone call her a female dog.

"Nothing, but lead the way," Lonnie said with a grin on his face, liking the way she looked from the back.

The field the kids played on was like half the size of a football field and covered with blades of grass tall as a toddler. Thinking it was cool for them to have an area designated for the kids and moms to bond and play, Lonnie couldn't understand why the chore hadn't been done sooner. Only because it wouldn't have made his work for the day backbreaking. After making sure all the sticks were stacked by the wall of the shelter, he mowed three or four rows back and forth, dumping the bag before the fifth time. Amanda was watching him with a close eye, and even Miss Humphrey had come out to check his progress. Lonnie felt like a modern-day slave.

Sweat was pour off his body. Taking off his shirt, he flung it across the fence so it could dry in the sun, then continued mowing the play area. He turned a shade darker and felt his skin sizzle in the heat, all the while never slowing up. The Adderall had him moving at the speed of a bullet. Feeling dehydrated and close to passing out, he finished the last row he planned on doing, then took a break for some water. Even his five-minute water break was monitored by Amanda.

Before going off break, Lonnie's cell vibrated in his pocket. He knew who it was without looking at the screen because since Kevin went to rehabilitation, no one had called except Trina. Digging the phone out, he nervously fumbled with it. The unknown nature of the call would torment him relentlessly if he didn't pick up. He had no choice if he wanted any sort of calmness in his already-confused mind. Lonnie didn't know if Trina was sitting in front of the cops, maybe to set him up. Nevertheless he said hello.

"Wow, after yesterday, I wasn't sure you'd answer." Getting straight to the point, Trina was slightly salty about Lonnie pulling his shake move. Not only had she felt dumb in front of the cops, but she wasn't able to stop thinking about him through the night. She'd been checking her phone relentlessly for the free minutes to load.

Her father, which they were close as daughter and dad just as Lonnie had been as son and mom, even noticed something was wrong with his first and only. Had he not been hooked up to an IV pumping out morphine for a pain he really didn't have and antibiotics for a self-inflicted wound, he would've given her an in-depth speech about how not to get caught up with a man. Trina's dad was more concerned with her surviving;

and in the meantime, helping him not fall further to the wayside. His daughter, although it was his God-given job to protect her from harm and provide for her, had stepped into the role as the protector-provider, and he didn't want to see her go.

"I broke out the other way when I saw you talking to the cops. You know black lives are at stake all over the globe, especially men," Lonnie played it off like he wasn't a monster. He figured if Trina was so bold, he could be just as bold.

Trina responded, "Yeah, they rode up on me asking me why I was holding the corner down. They let me go with a warning after it seemed like I was lying about waiting on you," she huffed and puffed. "But, I guess I get it. I would've called you last night, but my minutes were late reloading."

Lonnie didn't have time to dissect her story; Amada was behind him and tapping on his shoulder.

"Excuse me, Mr. McKay, but your break is up. You'll get another one in a couple of hours." She was rude, not even backing off to give Lonnie some privacy.

"Oh, my bad, I see you've got a warden over you as we speak. I'm hanging around outside if you get a minute to sneak off." Trina held her breath hoping Lonnie would tell her he'd be right out.

"Um, I'm not at that shelter today, but I'll call you back in a few hours. There's a snitch working, so I wouldn't linger around back if I were you," he snuck in a lie, not wanting Trina to find the dead woman he'd stashed while scrambling for food.

"Oh, snap! It's a good thing you told me because I was about to see if that wannabe uppity secretary threw out the uneaten donuts from this morning." Trina was disappointed. Popping the seal open of the cereal she'd gotten in the food box, she grabbed a handful and threw it in her mouth. Trina was hungry and had a taste for the donuts, but wasn't getting ready to risk getting caught by a snitch. "Call me later so we can chat it up or chill. My dad is in the hospital, by the way, so I could really use that callback."

Lonnie hung up, wanting to smack Amanda for not backing up. He had to bite his tongue to keep from telling the woman he was a grown-ass man. Lonnie's workday only got worse. He mowed the front lawn, cleaned graffiti off the walls in the alleyway, and took almost twenty boxes of trash to the curb singlehandedly. Feeling like a work mule with Amanda delegating his duties one by one, Lonnie wanted nothing more than for five o'clock to arrive. It's like they worked him as hard as they could for every single second that they could since he only came in one day a week.

With his time signed off for the day, he hurried out of the shelter and to the flowerpot he'd hidden his pills in. After working for the two less-than-pleasant women, Miss Humphrey and Amanda, he was ready to pop them before he even got home. Digging his finger in the dirt under the wilted red flower like he remembered, he didn't feel any pills underneath his fingertips.

"What in the fuck?" he said out loud in a panic, digging all around the flowerpot, even pushing soil onto the ground. "I *know* I put them in here!"

"Yeah, I know that you did too. That's why I came and got them out of there behind you," a woman's voice startled him.

Looking over his shoulder, Lonnie shook his head, realizing he was cold busted. It was the woman who'd let him in with a baby on her hip. He hadn't paid her a lick of attention earlier, but now he was forced to. This time around, the small child was in a flimsy stroller by her side, and her stance proclaimed an attitude with her hand on her hip. Climbing off his knees, Lonnie stood up and walked over to her so their conversation could be held in private.

With all of his attention on her, the homeless woman opened her hand up to expose Lonnie's pills sitting in her palm. "These what you're looking for, right?" Sneaky in her own right, she'd watched Lonnie walk out of the shelter earlier and every move he made around the flowerpot. She'd also made herself inconspicuous when he looked up and around to see if anyone was watching him.

"It ain't much I can say. You know more than I do; so how 'bout you tell me what's up." Lonnie didn't feel like playing games. Rationalizing the situation, he knew the woman could tell Miss Humphrey or Amanda about him hiding the pills and get him in trouble ultimately with the court. For that reason only, he was willing to hear the homeless woman out.

The homeless woman had no intention of carrying the information to Miss Humphrey, but to use it for her own gain. She wasn't interested in Lonnie sexually, or to play step-daddy to her baby, or for him to even be a friend since she didn't have a single one in the world. The homeless woman wanted more of the pills she'd found Lonnie hiding, along with some hush money. After finding the pills, then asking around about him, the homeless lady knew Lonnie would be desperate enough to pay off both of her requests without a fuss. At least she thought so.

"I don't want much. Just ten pills and twenty bucks each Monday you come. When your community service hours are up, so is our relationship." The homeless woman couldn't hold the secret over Lonnie's head forever even if she wanted to. Once he was done with the hours at the shelter, she was sure they'd never cross paths again. Little did the sheisty homeless woman know, Lonnie was on the verge to running back in the same down-and-out circles as her.

"Naw, I ain't gonna be able to work that out for you," Lonnie honestly replied. "I can't even guarantee myself ten pills and twenty bucks a week." He was being honest, but the homeless woman didn't care or question why he even had to do community service.

"Then I can't promise you I'll keep my mouth closed. You gonna have to give me something, homeboy. Now that I've got something on you, you've gotta do something for me. You know how this goes." The homeless woman, not used to having the upper hand, wasn't about to let up on the one person that she could actually get something for nothing from. Having sucked a lot of strange men's penises, stolen from stores for diapers and formula, and even stuck drugs up her coochie for a pimp, blackmailing someone didn't make her feel shameful but powerful. "Tell me what you trying to part with then, nigga. 'Cause I ain't walking away with nothing."

Thinking for a second, Lonnie thought about the stash he had at home and offered her ten of the pills plus some of the 1800. It wouldn't be a loss to him since it was first Kevin's anyway, but he wasn't about to give her all of his stash, leaving him fidgeting to get high. Nor was he about to make a deal he couldn't keep up. Lonnie had to get his way. He continued to play the woman. To make the offer sound sweeter, he told her he'd bring the pills she wanted back tonight. "I can be back before the shelter closes; and you won't have to wait a week to get a fix."

The offer, not as great as what she presented, sounded sweet to the homeless woman's ears nonetheless. At least the part about getting the pills later tonight did. Before accepting, she brought the money back up because she realized he hadn't. "What about the twenty? I'ma need that."

"What about five more pills? I'll double up on Tylenols to get by, but I ain't got no cash or nothing else to offer,"

Lonnie countered her request with that being his final offer. Not being difficult, stingy, or trying to get over on the woman who held a piece of his fate, Lonnie couldn't offer money he didn't have.

"Ten more, so that'll be twenty," she tried her luck.

"Five," Lonnie was firm, which shook the homeless woman into thinking his next response would be to forget their deal altogether because she'd pushed it.

Not wanting to miss the opportunity to get high altogether, she shook hands with Lonnie, giving him the pills back at the same time. "Don't play me. If you don't come back tonight, I'll be in Miss Humphrey's office bright and early by nine a.m."

Lonnie, hating that he was backed into a corner and being blackmailed by a homeless woman with less than him, knew he was about to do the woman the same way he'd done the homeless woman yesterday. "Don't worry. We've got a deal, and I've got you," he responded to her with ill intentions.

Satisfied with his answer, she spun around and tried opening the door while pushing the baby's stroller in at the same time. She bumped the wall, stirred the baby, and cursed for the little one to go back to sleep. Witnessing the woman being such a detached mother made Lonnie dislike what the so-called woman represented even more. He wondered where all the good women were at that his mom told him he'd one day find. Seeing the homeless woman struggle, Lonnie turned and walked the other way. He refused to lend one hand to help her manipulative ass. When he did lay a hand on her, it would be to kill.

CHAPTER TWENTY-SEVEN

Lonnie found himself at a gas station near the liquor store asking if he could pump gas for whatever people could spare. Only needing a few dollars to get a pint of gin, he wasn't planning on buying the bum his own personal shot but giving him a few pours into the cup he carried. Lonnie wasn't willing to be the bum's sponsor with his own addictions needing nourishment. After pumping gas, sweeping the lot clean of glass and debris for the attendant, and emptying the trash cans, Lonnie walked away ten bucks richer. It burned a hole in his pocket all the way to the liquor store.

At home, Lonnie drank and drank, then drank some more. With the bottle of gin he'd hustled up on almost gone, he drank it down till he couldn't get another drop out, then licked the rim. Lonnie had been lost in his thoughts and trying to stop the voices since getting home from the shelter. He couldn't control when they'd talk to him or for how long. All he knew was that they stalked him, screamed over each other, and made his head throb. He was back to doubling up on over-the-counter painkillers.

In front of the TV, he slid his hand inside his sweaty drawers and kicked back to relax. He tried to enjoy the peace of his apartment, even though he wasn't going to have it much longer. Serving his community service hours day in and out was like a prequel to the life he was about to live, back within the shelter and scrambling for the food in the soup kitchen. Relieving the nightmare of being cooped up with a bunch of men again shook Lonnie into a dark place.

Nothing about the day had gone right. First, taking a shot to get over the stress, humiliation, and anger he'd dealt with for six hours while Amanda watched over his shoulder, then went through his work with a fine-tooth comb. Lonnie then took a shot for how his day ended. Hours had passed, and he still couldn't figure out a way up out of the fucked-up situation other than to kill. Since the other woman hadn't been discovered, Lonnie felt confident that he could get away with committing the crime again.

No matter how hard he tried thinking the day away, time kept ticking closer and closer to eleven p.m. That's what time he had to meet back up with the lady from the homeless shelter this Tuesday night. To say he wasn't looking forward to it wasn't an explanation enough. He wished he hadn't taken the pills out of his pocket in the first place, especially since there wasn't a search done of his person as expected. Trying to outsmart the system, the slick young man ended up outsmarting himself.

Lonnie was downright pissed about the woman having something to hold over his head. He hadn't done anything the whole day but his tasks underneath Amanda's management, yet still found himself in the middle of some bullshit. Mentally adding her to the list of women whom he wished the worst in life for, Lonnie hoped that was the one wish the universe would grant him.

The caretaker's girlfriend, the daughter of the funeral home director, rat-ass Megan, the dean of students at the college, and even the judge all had something in common. They all had a hand in ruining his life. Not one time had they been nurturing to him like his mother told him the softer sex should be. Lonnie drank each time he thought about how each of the women played their roles of being completely heartless to him. Not once did they offer support, their condolences, or even a pat on the back accompanied by an encouraging word. They all had been completely heartless to him losing his mother, purposely being the worst possible human beings that they could be to him. All except Trina, who hadn't answered not one of his twenty calls. He was now almost out of minutes. He sank into an even deeper place. Crushing the can of liquor with his hand, he tossed it across the room feeling rage build up inside of him. If given the opportunity, he would've snapped all their necks.

Lonnie's mind drifted back to the day his mom died, how he felt at the hospital standing in the room with her dead body, and how she suffered so many months before living her last day. Tears gathered, then fell out of his eyes and down his face uncontrollably when he remembered how she would be bent over in pain, crying in agony, and then thanking the Lord when the worst part passed. Lonnie prayed she'd send down some of her strength, forgetting to say Amen. He wished he had Trina to talk to, since she knew firsthand how it was to lose someone to cancer.

The prescription pills he got illegally had Lonnie's personality splitting. He was up, then down; happy, then sad. The walls in his apartment began closing in. The air was stale and stagnant, accompanied by the musty stench lingering on him from sweating all day. Growing nauseated, Lonnie was making himself sick. With one hour remaining before meet up time, he showered and groomed himself as best he could, but really didn't care because he didn't have even the slightest interest in the broad. Part of him started not to meet up with her and let whatever would happen, happen. But Lonnie didn't want another woman dictating his future.

Dumping all the pills onto the nightstand in his room, he handpicked fifteen and put them back into the bag. To help his nerves, he popped an Abilify to help with the voices, and an Adderall to give him energy. Washing them down with water, Lonnie left the X-pill alone, as he wasn't attracted to the homeless woman enough to be horny or even want a piece of her ass. It was Trina he was stimulated by who was blowing in the wind.

This trip into the night was strictly to get a woman off head. Making sure the pills were in his pocket to lure the woman where he needed her to be, Lonnie grabbed the other things he'd need for the night: his music, the headphones, and the box cutter he now claimed as his own.

CHAPTER TWENTY-EIGHT

It wasn't until Lonnie was on the bus did he start feeling woozy and drained from all the liquor and pills he'd popped in such a short amount of time. Having a bubbling stomach, he feared he wasn't going to be able to make it to the shelter by eleven. A determined Lonnie pushed on, however, making it to his stop. It was then that he rushed to the nearest restaurant in sight to relieve himself in their bathroom and drink some water from their sink.

Lonnie rocked, strained, and grunted on the public toilet, but nothing came out. His stomach was burning as it tried digesting and moving food throughout its system but couldn't because the overconsumption of drugs had it malfunctioning. Lonnie was constipated to the point of making him sick, which was another side effect of him taking Adderall. Sticking his finger down his throat, he threw up forcefully into the trash can and felt an instant flush of relief. It took another ten minutes or so for him to get himself completely together. Not thinking he was getting the maximum effect of the Adderall, he decided to break half of one of the X-pills down to a half to help boost his high. Lonnie didn't realize his body was pushing for him to stop.

Calling Trina again, Lonnie punched the bathroom stall door when he heard the generic message say the caller couldn't be reached yet again. Although en route to handle his business, it was bothering him that she hadn't called.

"Yo, everything good in there?" a worker from the restaurant called into the lavatory after hearing a loud noise.

"Yeah, I'll be out in a second," Lonnie yelled back, then turned on the faucet, scooping up another few handfuls of water.

Walking from the restaurant toward the shelter, Lonnie made sure to keep his eyes and ears open as he was in an unfamiliar territory and surroundings. He hadn't felt uncomfortable in the daytime, but had a gut-wrenching feeling in the pit of his stomach that was making him feel nervous about being around there now. Digging his hands deeper into his hoodie pockets, he felt the pills in his right one for the woman; and his weapon in the other.

A few minutes past eleven, Lonnie lingered across the street from the shelter but in the darkness of the shadows so he couldn't be seen. They hadn't discussed the exact way they'd meet up; yet, Lonnie knew he wasn't about to walk up to the place he was ordered to be at by the judge with illegal narcotics on him to pass to a person living at the shelter. For him to have an addiction that he was breaking rules to feed was one thing. To be aiding the addiction of another person could come with circumstances the already-troubled youth wasn't ready to deal with. Agreeing to bring the homeless lady the pills in the first place was a bold—and bad—move.

Had Lonnie trusted women and not been disturbed by their kind constantly trying to destroy him, he would've told Miss Humphrey the truth and faced his consequences like a man.

Watching his surroundings and the shelter like a hawk, Lonnie didn't want to miss a footstep, a movement, or a mouse scurrying across the open play area for the kids. With the windows of the shelter cracked, he could hear the children playing inside as their mothers fussed at them to settle down for bed. Hearing the many versions of families, Lonnie thought of his own memories. He remembered his mom saying he was a ball of energy at night, but she appreciated the company even still. His mom. The thought of brighter days saddened Lonnie. If only he could live in the past.

Lonnie's phone vibrated. Moving his attention to the call, he saw that it was Trina finally calling him back. He huffed and started not to answer, but decided to anyway. "Well, hello, stranger," he said upon hitting the answer button.

"Nothing much but a whole lot of drama. You know how I told you my dad was in the hospital?"

"Yeah," Lonnie replied, looking around and wishing she'd spit out whatever it was she had to say.

"Well, he was faking an illness so we could stay somewhere warm and get food, but the shit ended up backfiring in the worst way imaginable. Come to find out, he's got some type of autoimmune disease and they're running a bunch of tests to determine which one. I couldn't even finish getting the 411 because the nurse caught me eating his food and put me out. I told you all of that to ask if you've got a couch I can crash on for the night." In tears and desperate, Trina was in a state of shock and simply wanted some companionship. Each step she took into the night alone, the more she feared she wouldn't make it until daylight. Always having her dad, Trina had never been on her own.

Totally thrown off by Trina's story about her dad, Lonnie zoned out into a trance about his mom and the day she got her diagnosis. The dreary feelings overcame him. Although Trina kept saying hello in his ear, Lonnie was too far lost in the memory. He recalled his mother walking into the doctor's office strong as an ox with a few sick days here and there . . . but coming out transformed into a sickly patient that required checkups every two weeks. Trina's life kept reminding him of his mom in some sort of way.

"I'm sorry to hear that, Trina. Hopefully, the doctors are quacks. Make sure you and your dad get several opinions," he offered her the same advice he and his mother were given and had been let down believing in.

"Whatever. I'm not trying to hear that bullshit. You and I both know that once they label you as sick, the coffin shopping might as well commence." Trina sounded grave but was keeping it real. "I'm sorry if it don't sound like I'm grateful for your kind word, but you know how it is." Full of emotions and spiraling out of control, Trina was starting to lose her composure. Not upset at Lonnie at all, but the fact that the man who stayed to raise her after her mother cheated and deserted them was sick with something incurable—All she wanted was for today to be yesterday and for the future to never come.

Lonnie sighed. "Had I only played the game like you're playing it and accepted the shit much sooner . . ." His tone was so low that Trina barely heard it. What she did hear was that he'd text her his address. Those words soothed her anxiety like a lullaby does to a baby.

Lonnie's voice was caught in his throat. The pill-popping teen was scared. Far out of his mind, his personality kept flip-flopping in between that of a good and bad guy. Knowing how the night hours were for him, he didn't know what type of monster would emerge. Yet and still, he was tired of being lonely.

CHAPTER TWENTY-NINE

The homeless woman saw Lonnie walk up. She'd been socializing and acting like she was watching television in the recreation room. Becoming excited and anxious for the pills Lonnie promised he'd return with, she bounced around the room to all the other women of the shelter begging if they could watch her son. No one was quick to help the woman. No one did, actually. Having made a reputation for herself, the woman was known to stay out past curfew just so she could have an excuse not to care for her bratty kid overnight. Her promises to be "right back" meant nothing to her peers. They waved her off saying they had their own kids they needed a break from, then watched her walk out with her baby on her hip.

Amanda, who was standing by the door ready to lock down the shelter for the night, held it open for the woman to walk out of. Amanda didn't bother telling her the rules, as she already knew them and was reminded of them when put on probation. She simply jotted her name down for Miss Humphrey to deal with her in the morning.

"You got that for me, I know," she said, breathing heavily as she ran over to him with her baby on her hip.

Lonnie looked at her like she had to be the dumbest woman alive for bringing her baby out into the night to cop pills. He knew killing the woman would be doing the child a favor so it wouldn't be neglected, mistreated, or left alone for days hungry 'cause the momma was someone stone-cold high.

"Yeah, I got a few on me but gotta go cop the rest from the spot around the corner. You and shorty wanna roll with me?" His intentions were to avoid sounding like the menacing, manipulative murderer that in reality he'd become. He wanted the woman to trust him. What he had planned would go much more smoothly if she bought into his act and took the suggested walk. If not, when it came down to it, he could care less how things popped off. Either way, he'd already made his mind up on the outcome. By hook or crook, Lonnie was going home tonight *with* the pills and another murder under his belt.

"Yeah, we can walk. That way, I can know where to score some when I get my coins up," the lady responded, repositioning her son on her hip, then taking a step showing she was ready to follow. "We're ready to go, so lead the way."

The two walked into the night, with the baby suckling on a pacifier. Lonnie made small talk, just to keep the woman comfortable until the time was right, while the woman soaked up every word. Left by the nigga who'd pumped her up with sperm and left the baby she was now struggling with on her own, the woman was blushing to Lonnie's simple words and corny jokes. Her mind started drifting off with the thought that maybe she and Lonnie could hook up and pop pills together sometime.

So caught up in what would never happen, the woman didn't realize they'd walked up the driveway of an abandoned home. Lonnie remembered passing the row of five when he walked passed, leery, not too long ago. When her voice sounded off as she finally realized where they were at, it was too late.

Grabbing her by the back of her neck, he pushed her against the brick wall and smashed her face against it. "All you had to do was mind ya' fuckin' business. Maybe tend to your child or some shit like that. But naw, you was too busy looking for a motherfucking problem. Now, you've found one."

Grunting in pain and trying to get Lonnie's weight off her, the woman tried sliding down the wall to maneuver out of his grip, but just ended up burning her face on the mortar. She cried, knowing there was worse coming. Holding onto her son tightly, she prayed his innocence was spared.

Muzzling her screams with the pressure he was applying, Lonnie then twisted a handful of her hair into his hand and snatched her head back as hard as he could. He heard her neck pop right before slamming her head right back against the bricks even harder than he'd snatched it back. On instant impact, her cranium split open and blood poured from it.

Lonnie felt instant gratification. The shrill from the woman's baby boy crying out for his mother as he slipped to the ground never woke Lonnie up from his psychotic trance. Killing the woman who was trying to blackmail him had him feeling too damn good.

"Shhh, li'l man, it's cool," Lonnie said to the child. "She wasn't gonna be a good mother to you anyway." Sliding his hoodie off, he flung it behind him and out of the way. He didn't care if blood got onto his T-shirt.

Flipping the body of the now fresh corpse over, Lonnie straddled her, then pulled the box cutter from his pocket. Uncaring of the blood, the rubbish that was in between the houses, or the still crying child, a heartless Lonnie pried the woman's mouth open and sliced her tongue out of it. Like the other homeless woman, this was his way of permanently silencing her.

Seeming like a vampire, Lonnie held the tongue up like a champion trophy and marveled at it underneath the dancing light of the moon. When he was satisfied with his small and sick celebration, he stuck it back in her mouth.

He then gripped her chin to hold her face still with one hand while cutting her lips with the blade of the box cutter right to left with the other hand. The repeated method of slicing and dicing turned him into a serial killer. When Lonnie was done, he stood up then leaned down over her body going through her pockets. He took the clothing voucher she'd gotten from Miss Humphrey, a ten-dollar bill, and a small bag of what Lonnie saw being sold at the trap house where he purchased pills from—blow. He wasn't gonna inhale the hard-hitting drug, but would sell it on the streets for either the ten it was worth or even for a few dollars less. Out of his rabbit-ass mind, Lonnie still had some sense.

Feeling supreme gratification, Lonnie grinned like the devil as he took one last glance at the dead homeless woman while exchanging his T-shirt for the hoodie alone. He then spun and left her sprawled out in the driveway. Now, he could finish his community service days at the shelter without worrying about the girl dropping knowledge to Miss Humphrey about him.

Or at least he thought so.

The woman's son was still crying, but much lower now. His tiny voice box was aching; his small chest and lungs couldn't handle all the emotion built up inside him because he was too young to be experiencing any of this. Unprotected from the rats, possums, and other rodents of the night, Lonnie left the baby where it lay as he disappeared into the night.

In and out of a deranged state of mind, Lonnie rushed up the street trying to get home. The voices in his head kept telling him to get there. He'd been fiddling with the box cutter he'd now killed two women with like he was anxious to pull it out and use it again. Lonnie's nervousness, anxiety, and paranoia not only came from him being scared over the consequences he couldn't endure if found out about, but from all the pills he was taking. Straight across the board—Adderall, Ecstasy, Abilify, Prozac, and Xanax all have similar side effects, with those three moods being the same. At some points during his travel time home, Lonnie couldn't figure out up from down.

Finally making it to his building, Lonnie dug through his pockets trying to find his key. Concentrating on getting in the house, he saw nothing else but the front door. He walked up the stairs and was about to go through the door when Trina finally spoke up that he'd stepped right past her.

"Long night? You didn't even see me on the stoop." Trina's voice made Lonnie jump, almost out of his skin.

Not paying attention to the fact Lonnie was jumpy, she was more anxious to get inside of his apartment and out of the streets she felt so unsafe in. Although her face wasn't currently covered in tears, she'd been crying the whole time she'd been waiting on Lonnie to get home. Not having her dad by her side meant a whole new life for Trina. The thought saddened her. Following him in like a zombie, she didn't notice his cold and blank stare into space.

Lonnie's mind was stuck in a dark place. Whereas he'd tuned out the baby's cry when he was only a few feet from him murdering his mom, the psychotic teen heard his wails loud and clear when he navigated his way home. His head was throbbing, his adrenaline was still pumping, and the Abilify he'd popped while navigating his way home only seemed to be making his depression worse. Lonnie wanted to close himself up in his apartment and start over on a new day. Yet, before him was Trina, vulnerable and not aware she was in the care of a killer.

Both of them were caught up in their separate messes of life, but had come together needing the space around them to be filled with the presence of another human being. In complete silence until Lonnie unlocked the door for Trina to enter the apartment, she broke the muteness between them with loud and continual awes.

"Awe, now *this* is definitely an upgrade from what I've been accustomed to as of lately. Thanks for letting me crash here." Walking into Lonnie's apartment, she felt ten times better even though her feelings were still in the dumps about her dad. A lot of the built-up anxiety she'd been experiencing while sitting alone with her thoughts had her paranoid her dad wouldn't leave from the hospital at all. Having only gotten control over her dreadful emotions a few minutes before Lonnie arrived, Trina felt that control slipping away again. The tears, fear, and even the pain she pushed down and bottled in from her aunt dying got caught up in her throat.

Lonnie recognized Trina's meltdown and for a minute, let her go through it on her own. He wasn't skilled in the art of consoling a woman. Wishing he had a sip of gin, 1800, or even a beer to offer her, he thought of the bag of blow in his pocket and wondered if she got down. Out of his element, Lonnie thought against offering her the drug and decided to offer her reassuring words instead. His words were a combination of what he wanted to hear Karisma's foster mother and even the caretaker's girlfriend say.

"All right, girl, you can quit all that crying and rest easy. My place is your place till you can come up on something better." He withheld the truth that she had less than thirty days. Ironically, Trina had come to him for a place to stay from the streets, and he was on his way back to them.

Showing her a few paces over to his couch, he apologized for not having any extra covers for her comfort. Trina shrugged it off and asked if she could take a shower.

"I don't care if you don't have an extra towel either. If I can't use yours, I'm sure you've got something around here I can wipe dry with, or I'll air dry." The wink she gave Lonnie told him she wanted to do something. Trina did. But only because she wanted to get the sad feeling of what was going on with her pops off her mind.

"It's cool that you're willing to compromise, 'cause I don't have an extra towel or washcloth. Being that it's only me, I only purchased one of each from the Dollar Store."

"Well, damn, Lonnie, is there at least some soap in there I could use?" She was serious but sounded playful.

"Now *that*, I've got."

"Good. Now, point me in the direction of your bathroom, and I'll be right back."

Peeking out of the window discreetly, Lonnie was trying to take in his surroundings for what might've been different or stood out. Similar to the day he stashed the dead woman behind the shelter, he was on edge. Had Trina not been here, he would've been still and hushed. Hoping the cops didn't come while Trina was here, he turned on the television to create some noise. Since he couldn't listen for them, he didn't want them being able to listen to him . . . if they did come.

Lonnie heard the shower water turn on, then Trina's singing voice coming from the bathroom. He didn't know what song she was singing; yet, he knew it was beautiful. It was something about being strong and overcoming, a Gospel melody. Sliding his hoodie over his head, he laid it on the card table he used a dining-room table . . . completely forgetting about the bloody box cutter still being in his pocket. Within a split second, his mind was back on

Trina and the possibilities of the night. Opening the bag of pills he'd promised the now-dead homeless woman, he threw the other half of the X-pill down his throat. Lonnie wanted to be as hard as he'd been the last few nights of jacking off; and even when Trina noticed his erection in front of the shelter.

Waiting on Trina to get done with her shower and the pill to kick in, Lonnie cleaned up a little and hid his documents from the court, along with his eviction paperwork in his backpack. He didn't want to be embarrassed by Trina seeing his business. Lonnie liked that he was mysterious to her and that she'd relied on him as if he was a real man. Since turning eighteen, Lonnie hadn't felt like the grown and mature man his mother told him she'd be proud of.

He wasted his energy trying to clean his space up so swiftly because Trina stayed in the shower for at least twenty minutes; and for each of those minutes, Lonnie paced and peeked out of the window. He even put some clothes at the bottom of the door so no one could glance in from underneath it. He planned on telling Trina that the neighbors were foreign and their food smells always seeped in and stunk up the place.

Finally out of the shower, Trina walked into the living room with her hair dripping wet and Lonnie's towel wrapped around her body. In the shower, she thought about all of her options and what she'd do if her dad's condition couldn't be treated. Then she thought about his basic state insurance and if they'd even pay for all the scripts and doctor visits he might need. The one thing that brought Trina to tears was that she didn't even know how she'd bury him if whatever he'd been diagnosed with was terminal. At her lowest and done crying underneath the mildew-covered showerhead, Trina had climbed out with the intention of making her pain go away.

"Damn, you look good as hell," Lonnie blurted out, feeling his penis harden.

"I was hoping you'd say that." Trina was trying to sound sexy. Walking toward Lonnie, she let the towel fall right before approaching him, and then pulled him in for a hug. "Let me show you how much your friendship means to me. How much I appreciate you looking out for me," she whispered in his ear, licking it, then nuzzling up to him.

With the X-pill in his system, Lonnie was ready to go wild with her body. Grabbing her by the hips, he then used his hands to roam all over her curves. Using the moves he'd picked up from watching the porno, Lonnie was getting a positive response from Trina as she moaned and yelled out his name.

Trina wasn't a virgin in the sheets. She'd been cuddling up to niggas on a regular basis if the dollar amount was right. She wasn't a prostitute or a whore by any description of the word, but a hustler to make sure she and her dad at least ate. Only realizing she had herself to count on, fucking Lonnie was her way of making sure she could come back night after night.

"I told you it ain't no thang, but I'm willing to see what you workin' with," Lonnie remixed a line he'd heard Kevin run on a girl at one of his last parties. With the X-pill in his blood, unlike how he was with Megan, Lonnie's manhood was at attention and poking Trina in the belly button. His reaction was different than it was the other day when he hid his erection. Lonnie was standing firm, cocky, and proud. "You see what tip he's on," he said, referring to his dick. Taking Trina's hand, he placed it on top of him and moved his hand until she started jacking him. Lonnie then slid his finger inside of her wetness, going crazy over the feeling of her juiciness. He was about to cum just from them basically feeling on each other.

All the tension Trina was carrying around about her dad melted as she creamed on Lonnie's finger. For the first time in her young life, she actually felt a connection with a man other than her father. Damn near jumping in Lonnie's arms when she felt her body getting ready to erupt, Trina screamed his name as loud as she could and without control.

Out of breath, she leaned against the boy who'd just fingered her into an orgasm and tried gaining her composure. She was spent, but definitely ready to see what Lonnie's stroke game was about. Getting ready to open her mouth and ask, her phone rang and killed the whole mood.

"Hold on a second; it could be my dad," Trina said, breaking away from him.

Watching her ass jiggle as she ran across the room, Lonnie wanted to run behind her and tackle her onto the couch. Never before had he wanted a woman so bad.

"What? Oh my God! I'll be there in a second," Trina shouted out after listening to the caller. Dropping her phone in an absolute panic, she ran around Lonnie's apartment frantically. "My dad, Lonnie, oh my God, I'm so scared." Trina tried gaining her composure while remembering where her clothes were at. "That was the nurse. They just had shift change, and she told me to come back. She said my dad's not taking to the medication and is somehow getting worse. Lonnie, he ain't walk up in that motherfucker sick for real, and now he's about to die. Oh my God," she was screaming, crying, and hyperventilating.

The voices in Lonnie's head returned. Trina talking about her father's hospital experience sent him straight back into the past about his mom. Now in a dark place, Lonnie didn't care about busting a nut in Trina, but swallowing some more pills.

Leaving her in the middle of his living room with a look of hurt and question written all over her face, he went into his bedroom and slammed the door uncaringly. Lonnie was in search of where he'd hidden the pills. Finding the bag and swallowing two without paying attention to what they were, he fell on the bed angry.

Trina, on the other side of the door, felt crushed by Lonnie's display of insensitivity. She felt that he should've offered some encouraging words, even if he didn't believe in them or know any of the details. She was disappointed that he hadn't rushed to hold and caress her tenderly till she felt better, especially since he'd just been groping her body without restraint.

She stood frozen in disbelief and pain, not able to break her stare from the door. She thought the doorknob would twist and Lonnie would walk out, or even that she'd hear his voice explain why he'd dismissed her. Sadly, she was let down and left more confused than ever. Being that he'd lost a mother and claimed to have been a good guy, Trina felt bamboozled.

She was tempted to knock at the door herself or bust in and demand answers. Had the nurse not called saying her father's condition had worsened, that would've been her plan, and she wouldn't have hesitated for not even a second. However, as always, she put her father first, because doing anything else would've left her with a guilty conscience.

Trina rushed into the bathroom where her clothes were and quickly put them all back on. She didn't care about having a come-sticky coochie or even built-up sweat from the heavy make out session she'd just had with Lonnie. All she wanted to do was be out of his presence and apartment. She didn't know what his problem was and why'd he'd acted like an asshole out of nowhere; but she was mad as hell that he had.

Moving through the apartment swiftly, but while watching over her shoulder just in case Lonnie opened his bedroom door, a homeless Trina took something to eat out of the fridge and stuffed it into her backpack for later. She was starving and had already gotten put out of the hospital for eating her father's food, and she wasn't trying to go down that path again. Feeling her stomach churn, anxiety started building up about what the future held for her. The one thing she hoped would one day change was being homeless. It was obvious to her she wouldn't be on Lonnie's couch for the night. Because of that, she hoped she at least got to stay at the hospital until the sun rose. It was already too late for her to find a bed at any shelter within the city.

Getting ready to go in Lonnie's hoodie pocket for some money or some change, she heard Lonnie opening his bedroom door. Not wanting him to see her panic and figure out what she'd been doing, Trina quickly darted out of his front door and down the stairwell, almost tripping over her feet. One second longer to snoop and steal, Trina would've found the box cutter he sliced women's tongues out with. She also missed the chance to hear Lonnie apologize and tell her why he reacted the way he did.

Staying completely still in one spot for most of the night, he didn't make any loud sounds someone on the outside could hear. After Trina stormed out pissed at him, he shut his apartment down the way it would've been had she not needed a place to crash. The television stayed off because he was afraid to see a picture of himself pop up underneath the large bold word *"Wanted."* The more Lonnie prayed, the more he swore he heard God tell him to shut up and suck it up. Left with his thoughts and the voices in his head, he now heard the last woman and her baby crying out for him to stop . . . and that's what drove him insane.

CHAPTER THIRTY

All the unmonitored dosages of pills Lonnie had been popping into his mouth like candy over the last few days had absorbed into his bloodstream in the worst possible way. The Xanax and Abilify pills he'd nicknamed the "Happy Pills" cheered his mood up from whatever depressive state he found himself sunken into. They also helped Lonnie sort out the voices. Mixing Tylenols, Motrins, and sometimes Snapbacks, Lonnie never thought twice about the daily dances he took with death. In his mind, he was soothing his misery.

Not only had his mind split into two totally different personalities, his irresponsible consumption had wrecked his immune system as well. Constantly high off drugs and not consuming much food, he wasn't even aware of his digestive system slowing down. Lonnie didn't notice the vices were the reason he seemed to be functioning normally. His body had gotten accustomed to getting fed a liquor diet of either beer or something heavy hitting if he had some money. The moment he stops, will be the moment he drops.

The X-pill and Adderall kept him energized and feeling euphoric; yet, the emotionally damaging Ecstasy pill was actually making his already-flawed mental condition worse. Whereas it made him feel good for a short amount of time, maybe even for a few hours, the long-term effects of overusing it is part of the reason why Lonnie kept having psychotic episodes.

Completely addicted and oblivious, he continued to feed himself the pills like they were helping him cope with life. The truth of the matter was that Lonnie was self-destructing and ruined his own life. Before giving into temptation from Kevin, the counted-out teen had risen. Yet now, he'd fallen to the wayside and was barely even a statistic. Not only was the world fighting against Lonnie, at least as it seemed to him, but now his body was attacking him from the inside as well. Similar to the cancer that killed his beloved mother, his pill habit was killing him.

Forty-eight hours had passed, and Lonnie was fresh out of pills and liquor. There were so many voices in his head each second of the day that he'd tried drugging himself into a coma so they'd stop. They kept telling him to kill again. They kept encouraging him to go out into the night with his box cutter and evil intent. Lonnie's hands were covered in blood with bodies. He was the Grim Reaper of the streets.

Walking out of his apartment building into the bright sun, he squinted his eyes at the daylight. Lonnie had been like a vampire, having been locked up in his apartment with the blinds closed. He'd isolated himself from the outside world and would've continued doing so if his pill stash and liquor supply would've withstood for a longer time.

All Lonnie did on his binge was pop pills, sip liquor, and roll the bag of blow around in his hand, tumbling around with the idea of breaking the seal. He also tried calling Trina a gang of times, but she did not answer. Lonnie knew he deserved the cold shoulder for how he played her when she got the call about her dad; however, he stopped giving a fuck about apologizing when he ran out of minutes. In such a short amount of time, Lonnie had spiraled down into the dumps and lost total control of his life.

Pulling the hood of his sweatshirt further over his head, Lonnie kept his head low as he walked toward the bus. Not having Kevin as a connect meant he had to score pills on his own. With his headphones nestled in his ear, he was oblivious to what everyone around him was whispering about. So much had gone on in the world while Lonnie was binging and telepathing himself into a different realm that was controlled by drugs. Two mutilated bodies of women had been discovered; and what had the whole nation looking at Detroit with a shaking head and sad eye was that a baby was found halfway dead a few feet from his dead mother.

Had Lonnie been in his right mind and not concentrating so hard on how the three dollars he had left from the ten he'd stolen would buy him enough liquor to last him for another binge, he would've seen the woman on the bus that noticed his face from the picture the news put up with the story it ran. A working woman with kids herself, she paid attention to crimes of that nature because she often traveled alone. When she snapped a picture of him on her phone, posting it on her Facebook site with the question, "Is this the guy?" Lonnie was completely oblivious that she'd done it and that he was smiling. In his mind, he'd figured out a winning plan on how to spend the ten and sell the blow.

The blocks Lonnie walked to the trap house looked a lot different in the light of day than it did at night. Still halfway deserted, there were a lot more hustlers and bums out, lurking for come ups. Lonnie walked with his hands stuffed in his pocket wrapped around his trusty weapon. He didn't think anyone would try him, but knew he had it in him to kill, if need be.

Finding his way back to the trap house without a problem, Lonnie was thankful the old homeless man from the store put him on to it. Walking up to the door, he knocked and was let in just like he was before.

"What up? Whatchu' looking to cop?" the hustler asked Lonnie, ready to make the sell and put the druggie out. The few trappers of the house had a Madden competition going on, and he wasn't trying to miss a play. There were three of them total, and they'd been taking turns serving custos at the door while two stayed and played.

"Hey, I need some pills, but all I got is this bag of blow. You think I can exchange it?" Lonnie asked. Having gone over the question a million times in a million different ways, he felt confident about the way he intended on getting rid of the bag and getting the pills until the words were actually said to the trapper.

"What in the fuck? Say, word? Yo, nigga, step the fuck up outta here. This ain't no motherfuckin' Walmart. We ain't selling drugs with receipts. Get the hell on till you come up with some cash," the trap star clowned Lonnie, then collared him up and pushed him out the door.

Lonnie stumbled on his feet and fell to the ground. The trap star laughed before slamming the door and retreating back to the living room with his friends. Unfortunately, the fall didn't knock Lonnie's sense into him. It actually made him more determined to get the money for his habit by any means necessary. Climbing off the ground, he walked around from the trap house, then around the neighborhood aimlessly. He was trying to think and plot about everything he could do to come up on a few dollars. Needing twenty dollars to at least stay tucked away for a few days, he was willing to settle for ten. Lonnie wasn't going home empty-handed, for sure. He'd promised himself that before walking out the door.

Lonnie thought about busting out a car window, but didn't because none of the cars looked to be worth the twenty he wanted to at least think there was that type of cash in them. Then he figured the people around the hood were hard up like him and not going to leave money laying around. At that moment, Lonnie's eyes lit up like a lightbulb really had gone off in his head. He got the idea to rob somebody. Since most people carry their life savings with them everywhere they go, he cursed himself for not thinking about the idea sooner.

Lonnie chose to tuck himself away near the in-house restaurant the bum had gone to for a burger. He remembered there was a lot of traffic going in and out of their door in the nighttime and was giddy over the thought of how daytime's food traffic would be. He could barely contain himself when he saw the house was slapping with customers. Lonnie wished he was a burglar, 'cause he started thinking about how much money had to be in that house with them doing business in drones the way he was seeing.

Lonnie watched the people for who looked to be alone. He wanted an easy target, someone that couldn't put up much of a fight but didn't look like they were spending their last. He needed a person on foot. After casing the spot for about thirty minutes, he finally saw a young girl walk away alone. Coming toward him, she was too caught up in her delicious burger to notice Lonnie lurking by the corner for her.

As soon as the woman hit the corner, she stopped and looked both ways to see if a car was coming before she crossed. She was cleared to go from the left; then two nibbles of the burger in and a glance toward her right, the woman choked on the remnants of burger going down her throat. She tried spitting the burger patty, and toppings out to the ground, but Lonnie had her mouth covered with his hand and was slow walking her up the block. There was an alleyway a few feet away he'd planned on eventually robbing her at.

Kicking, twisting, and flinging her arms, the young girl wasn't trying to get away from Lonnie, but get his hands off her mouth. She was panicking and having an anxiety attack, about to choke on the mouthful of food she couldn't swallow or spit out. Each step Lonnie took without letting her go, the more she felt her life slipping away. Getting marched into the alley, not knowing what the crazed man was about to do to her, the woman hated she hadn't listened to her grandmother.

The old wise woman who ran the at-home restaurant had just warned her granddaughter about wandering the neighborhood alone, day or night. The young girl might've only kept up with her Facebook feed, but her grandmother watched the news religiously and knew there was a serial killer at large. Had she known her family member was in the horrible predicament she found herself, she would've been out of the kitchen from mixing up her special seasoning that kept folks coming back to her hood business.

"Calm yo' ass down," Lonnie said to the girl in a cold, raspy voice.

Once in the alleyway, he'd seen the back door of an abandoned house either open or completely off the hinges. He knew for sure it was empty because the curtains that once kept the family's private life in was now hanging out of the open window—those that weren't busted out. Lonnie, walking backward, dragged the girl in by her face, a few times stumbling over his own feet.

"I said calm ya' fucking ass down before you make shit worse for yourself," Lonnie warned.

The girl didn't listen. She figured if she was going to die, she was going to fight one helluva fight doing so.

She reached her hand back and clawed his face with her acrylic nails, feeling small pieces of skin underneath her nails. Then she tried her hardest to pry his fingers back from off her mouth.

Lonnie, desperate for the pills to feed his addiction, had grown tired of tussling with the woman. He might've gotten off on the woman tussling if it was in the middle in the night and he was fresh off pills, but his high had already spiraled down. Lonnie simply was ready to get the attack over and get back to the pill house. Without wasting another second, he tightened the grip on her mouth and used his other hand to snap her neck. The sound of it popping sent shivers down his spine.

Lonnie let the girl fall to the floor—if not dead, within the last breaths of her life. He hadn't intended on killing the woman, only robbing her. But her spunk had worked against her. With another murder under his belt, Lonnie felt invincible.

Reaching for the box cutter, he only sliced the girl's lips left from left to right. He left her tongue intact and in place in her mouth. Unlike the other murders where he crept off in the middle of the night, this murder had taken place in broad daylight with people out and about within the community. Whenever he did leave from the abandoned house, reality would be waiting on him.

Leaning over the girl, Lonnie searched her pockets but didn't find a thing. He'd done all that for her not to have a dollar or even fifteen cents! He wished he had an X-pill to get him horny so he could've at least had sex with the girl and got some form of satisfaction. Not walking away empty-handed, Lonnie took her cell phone and school identification. He knew he could at least get a few dollars for the cell phone. He was ready to give it away for free, if free meant a couple of dollars.

So close, yet so far from feeding his addiction, Lonnie ran out of the abandoned house and all the way to the liquor store where he'd met the bum at. It was a neutral place for him to sell the phone and maybe even the bag of coke.

The bum who'd been struggling in the worse way trying to fight off his past addiction was happy to see Lonnie running up. Liquor is what helped the bum stay clean. He knew the young boy was good for at least a shot, although he was going to push his luck for a whole bottle. Or at least another burger from his wife's in-home restaurant. The bum knew he had a chance to clean up his life and go home one day; otherwise, the woman would've gotten a divorce years go. It's that thought that keeps the bum functioning off liquor and not the crack rock he loved to love.

"If it's not my favorite young friend. What's good, partner?" the bum asked Lonnie as he approached, glad to have some company. As long as the bum kept someone around him to talk to, he didn't fall victim to the white powder floating around that would kill him.

"Nothing but some more problems, O. G.," Lonnie responded. "I need your help with something else, and I'll give you a little taste of the come up if you can help me," Lonnie cut into the homeless man, feeling pressed for time and frantic for some pills.

The bum didn't wait to say yes. Before even hearing what Lonnie's plan was to come up, the bum was already plotting on how he could take a few dollars over to his wife. She cursed him out each and every time he came around with crumbled-up cash looking for some food, yet always gave him a meal. That's another reason the bum was so quick to say yes. He wanted a reason to visit his wife.

Lonnie pulled the bag of blow and the cell phone from his pocket, but dropped something else he didn't pay attention to. "Who can I sell these to?"

Seeing the blow made the bum's dick hard. The high he'd been hiding from was now right in front of his face. Lonnie was dangling the bag back and forth in front of the bum, hypnotizing him with the thought of what it tasted like. Looking down, trying not to give into temptation, the bum saw what he'd seen fall out of the Lonnie's pocket and went down to pick it up. He wasn't trying to be slick on any level, simply trying to do anything other than take ten steps backward.

"Hey, you dropped this outta ya' pock—" the bum said, as his eyes locked in on the piece of plastic beside Lonnie's feet. The last word hadn't gotten out of the bum's mouth before he started a whole new sentence. "What in the fuck are you doing with my granddaughter's school ID, li'l nigga?"

Already on edge, the bum's words fucked Lonnie up even more than he already was. Lonnie didn't speak. He couldn't think of a lie good enough to say. In all of the chances, coincidences, and women in the world, he couldn't believe he'd killed the granddaughter of the bum. Not knowing what other threat the bum could pose to him but to call the cops, Lonnie still felt the urge to attack. He wasn't about to fall victim by the hands of a homeless, drinking bum.

Gripping the handle of his trusty box cutter, he whipped it out of his pocket and viciously sliced the bum across the face. From the lower left side of the bum's chin to his right temple, blood dripped from his face as he screamed out in agonizing pain. In what seemed like a mere blink of an eye, that heinous moment in time was history. Stunned, the bloody bearded bum had failed to see Lonnie even produce the jagged-edged blade as he struggled to speak.

Grabbing at his face, he leaned his head back facing the sky with his mouth wide open to scream "why." Before he got a chance to send another menacing scream out into the air, however, Lonnie sliced his neck from the left side to the right side like an experienced meat cutter. The serial killer was now an expert with his winning weapon.

The bum's body fell to the ground. Lonnie didn't bother standing over him as he squirmed and bled to death, cut his tongue out, or go through his pockets because he knew he had nothing. Instead, Lonnie picked the girl's cell phone up off the ground, along with the small bag of coke and the identification card.

Feeling a rush and not thinking about the consequences of his actions, young, dumb, and stressed Lonnie ripped the bag of coke open, poured some out into a line, and then sniffed it up like he'd seen Kevin's friends do. The instant rush of the drug entering Lonnie's bloodstream made his eyes pop open when it hit his brain. He then licked his finger, swirled it around in the bag, then rubbed the coke on his gums and the tip of his tongue like he'd seen Kevin's friends do. The bitter taste was a turnoff, but the euphoric high the blow gave Lonnie was the best he'd ever felt. It felt ten times better than being on Adderall. Wiping the residue from underneath his nose, he stuffed the bag and ID in his pocket, then took off running in the opposite direction.

Sprinting like he was a lion running through the jungle, Lonnie felt untouchable and free as the air smacked against his face. Instead of the breeze waking him up, it only excited him more. Reaching a low he never thought he'd stoop to, Lonnie was now addicted to heavy-hitting drugs and experiencing a side effect of cocaine described as the feeling of supremacy.

CHAPTER THIRTY-ONE

A fresh fish on cocaine, Lonnie's heartbeat was pounding. He couldn't calm down and felt anxious, like he was going to pass out when it was hard catching his breath. Thinking it was because he'd run for so long and was tired, a misguided Lonnie was wrong. The abnormal heartbeat he was experiencing was because of his intake of coke, nothing more. Luck was on his side, but Lonnie didn't know it. He was outsmarting death . . . for now.

Having two new murders on his résumé, Lonnie was ready to get out of the world and back within the confines of his apartment. Once inside, he sat at the card table and poured out some of the coke onto it. Burying his face into the pile, he snorted up each piece of white dust until his nose ached and his teeth throbbed. In a matter of seconds after that, his nose went numb as well as the back of his throat. He almost panicked at the feeling of not being able to swallow. Closing his eyes, Lonnie rode out the different waves of odd sensations and reactions. He'd become angry at himself for not trying the drug sooner. Unlike all the other times he'd popped pills and only felt a little better about himself or certain situations, on coke, Lonnie felt like nothing in the world mattered. It was an indescribable feeling that he never wanted to go away.

Putting his headphones on, he turned some rap music up as loud as the volume would go and was dancing like he was at a college party. He even started rapping some of the verses loudly. Lonnie had tons of energy and felt good about himself. Not used to the foreign feeling, he couldn't calm himself down. All the fear of the cops coming melted the higher Lonnie got on coke. He literally felt on top of the world.

Ducking and hiding in a corner, Lonnie's eyes got wide as saucers when he suddenly heard someone pounding at the door. The song had ended and was changing to the next one; that was the only reason he'd heard and turned the old phone's music player off. A paranoid Lonnie covered his mouth, like he was trapped in both his words and his breath.

"Lonnie! I know you're in there because I heard you rapping a few seconds ago—so open up," he heard a girl's voice, one quite familiar to him. He smiled. It was Trina.

Not thinking about his current condition or checking through the peephole to make sure it was indeed her and she was alone, he bounced across the room and opened the door. Trina grinned at him, then rushed in before he had a chance to send her away. She'd mustered up too much courage to pop up at Lonnie's apartment to not at least run down the speech she'd been going over for two days.

Her dad was still undergoing tests, but they'd diagnosed him with an autoimmune disease called lupus. In a nutshell, that means that his body is fighting itself on the inside. The doctors told her dad to expect excruciating pain, unexplained nausea, skin rashes, and exhaustion that comes from out of nowhere. They also briefed him on at least five medications he'd have to start to help combat the illness. Trina didn't think it was fair, but she was happy that it wasn't cancer. Not breaking any hospital rules because she promised the staff that she wouldn't, Trina stayed with her dad around the clock learning how to help him, about his diagnosis, and praying over him for a speedy recovery. Now that he was out of the woods,

Trina wanted to check the shit out of Lonnie for how he'd treated her.

Lonnie read Trina's expression, although he didn't have to in order to know what she was thinking. He already knew he was dead-ass wrong for making it seem like it was fuck her, her dad, and her feelings. Feeling supreme, untouchable, and disconnected from every problem he had in the world, Lonnie didn't address the elephant in the room, but reacted per the coke in his system. He felt like if he wanted his way, he could have his way.

Not missing a beat, Lonnie moved toward Trina and pulled her in like he'd done days before. She moaned, feeling tension melt from off her shoulders. The heaviness had shifted into her panties. Her private part was thumping for Lonnie's attention again. Trina was mad as hell at him, yet still lusting. In between talking to nurses, doctors, and social workers about her father's condition and their circumstances of being homeless, Trina found happiness getting caught up in thoughts about the way he tickled her coochie into cumming, then how hard her body shook and quaked.

"You came over here for this dick? Huh?" Whipping it out, he rubbed it against her stomach, then asked her if she wanted to feel it. The voices in his head kept telling him he was great and she'd be privileged to feel his strokes.

She nodded like a nervous schoolgirl but was soaking wet between her legs. Grabbing Lonnie by his manhood, she gently tugged at it, letting him know she wanted him to follow, then sat down on the couch when her heels hit the front of it. Doing what he didn't get to do with Megan, Lonnie stuffed his monster deep into Trina's throat and viciously fucked it until he felt himself about to lose it.

An experienced Trina could tell Lonnie was about to shoot off down her throat, so she moved with the quickness to pull it out of her mouth. She wasn't ready for him to cum so she controlled his orgasm by holding out. From the example of the few other men she'd slept with for a mere sandwich, a few bucks, and even the police officer she'd sucked clean to prevent a petty theft charge, Trina knew the power of her mouth. She also knew that making Lonnie hold out longer would make his attraction and need for her greater. All Trina wanted to do was feel secure.

What Trina didn't know, because she prided herself on staying drug free, was that Lonnie wasn't only crushing on her, but cocaine as well. Finding the small bag of white powder had him horny, thinking recklessly, he grabbed Trina by the neck, forcing her up against the wall. The intense attraction each one of them had for the other quickly turned even more intense, but in a cold and demonic way.

"Ain't nobody tell you to stop." Sticking his tongue down her throat, Lonnie kissed her deeply and passionately, just as he'd seen two porno actors do. It had been gross to him as those people are paid to have sex and do vile things to a ton of people for cash, yet completely understandable now that he was forcefully kissing Trina.

Trina hit him in the back with her fists, totally turned off by the kiss. His mouth tasted dirty, bitter, and like he'd been sucking on red onions all day. She was an experienced fucker, not kisser, which meant Trina didn't know how to play it off like it felt good or satisfying until the kiss was over. She wanted him off of her, not even sure she wanted to lie down at all.

Lonnie, however, wasn't coming up for air. The harder she fought against him, the harder he fought to keep her close to him. He had snorted up too much coke in such a short amount of time. Whereas the drug already gives a person a heightened sensitivity to touch, snorting up so much of it had Lonnie tingling all over. He couldn't stop—didn't want to stop. Matter of fact, the voices he'd gotten comfortable and acquainted with all started talking at once. Lonnie tried shaking his head to shake them quiet, but that only made their voices louder and in unison.

"Kill."

"Kill."

"Kill."

Lonnie tightened his grip around Trina's neck. Her fight was his thrill. With one hand she was held against the wall, and with the other, he slipped it inside her panties again.

"Shhh, I'ma make you feel good. I know how you like it," he said, referring to when he'd pleasured her to cumming, Lonnie was ready to make both of them feel good. He felt his dick bulging and jerking, ready to explode.

"Let me go! I can't brea—" Trina tried telling Lonnie, but felt her air passageway constricting. The harder he flicked her clit, the tighter he squeezed her neck.

"Shhh, just settle down and cum. I feel it swelling up on my fingertip." Completely possessed, Lonnie rammed two of his fingers up in her wetness at the same time. "Let 'er rip!"

Trina never recognized Lonnie as the pillhead he was. She never connected the dots of his erratic behavior. She hadn't asked enough questions, just those that were important to her coming up. So caught up with the health drama concerning her dad, Trina hadn't seen her fate coming. Now erupting all over Lonnie's hand once again, she wished she could take everything back. She wished she would've run like the speed of lightning out of the alleyway when she'd heard someone coming out of the shelter. Trina regretted taking the food box the first day, calling him later that night, and most importantly, she regretted coming to his house after she'd already made it out and away. Taking a deep breath at the end of her orgasm, she didn't know it was gonna be her absolute last.

In a coke-induced craziness, Lonnie had choked the life out of her body. It wasn't until he'd felt the fight she'd been putting up slip from her body did Lonnie know he had killed his friend. The only friend he had left in the world. Not feeling remorse, Lonnie finally let her neck go and dropped her to the floor. The voices . . . They were loud, clear, and controlling him.

With Trina's body sprawled across his floor, Lonnie left her there and went to sit down at his card table. He want another lick of coke. Doing a bump, he then rose, feeling on top of the world again. Pulling his still bloody box cutter from out of his pocket, he marched over to Trina's body and sliced her the same way he'd done his other victims. He cut her tongue from her mouth, then sliced her upper and bottom lip until they spit open. Had Trina not been dead, she would've drowned on all the blood spewing from her. When he was satisfied with the kill, Lonnie left Trina again; but this time, to take a shower.

An hour had passed, and Lonnie still felt like he was a king. Every time he felt the feeling fading, he'd do another line or wipe some of the powder on his gums. He'd already made up in mind that he wasn't going back to pills. Lonnie had officially graduated to being a full-blown addict. In less than two hours, he'd consumed more cocaine than the richest walking-alive junkie. Being that his body was trained to withstand all the drugs he was pumping into it, he'd yet to overdose. Lonnie wasn't worried about the future and didn't plan on it until the bag of blow was emptied.

He was high as hell sitting in front of the television with his hands in his pants. With his eyes roaming back and forth from Trina's body to the TV, he thought about putting a porn on and having sex with the corpse. Right when he was getting ready to change the channel to pick up the DVD player's reception—his eyes widened like saucers, and he threw up all over himself.

"The citizens of Detroit, women in particular—please be safe and travel in pairs. Another woman has been found mutilated in the exact same fashion as the other two women Detroit police discovered earlier in the week. And also, a few miles away, a well-known homeless man of the community was also murdered. Tips from witnesses lead the cops to believe both murders are related and committed by the same person. They are working on the case diligently. Please stay safe, on guard, and aware of your surroundings as this man is armed and inhumanly dangerous. Stay tuned as we'll report any updates as they come in. For around-the-clock news coverage, follow us on Facebook, Twitter, and Instagram."

In addition to seeing the mugshot picture of him from when he was arrested for the DUI on the screen, the newscaster's report sent Lonnie into a frenzy. Not only had they discovered some of the women he'd killed, they had identified him as the serial killer. It never crossed his drug-fried brain that the cops already had his prints, address, and how to find him on file since he was in the system. When killing the people, the voices never told him he was leaving his prints everywhere.

Knowing he wasn't going to be able to outsmart the cops for long, Lonnie hurried throughout his apartment getting all the things he wanted and saying good-bye to all the things he'd never see again. He also gave Trina a good-bye kiss. With his book bag on his back full of the few things he'd salvaged from when the caretaker's girlfriend started his love-to-hate-women affair, his intention was to do one last thing while free. Snorting up another line of coke, Lonnie felt the powder give him the adrenaline boost he desperately needed; then he rushed out of his apartment door for good.

CHAPTER THIRTY-TWO

Having a panic attack, he ran down the stairwell and almost tumbled over his feet and all the way down. He heard sirens. Unsure if they were from a squad car or ambulance, he didn't linger around to find out. Gripping the straps of his book bag, he flew out of the exit door and down the street like he had a cape on his back instead of a book bag. Lonnie truly wished he was a superhero so he could have powers to disappear, go back in time, and get away with killing . . . even if he wasn't killing bad guys.

Halfway up the block from his apartment building, the cops zoomed right past Lonnie. Only focused on the boy's address, they were suited up with bulletproof vests and extra clips for their weapons on their waists. The goal, given from their captain that they planned on executing, was to apprehend Lonnie Eugene McKay and save the day.

The longer the serial killer roamed the streets, the worse off the Detroit Police Department was. Not all press is good press, especially for those of the judiciary system. If the citizens feel like they aren't protected, the cops aren't doing their jobs or are qualified to handle crime, and all hell could break loose. The captain had gotten strict orders from the mayor, who was tired of his city getting negative shine, especially with an election coming up. The two cops headed to Lonnie's were at the bottom of the totem pole and doing the dirtiest work. All they wanted was their paychecks and to get their captain's foot up off their necks.

Lonnie stopped in his tracks and spun around to see if his fear was right . . . and it was. The squad car swerved in front of his apartment building; then the two cops leaped out with their pistols drawn. Lonnie's heart was pounding so hard and fast that he thought it was going to pump out of his chest. Ducking down behind a parked car with his eyes glued to the cops pounding on the main door and ringing every bell, he snickered; knowing they were only moments away from finding Trina. He didn't wait on them to search his apartment or for the coroner to arrive and carry Trina's corpse out. Lonnie stood up, took a deep breath, and then ran as fast as he could, getting the fuck out of Dodge.

Over leaves, trash, and dirt on the ground, Lonnie walked through the cemetery looking for his mother's grave. He saw gigantic marble headstones, benches customized for loved ones, and even regular tombstones with loving messages etched on them—all noting the resting places of deceased people who must've been better off than him and his mom. The cheapest plot he could afford only noted his mother's last name and year of death. Sitting down on top of where she was buried, he then lay down and stared up at the sky. As her body was in the ground, Lonnie believed her soul was looking down on him from heaven.

"Ma, I'm so sorry." A broken-down Lonnie, full of tears and pills, wasn't apologizing because he wasn't able to bury her properly, but for being a disgraceful son.

Just like when he used to sit in her room on her bed and talk for hours, Lonnie curled up on the ground and lay his head on her gravestone like it was a pillow. Like a little lost boy, he wanted his mommy. If he could've, he would've gotten a shovel and dug six feet down to his mother and got inside the casket she was resting within. Dumping some coke out of the bag onto the flat granite engraved stone, he leaned his head over just enough snort it up.

"Ma, I killed some people, mainly women. Four women and one man is who they found, but a couple they didn't. There's still more out there." Lonnie was talking frantically like he was speeding against time. "It's not my fault, though. I swear it's not. It's like these voices, Ma—they tell me to kill. I even heard you tell me one night everything was gonna be all right. Was that really you, Ma?" The tears that were gathered in Lonnie's eyes began falling freely. He sniffed and sobbed, then cried loud and hard. "Do you hear me, Ma? It's not my fault. Do you know what I've been through since you died? It's been nothing but pure hell. Why didn't you take me with you? Why did you leave me here to struggle?"

Lonnie's emotions were bubbling over. High off the new drug, his body was experiencing a euphoric feeling it's never felt before; yet, it was breaking down at the same time. He was none the wiser.

Calling himself confessing, he started talking aloud telling her about everything he went through from the time she died, starting with the caretaker's girlfriend. He even told her about Kevin, the X-pills, and how he couldn't keep his manhood up to have sex. Lonnie divulged every detail of how the pills made him feel, how he killed each woman, and how the power he felt after killing them made him feel like a man. He then told her about Trina and the strong connection he had to her. He told her from start to finish about their relationship, all the way down to the bitter end. He swore he saw lightning and felt the earth beneath him shake. The more Lonnie talked, the more Lonnie snorted. Then he started hearing voices telling him to kill himself, so he tried.

"See, Ma, I told you they talk to me. Can you hear them?"

Taking out the still bloody box cutter he'd killed all of his victims with, he sliced a line on his own wrist, then snorted a little more blow. He then cut himself again, but a little deeper this time, followed by snorting a little bit more blow. Wanting to go for the gusto, Lonnie stuck the bag up to his nose and inhaled as hard as he could. As soon as he put the bag down and lifted the box cutter up to slice at his wrist again, his fingers trembled and got numb. Two seconds later, his entire body shook in an intense spasm, and Lonnie's head hit his mother's gravestone before he passed out.

Lonnie Eugene McKay had overdosed.

CHAPTER THIRTY-THREE

Lonnie sat blank faced until the judge's count got all the way to "three" from her countdown. His lawyer had been trying to get him to rise out of respect to hear the verdict, but Lonnie didn't give two shits about respecting a woman or what the verdict said. His utter disregard for women is what had eighteen-year-old Lonnie facing natural life behind prison without the chance of parole. Lonnie knew he wasn't walking out of the courtroom a free man, so he didn't understand why he needed to kiss the judge's or jurors' asses.

The judge smiled like she was the devil's partner in crime, if he had one. She reveled in the fact she was about to send one the most notorious serial killers of Detroit's history away. The case had gotten news coverage all over the nation, wanting to know the mind of a criminal as brutal as Lonnie had been. They all wanted to know why he targeted women. Beside the bum, who was still connected to one of his victims, Lonnie had killed a gang of women. With them finding five of the bodies on their own, there were still a few spaced around the city he wasn't sure they'd ever find. And Lonnie sho' wasn't gonna lead them to their bodies. He smiled strangely at the thought of maggots eating them and them rotting.

See, Lonnie was on a whole new set of pills.

The undertaker, while doing his rounds of the cemetery, found Lonnie overdosed on his mother's plot. He recognized the boy's face immediately from when he buried his mother since he had been required to hold her body for such a long time. And especially now because his face had been plastered all over the television. Instead of waking the boy and telling him to run for his freedom, he called 911 on his cellular device and said he wanted the finder's fee for the tip.

Lonnie woke up to the cops reading him his rights while putting silver bracelets on his wrists. It was after booking that they sent in a psychiatrist to analyze him. He was labeled a druggie, a manic-depressive individual, a ticking time bomb, and a whole bunch of other stuff that meant the jail got to keep him heavily sedated, and he remained by himself. Alone, away from the rest of the population while awaiting his trial, Lonnie went even crazier. He was forced to quit coke cold turkey, which sent him in sorrowful places more times than he could count. He'd even tried committing suicide while behind bars, only gaining himself a "weak man's" reputation.

Locking eyes with the judge with a sinister smile as she smiled back, they were smiling for two different reasons. Lonnie was now thinking about how sweet it would be to slice and dice her. The cameras zoomed in, snapping pictures and taking live footage of Lonnie and the judge. She was getting ready to be famous and loved it. No one wanted to miss a beat or speak a syllable. Tension was radiating throughout the courtroom.

"Lonnie Eugene McKay, as you stand in front of me like I stated before, I am sad to be here; we all are. However, here we are. Once again, I beseech each and every person inside this courtroom to refrain from any outbursts." Upon opening the envelope, the judge read what was written on the paper. She raised her head and read out loud, *"Lonnie Eugene McKay, you have been found guilty—"*

Not giving her a chance to finish fully reading the verdict, going against everything she'd just said, the families cheered loudly, creating an uproar within the courtroom. The judge, trying to keep her composure and remember she was sitting high on the throne within the courtroom and couldn't celebrate as she truly wanted, finally banged her gravel. "Order in the court. Please, calm down. I need order in my courtroom now."

With everything going on in the courtroom around him, Lonnie continued to stand unmoved and unfazed. He didn't care about the guilty verdict, but the way the judge was mocking him. Like the women he'd killed, she too was deserving of his wrath. Wriggling his fingers, he wished he weren't handcuffed. Not hearing a word his lawyer was whispering in his ear, Lonnie could only think about how good it would feel to kill one last time.

There wasn't one person within the courtroom with a hung head. All the families there were mournful over their losses, even though their losses had been like trash and in homeless shelters. Except for the granddaughter who'd been in the wrong place at the wrong time, Lonnie couldn't understand why the others were crying like they cared. That's why he was completely uncaring and heartless of them telling him how evil, coldhearted, and heinous he was.

Looking over the crowd of people in motion, it's like the room silenced and all movement froze when the oversized courtroom door opened and a man in a wheelchair Lonnie thought looked familiar was wheeled in. Staring at Lonnie with the look of death in his eyes, Lonnie stared back just as hard but also with curiosity of who the man was. Lonnie didn't realize who he was until he was wheeled right behind him and an arm's length away.

"I hope your cell mates rip your asshole apart, motherfucker. My daughter liked your pathetic ass. I hope she haunts you every day of your miserable life—then you die a slow and painful death." Trina's father wished a living hell on his daughter's killer. Finding out about Trina in the hospital sent the old man into a flare-up. He got even sicker when he was forced to cremate Trina because he couldn't afford to bury her. He planned on finding a man behind bars with Lonnie who'd be willing to make the teen suffer just as much as his daughter did.

"I got news for you, sir; I've been living a miserable life for the last few years. If you can make sure I die tomorrow, I'll thank you right now." Lonnie refused to apologize, even though an apology wouldn't have done shit.

Trina's father tried swinging his fist and punching Lonnie, but the guard grabbed his hand and ordered the man's caretaker to wheel him out of the courtroom. Emotions were high. Lonnie laughed loud and devilishly, bidding Trina's father farewell.

Two officers came over to escort Lonnie out of the courtroom. They too were wearing smirks, for they loved their jobs of locking criminals up. Looking at the court TV cameras for their few seconds of fame, they moved to grab Lonnie's arms, one on the left and one on the right. Neither of them had any idea Lonnie had one last act of craziness to show them.

"You're gonna rot for the rest of your life, you scumbag motherfucker," the guard said, but away from the camera so only the crowd could read his lips. Like the judge, he didn't want to get in trouble for expressing his true feelings about the case. Both of the court officials had to keep their jobs. Their celebration would occur once the room was cleared.

Lonnie, however, was motivated by the cameras. Not liking that everyone was cheering, jumping for joy, and filming him at his lowest point, he felt his adrenaline surge once again. This time, it wasn't from an X-pill, Adderall, Abilify, the liquor mixture, or the coke he missed the most; it was pain and frustration he'd been pushing down and self-medicating. Taking a deep breath, he looked over at the security guard with so much mouth, pulled his head back to make the blow more powerful, and then rammed his forehead directly into the officer's. Not expecting the mighty blow, the officer's legs crumbled, and he fell to the floor.

"Order in the court. I need order in my court," the judge yelled over the crowd's explosion over what just happened. "Bailiffs, clear the room and get this piece of scum the hell out of here. I want his ass locked in the hole, never to see the light of day again. Lonnie Eugene McKay, you disgust me. I know your mother is looking down on you from heaven shaking her head." She didn't care about the rules she was to follow as she spat venom on Lonnie. The judge's words were led by emotion because she was a woman who'd just presided over a court case that unveiled so many atrocious acts on women. She wished she could haul off and kick his ass herself.

"Hey, Judge, you better make sure I stay locked in that hole these pasty-white cocksuckers are about to take me to. 'Cause if I ever get out, *you're* the first chick I'm gonna be looking for."

THE END

Also Available July 2016

***From Ms. Michel Moore
and Marlon P.S. White***

I Can Touch the Bottom

CHAPTER ONE

Years up in that motherfucker; straight wasted. Caged up like some wild animal that's used to roaming the streets. Alienated from my people like a nigga had the plague or something. I swear, I hope the garbage-mouthed rats that sold me out rot in hell. You don't turn your back on a real one like me; we a dying breed, and that's on everything. Yup, hell, yeah, them bastards tried to hold me up. And yeah, they slowed me down, that ain't no lie. But fuck outta here. I'm back on the block in full swing on some O. G. shit. On top of my game where a guy supposed to be. Now if that ain't God blessing my hustle, then I don't know what the hell you call it. Stack was tipsy, feeling good as he turned up the sounds in his truck. For him, everything was lovely. He'd done his time in the penitentiary, and now it was time to live like a king; stress free. *Yeah, tonight was a good-ass night for me! Matter of fact, the entire day was off the chain. The streets was acting right with my money, and them dusty females at the club was acting like they never seen a dude as polished as me. Shit can't get no better. Now all I need to do is get my stomach off craps, and I'ma be all the way a hundred.*

Stunt profiling in the butter-soft leather seats of his truck, all was well with Stackz as he reminisced. Blasting the rhythmic sounds of jazz, the music flowed out of the custom-installed speakers. Each beat of the multiple instruments seemed to be felt deep in his muscular built bones. Content with life, his fingertips tapped on the side of the steering wheel. Off into his own world, the semiwasted young-style gangster with an old-school mentality wanted and needed something hot to put on his empty stomach. After throwing back several double shots of 1738 at Club A.F.S.C., short for another fucking strip club, he was about spent.

Fighting the beginning numbness of a slight headache, he felt the rumbling movements of his ribs trying to touch his spine. Realizing he couldn't fight the need for food to soak up some of the liquor in his system any longer, he knew he had to get right. Stackz finally turned the radio's volume down to focus. Slowing down, he hit his blinker and busted a quick U-turn. Knowing relief from hunger was only minutes away, he pulled up to a local favorite late-night spot. They served breakfast twenty-four/seven which always came in handy when the pancake and scrambled eggs with cheese munchies kicked in. Stackz and his close-knit crew were semiregulars at the greasy spoon. They often stumbled in there to get their grub on after clubbing or getting wasted. But this time was different. Stackz wasn't crewed up with his team of menacing cohorts. He was rolling solo.

Looking through the huge neon-lit window, he immediately took notice that the "hood" restaurant was unusually empty for that time of night; a perfect setting for the impossible to be made possible. Any and everything was subject to jump off after 2:00 a.m. in Detroit, and no one, not even the toughest gangster, was exempt from getting got if caught slipping. Being cautious, Stackz had second thoughts of even stopping at the hole-in-the-wall, yet his stomach growling once more made up his mind for him. Stackz wasn't scared of the crime-plagued city at all. Matter of fact, he felt the city oughta be scared of him. He'd just come home after serving time in prison and was still on parole. But that wasn't going to hinder him from being the man he was on the streets or handling business on a daily basis; legal or not. And on that note, Stackz reached over to the passenger,s seat, grabbing his pistol. After putting one up top, he placed it on his lap.

Fuck that ho, a motherfucker don't wanna act a fool tonight bullshit; a nigga straight hungry as hell. Chili fries with cheese is just what a brother need to get me back right, Stackz thought as he pulled to the side of the building.

Stackz put his vehicle in park. With no worries, he jumped out of the triple-black Jeep Commander, gun in hand. Like a hawk hunting for prey, his eyes searched the general area, being mindful of his surroundings. Tipsy not drunk, the trained street soldier was on high alert and on point. Pausing momentarily, he tucked the rubber-gripped .45-caliber thumper in his waistband, adjusting it. He was a hood sniper when it came to automatics, so the fact he had his "li'l act right" with him, he was all good. Pulling his shirt down in an attempt to conceal the illegal peacemaker, Stackz reassured his still-disgruntled stomach that satisfaction was shortly on the way.

Shutting the truck door, he hit the lock button on his keychain. Checking the lot once more, he headed toward the restaurant entrance. As he made his way past the window, Stackz took notice of the people inside; three guys who appeared to be silly and harmless and two young females. Listening to their laughter from the outside, he assumed they were here on the same buzzed mission he was: needing a greasy fix.

With confidence, Stackz pushed the glass door wide open, stepping inside. It was whatever. On some Martin Luther King shit, tonight, he was fearing no man. As if on cue, all the laughter he'd overheard while walking up abruptly ceased. It was as if Jesus had jumped off the cross or Tupac's ghost had appeared for a final ell concert; all eyez were on him. After a few brief seconds of uncomfortable silence, the three initially-perceived-to-be-harmless dudes took on the form of pure thirstiness. Although Stackz felt he was outnumbered when it came down to it, he knew he was good with the hardware and would put in work, if need be. Maybe it was the 1738 flowing through his bloodstream making him paranoid—and maybe not. But whatever the case, Stackz immediately felt like the trio of guys possibly had some bullshit brewing and put his game face on.

Making eye contact with both of the girls, Stackz had the ability to quickly study people's body language and act accordingly. It was a gift that his grandmother passed down to him; one he often used to his advantage. The lighter skinned one with all the weave appeared to be wild. Smacking on her gum, sucking her teeth, and talking loud, she was everything that Stackz didn't like in a woman. He might have been locked up for some years, but he knew she was out of order. Her clothes were too tight and definitely too revealing for his taste. Whoever she was, Stackz could tell she was trying too hard. Not wanting to stare at the group of people too much longer, he quickly glanced at the other female. Immediately with ease, he read something in the caramel-complexioned female's mannerisms that said she wasn't down with the clown antics her group was into. Stackz made a mental note that although she was cute in the face and had potential, she was dumb as hell for hanging with dudes that appeared to be bottom-feeders.

"Hello, there, can I help you?" the girl behind the security glass asked, pen in hand as he approached the counter.

"Umm, yeah, dear, let me get some chili fries with bacon, Swiss, and American cheese, along with fresh chopped onions," he calmly responded, still being aware of the eerie silence since he'd come inside the building.

"Will that complete your order?" she leaned closer to the bulletproof glass, getting a whiff of Stackz's cologne that had somehow floated through to the other side.

"Yeah, sweetheart. That's it," Stackz replied, taking his money out of his pocket. While waiting for the total, he stared down at her name tag which read Tangy. He thought he knew her but couldn't call it for sure. Although he and his boys were semilate-night regulars, the virtually unskilled cashiers working the graveyard shift changed like clockwork. Waiting for the female who seemed somewhat familiar to give him his total, it suddenly hit Stackz where he remembered her from. She was T. L. people; his young soldier who he'd raised from a youth. He ran with a lot of chicks, but this girl's cat-shaped eyes were what he remembered.

Tangy had run with Stackz's protégé a few summers back and easily knew who he was. As soon as he had walked through the door, her heart raced. Tangy hoped her hair was on point and wished she'd worn her good push-up bra. She always had a secret crush on Stackz, like most females from around the way, even if they were banging one of his boys. Stackz always dressed nice, stayed driving good, and most importantly, was rumored to have a big piece of meat between his legs he knew how to work. She wanted nothing more but for him to sit in the dining-room area and eat his food, but with the three stooges and their girls still tucked away in the corner of the restaurant acting a fool, Tangy knew that would never happen. She was disgusted, constantly giving them the side eye as she rang up Stackz's order.

No rookie to the streets, Stackz peeped her unease and body language. He felt like something was up and knew right then and there he should get ready.

"That will be $5.37, please, Stackz," she quietly announced, seductively licking her lips.

Like Stackz thought he knew who she was, the fact she called him by his street name confirmed he was right. Tangy did, in fact, used to run with T. L. Nevertheless, Stackz was used to females openly flirting with him so he paid her no mind, especially at this moment. Without hesitation, he pealed a twenty-dollar bill off his medium-sized knot and slid it to her, insisting she kept the change. Just then, Stackz overheard the biggest of the three guys posted in the far corner try to go hard.

"Who in the fuck this pretty-ass nigga think he is! All fly guy and shit with his red Pelle on and rocking them overpriced Robin's Jeans. He must not know where the hell he's at. He gonna mess around and get all the shit ran, plus that truck he drove up in."

Stackz clearly wasn't moved by his hating punk-ass comment. He knew just where he was; in the heart of the city; the city that he got hella money in. Stackz had already killed the nigga with all the mouth and his homeboys eight different ways in his mind before he could blink twice. *Got me a few to go, I see. Any sign of fuckery and they people ain't gon' be able to sell enough fish dinners or raise enough money in a GoFundMe account to bury they asses quick enough.*

"Stackz, you heard that right?" Tangy asked on the sly.

"Yeah, baby girl," he grinned, winking his eye. "I know where I am; just where the fuck I wanna be." Casually, he turned, looking over his shoulder at the trio, especially the one with the big mouthpiece. "Listen up, you ho-ass nigga; this ain't what you want. This right here ain't what you looking for tonight; none of y'all. So fall back with them bitches and relax. Don't tempt me to show out."

Overly intoxicated, the three drunk wannabe thugs huddled together, obviously getting their courage up to attack. With ill intentions of going for bad, each kept looking over in Stackz's direction, hoping their intended target was just talking that ballsy shit to convince himself he wasn't about to get got.

Stackz had already sized the dudes up when he first stepped inside the restaurant and knew if and when the time came, he'd lay all they asses down; the two groupie skanks also, if need be. In Detroit, females were known for having "gangster moments" too. So fuck all that "I'm innocent and was just with him because" bullshit. In Stackz's eyes, everybody could bleed blood if they jumped into the murderous street arena; hoes included. Holding his own, like the O. G. he was, Stackz stood by the counter. With his phone in one hand and the other ready to whip out his .45 and go to work, he was hyped.

"Dang, why y'all always stay on some unnecessary crap?" one female remarked loud enough so Stackz would hopefully hear. What she was really doing was dry snitching on the always drunk, belligerent clowns she was sitting with. She'd been around them long enough from time to time to know they were seriously out of their league where this guy was concerned. The way he stood and carried himself, Ava knew dude was right; trouble with him was definitely not what they wanted. "Look, Leela, I'm ready to go right fucking now. Fuck this dumb shit! Y'all tripping!"

"Naw, Ava, slow down—chill; we good. You always acting like you too good to hang out with me and my friends," Leela smartly replied with a look of disdain.

"Yeah, and creeps like these right here is the reason why I don't fuck with your ass on the regular." She stood to her feet, leering over at the plotting haters with disgust.

"Creeps, huh?" Mickey had been called worse in his life so he let that little insult roll off his back like water but took offense to her trying to cause a scene. "Yo, Leela, shut your sister the fuck up," he urged in a hushed tone as to not be heard by their soon-to-be victim. "Calm her uppity-acting ass down; all loud and shit. She gon' spook dude before we even get a chance to run his pockets."

"Oh, hell to the naw," Ava loudly clapped back at Mickey, not caring who heard her. "I'm out of this moth-erfucker for sure! I ain't into catching no cases or bodies for the next dummy; especially your thirsty-trapping ass. Y'all do y'all!"

"Dang, sis, hold up for a few," Leela cut her eyes. Reaching over in an attempt to grab her little sister by the arm as she tried heading toward the door, she knew things were about to get out of hand.

"Yeah, hater, listen to Mickey and your sister. We on to something big right now, so chill! You can break out when we done and not before."

"Fuck your bum ass," Ava instantaneously snapped on Devin, the biggest in size of his wannabe tough crew; the one with all the mouth Stackz had overheard. "You might run Leela's simpleminded self 'cause y'all fucking around, but you ain't running nothing this way. You can bet that much." Still protesting her readiness to leave and the fact she wanted no part of whatever they were on, she pulled away from her older sibling's grip.

Devin grew heated. He hated to be contradicted, and hated even more for Ava to talk down on him and his boys. She had a bad habit of behaving like her shit didn't stank and she wasn't born, raised, and still posted in the same part of the city as he was. He didn't want her hanging with them anyhow tonight, but in between Leela wanting female company and Mickey always hoping he could one day get on, here Ava was; going against the grain, as usual. "Look, girl, I swear on everything I love, I'm straight bulldogging and skull tapping that ass if your people blow this lick for me with that bad luck mouth of hers."

Leela wasn't gonna front and act as if Devin's wrath meant nothing. Those ass kickings she received at her man's hands leisurely were taking a toll on her body. With that in mind, she once again pleaded with Ava to stop bugging. Leela tried reasoning with her that it was just about to be another simple strong-arm robbery that was about to take place.

So she believed.

Stackz was no fool by a long shot. He knew his own pedigree in the grimy streets he ran in. Real gangsters move in silence. So he didn't say one word, because if it came down to it, he didn't mind being the suspect in the interrogation room on the next season of *The First 48 Hours*. Unbeknownst to the three drunken thugs, Stackz had firsthand experience with cold-blooded murder and had no problem whatsoever sending them on their way.

"Here you go. You have a good night and be safe out here," side eyeing the thirsty trio yet again, Tangy gave Stackz a brown paper bag containing his chili-cheese fries.

Sensing some sudden movements from behind, Stackz was fast and on his 360 spin. Having already grabbed his food with the left hand, he swiftly reached behind his back with the right. Whipping out his .45 upping it as he turned around, it was on. Game time. Meeting the big man Devin's mouth with the pistol, he stopped him dead in his tracks as he brought it crashing down into his dental. The steel barrel shattered a few of Devin's teeth and busted his lip. Stackz was now in his zone. He'd stepped over into the dark side. With a menacing look on his face that read *I'm about to catch a case on that ass,* his heart raced.

"Arrggh." Blood ran out of Devin's mouth, dripping all over his once winter-white shirt. Feeling as if he was done before he even got started, Devin held both hands up in the air like the Mike Brown protester with his eyes closed. Bracing himself for the worst that was evident to come, the other would-be robbers jumped up ready to come to his aid.

Stackz was stern in his demeanor and words, dropping his much-needed bag of fries to the ground. He wasn't with no games, and he made sure everyone understood that much, shoving the gun's barrel in Devin's mouth as hot piss flowed down the wankster's pants leg. "Yup, come on with it, and I'm gonna send this here fat nigga to the upper room first. Then I got sixteen more 'li'l friends' to make sure you lames catch up with this big pissy bitch before he reach Jesus' front door. So what in the fuck it's gonna be, fellas? We rocking out or what, 'cause my food getting cold?"

Rank and Mickey straight-away stopped. They stood perfectly still, taking in all what Stackz had just said. It was as if they were frozen in time. They both considered their fate if they took another step, as well as Devin's. Confused and concerned, they turned to each other, not knowing what move to make next. Stackz was not in the mood to play around as his stomach was still growling. Ready to put an end to this entire failed attempt of them playing at being gangsters, he helped them decide. Snatching his burner out of Devin's bloody mouth, he pointed it at the defeated voiceless duo. Motioning his peacemaker toward the booth where the females were still posted at, Rank and Mickey quickly got the idea and politely sat back down.

"Oh my God," Leela gasped on the verge of tears, seeing her meal ticket getting his ass handed to him.

"Okay, back to you, fat boy." Stackz turned his attention back to Devin, "Mister, I'm the winner of the ho-ass nigga of the night contest." Not done with showing these fools that if you play with fire you *will* get burnt, Stackz gripped up tightly on his gun. With brutal force and an overwhelming taste for violence, he smacked Devin across the top of his head with the butt of the pistol. An echo rang throughout the walls of the restaurant. Cracking Devin's skull, blood started to leak from an instant deep gash. He was dizzy. The room was starting to spin as smells of bacon, cheeseburgers, and chicken finger aromas filled his flaring nostrils. Stackz had proven his point just as he claimed he would. Tangling with him wasn't what Devin or his crew of cowardly misfits wanted. "Now, okay, motherfucker, you see what it really is and what's really good. So we done here tonight, or you wanna go a second round?"

Devin tried to stand strong but couldn't maintain his balance. His knees buckled as his heavy frame dropped to the ceramic floor. Speechless, Mickey and Rank were in shock. They had never seen their peoples so humiliated by the next manz. It was like Devin was nothing to Stackz but a small child being punished for speaking out of turn.

With their mouths wide open in disbelief and horror, Ava and Leela held each other tight. The different-as-night-and-day sisters stayed at each other's throats, but at this point, they were as one. What started off as a late-night run to the restaurant to grab a bite to eat and hang out had turned to them being terrified to move an inch. Motionless, afraid for their lives, the girls did what most females would do in that situation.

Cry.

Praying they would make it out of there alive, Ava searched Stackz's eyes for any small glimmer of mercy he was willing to grant them. In between hoping she and Leela would see daylight, Ava was secretly elated Devin and them had finally met their match. They had a bad habit of thinking the world owed them something so Mickey and Rank getting ordered to go sit in the corner like some punk bitches was priceless. And as for Devin's big-mouthed fat ass sprawled across the floor, mouth busted, drenched in his own piss, that was nothing short of Christmas, her birthday, and tax refund time all rolled into one. Ava wanted to do cartwheels across the restaurant and break out in a cheer celebrating Stackz, but the fact he was holding a gun on her and her sister thwarted that thought. As crazy as it seemed, Ava was turned on in a sexual way. She was mesmerized seeing this fine-ass mystery man in total beast mode. Her pussy ached and tingled with every word he spoke and movement he made; even when his rage was directed at her.

"Okay, you two silly, sour-faced broads, bust the fuck up; get the hell on before I change my mind," Stackz irately ordered, giving them the opportunity to leave unharmed.

The fact they had come with the plastic thugs meant nothing. This was not one of those all for one, one for all moments. This game would be played solo, if need be. Terrified Devin's fate could easily become theirs if they got too close to the man didn't stop them from taking Stackz up on his offer before he did actually change his mind. Hauling ass toward the door, Leela was surprisingly first in line. Rushing by Stackz, who was towering over a bloodied mouth and head Devin, Leela's body trembled with fear. Lying on the floor holding his open wound, Devin tried to slow down the loss of blood. While he begged for his life to be spared, Leela never once made eye contact with her so-called man. Instead, almost knocking Ava to the ground to get by, she pushed the double exit doors wide open. Fleeing into the parking lot, Leela disappeared into the darkness of the late night not looking back, with Ava trailing closely behind.

CHAPTER TWO

Tangy was all in. Stackz had just become her hero. Watching him regulate not one, but three thugs at the same time, he'd definitely be her new man crush Monday on Facebook. Just as Ava was feeling some sort of weird sexual tension seeing Stackz boss up, so was Tangy. Working the graveyard shift in the hood, Tangy had seen just about every type of crazy shit pop off and heard the unimaginable. But tonight was the icing on the cake of them all. The dude she'd been crushing on since the first time she'd seen him was full-blown flexing and making that shit seem easy. T. L.'s mentor was holding court on the wannabe thugs that'd been trash-talking and intimidating customers all night. The guy Stackz had laid out on the floor had called Tangy out her name repeatedly. He also had his girl threaten to beat her ass not more than twenty minutes prior. So in Tangy's eyes, it was like *fuck him*. He needed some act right in his pathetic life.

The foreign cook felt the exact same as Tangy. He didn't want any trouble so he kept his head down, working on peeling potatoes. To him, it was just another normal late night at work. Since he didn't have his green card yet, he wanted no one from any of the two sides to even look at him as if he was interested. Barely speaking English, he was there to cook food and go home to his wife and four small children. He saw nothing; knew nothing; and cared about nothing.

"All I wanted was some damn chili fries. Maybe swing by a freak bitch crib to get some pussy and head and call it a night. But, naw, y'all thirsty niggas wouldn't let that shit go down like that. That shit was too much like right. Y'all wanted to see what it was like to go toe to toe with a dude of my caliber. Y'all was looking for this heat, so now you got."

"Whoa, hold on, bro," Devin spoke out as the room continued to spin from the blow on the head he'd suffered.

"Naw, shut the fuck up! Ain't no 'hold on' or 'time-out.' This shit is all the way live, and it's gonna stay that way. And for the record, I ain't your bro," Stackz announced, enraged what a simple stop at the local late-night food spot had turned into.

Devin did as he was told. He knew he had no win with Stackz at the moment. Dropping his head with his hands up, as to say okay, whatever you say, he prayed he could get to his gun. He looked over at his homeboys with a look of shame on his face. He wished Mickey and Rank would've backed him up when he originally made his move on their intended victim. Maybe then, things would have flowed differently. The tables would definitely be turned. Stackz would be half dead on the black-and-white dirty tiled floor, begging for his life instead of him.

Realizing it was time to bring this situation to an end, Stackz had to break out. A born thinker, especially in chaotic bullshit such as this, he formulated his next move. With only one way out of the restaurant, he knew what he had to do. Staring down at Devin, he let him know that for every action, there was going to be a reaction; some reactions worse than others. With those words of hood wisdom being bestowed upon Devin, Stackz then kicked him directly in the face. Just to make sure he got his point across, he then callously stomped the side of Devin's already traumatized head. The crispy fresh wheat Tims he'd coped earlier in the day now had bright red splatters of blood not only on the toe area, but the sides as well. Taking in account the door was at least ten or so feet away, Stackz slowly inched his way to the exit. Keeping his eyes focused on Rank, Mickey, and Devin, he wasn't sure if the thus far cowardly trio had guns on them or not. Raised in the streets of Detroit, he cautiously treated the situation as if they did.

Just as Stackz was nearing the front door, Tangy came from behind the bulletproof glass. Stepping over Devin like the piece of nothing nigga he was, she smiled, handing Stackz another bag. "Here you go, bae, some fresh chili fries on the house."

Stackz happily accepted the fresh hot food, almost forgetting the reason he'd stopped in the first place. "Good looking out, girl," he winked, backing up slowly toward the doors. Watching his would-be attackers like a vicious pit bull ready to pounce in a dogfight, his finger stayed on the trigger. Finally arriving at the exit, Stackz placed his back against the door. Using his weight, he pushed it wide open. Gun in his right hand, food in his left, in a quick movement, he tucked the brown paper bag food under his arm. With that now free hand, Stackz reached down in his pocket. Pulling out his keys, he pushed UNLOCK on the multibutton pad. In one click, the driver's door of his Jeep Commander popped up. Safely in the parking lot, the victorious warrior momentary stood at the side of his truck. Looking back into the Coney Island, he saw a lot of movement.

Making sure they were well out of harm's way, Mickey and Rank ran over to their boy's side. Lying on the floor both severely beaten and bloody, Devin moaned out in pain. Bending down, they aided him to get on his feet.

"Dawg, come on, get up! Get up! Let's go get on his ass before he dip." Mickey was now brave hearted in words, gripping the big man's elbow as he stood. "I'm gon' kill that pretty-ass nigga. Look what he did to you."

Almost in tears, Devin desperately fought to catch his breath. Suffering from high blood pressure, the over-weight ruffian was already two or three cheeseburgers away from a heart attack or stroke. Stackz's rough house blows to his face and side of the head had him still dazed even after the fact. Being helped over to a nearby booth against the wall, Devin sat down, looking as if he was moments away from passing out. Barely having control of himself to sit upright, he told them to go handle Stackz as he slumped over on his side.

Mickey and Rank stood tall. They didn't have a choice if they wanted to save face and have any sort of dignity left. Finally revealing their weapons from underneath their shirts, each ran outside. With guns drawn, the pair sought Stackz out to deliver a little bit of payback for his disrespectful treatment of Devin. Revenge would soon be delivered in a deadly fashion. Easily finding him at his vehicle, Rank knew they had to act fast seeing Stackz already had one foot inside his whip with the rest of his body soon to follow. Raising both pistols, the calmness of the late-night, early-morning air was interrupted as shots rapidly rang out.

Round after round was recklessly let loose. One, two, three. Eight, ten, twelve. It seemed like the hail of gunfire would never let up.

"Fuck, naw," Stackz mumbled as bullets whizzed past him, rocking his Jeep.

Posted side by side, Mickey and Rank were going all-out commando-style. Close up enough to see the fruits of their ill intentioned labor, the menaces' courage increased, seeing the bullets rip through the truck's rear door and shatter the thick, tinted glass hatch.

"What up, doe, now?" Mickey shouted, directly hitting the driver's side mirror.

Rank then chimed in, promising the ultimate revenge while doing his own equal amount of damage to the washed and triple-waxed Commander, "Whack pussy-ass nigga, yous as good as dead! Dead as a motherfucker!" Squeezing the trigger of his .45-caliber automatic, Rank held his firearm sideways like you see hooligans do in a bad, low-budget hood movie.

Stackz was heated; beyond pissed. Never mind the fact bullets were zipping around his body barely missing him. Of course, he was mad they were shooting at him; that goes without saying. But he was even more so enraged because his ride, his baby, was being abused, taking in huge gaping holes left and right. Simple Street-olgy 101; the worst thing a player in the game can do is shoot up a nigga'z ride. Especially if he had money invested in it.

Stackz wasted no time snapping into defense mode. His fury reached a hundred in no time flat. Automatically diving all the way in the truck, he ducked down, taking cover. Tossing the damn bad luck food in the brown paper bag aimlessly inside the truck, he listened to the ear-popping sounds of round after round being let off. Crouched over, Stackz reached into the driver's side door compartment where a normal person would often keep meaningless bullshit. Thank God, Stackz's DNA dictated that he was far from normal. Retrieving an extra clip he kept fully loaded, ready, just in case for situations like this, he was ready to go to war.

Climbing over to the passenger's seat, he quickly put the clip in the back pocket of his jeans. Pulling the handle out, he swung open the door. Staying low, he positioned himself behind the car door. Stackz peeked with caution from behind his makeshift barrier. He knew from firsthand experience, the longer he stayed in one position, he'd be more likely to be a sitting duck, and one, if not both, of the amateur marksmen may get lucky. As the bullets continued to rock his truck from side to side, gaping holes started to appear in the door he was behind.

These young boys want it . . . Well, they 'bout to feel me. 1, 2, 3, he counted to himself, then brazenly made a mad dash toward the rear of the vehicle, gun blazing. Once making it there, he started to return fire more deliberately aimed at Mickey and Rank. With the first volley of shots, he aimed high at their faces. Stackz's motto was if you kill the head, the body will surely follow. In a matter of a few brief seconds, Stackz introduced them to what it was like to do battle with a real-life gangster.

Mickey's courageously tough-guy stand was abruptly cut short. His upper body jerked back. Instantaneously, his shoulder cap exploded on impact from the .45-caliber slug Stackz sent his way. "I'm hit! I'm hit! I'm fucking shot," he agonized before being struck once more. This time, the force of the bullet spun him completely around. As he dropped to his knees and fell to the pavement, Mickey held his shoulder. Bleeding profusely from the two wounds, he crawled behind a huge green metal trash Dumpster located in the rear of the restaurant. Almost in shock, Mickey started to pray, begging God to spare his life.

Having no focus or discipline, Rank was blindly shooting at Stackz, hoping to hit his mark. The more rounds he let loose, the more he realized it was as if Stackz were superhuman. None of his bullets struck the polished player, even though he'd emptied his clip. Taking cover behind a car also parked in the lot, Rank was terrified, feeling some wetness in his head. Reaching his hand up, he brought it down to his face. Rank wanted to pass out. It was blood. Like his cohort Mickey, he'd been hit as well. Hearing footsteps, he braced himself, knowing death was near. Fortunately, he heard his boy Devin's voice yell out.

"Yo, nigga, you think you just gonna do me like that up in that motherfucker, and shit gonna be all sweet? Naw, dawg, shit ain't going down like that. You gonna pay, homeboy." Gun in hand, Devin stumbled out of the restaurant door in search of Stackz. As blood from his open head wound dripped down onto his face, he went on with his impromptu rant, vowing retribution. "Yo, Mickey, Rank; where y'all asses at? Posse up, niggas! Let's bury this bright-skin faggot!"

Turning his head for a split second to the right, Devin caught a quick glimpse of a terrified Mickey lying slumped over behind the Dumpster. Unfortunately, for bad-boy-to-the-end Devin, it was the last thing he'd ever see. One of Stackz's bullets ripped through Devin's neck. The next slug tore through his left ear, exiting the right side of his face. Devin's brains showered the already filthy glass of the window's restaurant. His body collapsed onto the pavement. His pistol fell out of his once-closed hand and slid across the asphalt.

An eerie silence filled the air. Stackz had counted the rounds each shooter probably had and realized unless they had an extra clip like him, they were out of ammo; hit; tapped out. Stackz hoped they had seen what just took place with their appeared-to-be leader and scattered out of Dodge. On parole, the eager-to-stay-free Stackz had no intentions whatsoever to wait and find out if his calculations were correct. He wasn't a fool. He knew it wouldn't be long before the Detroit police either crept up on the fresh murder scene or were dispatched there. Either/or, it was time for him to do what he was trying to do before aggressively interrupted by Devin, Mickey, and Rank; go home. If the two survivors turned out to be rats and told the cops what they knew or bossed up to be loyal to the game and wanted street justice remained to be seen in the days to follow. Stackz would have to deal with either play they made next.

He took in mind everything that had just popped off in slow motion. He didn't panic before, during, or now. This wasn't his first shoot-out with wannabe assholes who mistakenly believed they were about that life and the way he lived, Stackz surely knew it wasn't his last. Running down the list of things he had to do next in his head he took a deep breath. *#1 Get away from the scene as soon as possible. #2 Get rid of the murder tool after making sure his prints were clean. #3 Call T. L. or Gee for damage control,* and lastly, but most importantly, *#4 find out who these three clowns are and who their people are.* If their folk were in the game, or even dreamed about being in the game, they might have the notion of getting revenge. And if they did feel ballsy, then the body count would have to go up; no questions asked.

Searching the now-seemingly deserted parking lot with his eyes, Stackz wanted nothing more than to go over and spit in Devin's face but had watched enough episodes of *CSI* while locked up to know his DNA on the deceased would be like signing his own arrest warrant. Climbing up in his bullet-riddled truck, he prayed it would start. Once again, blessed by the hustle gods, it did. Gun still in one hand, he threw the metal warrior in reverse. Backing out of the lot like a normal person that'd just picked up their carryout, Stackz played his departure cool, seeing how his rear window was shot out.

Driving maybe a good few miles or so, he stumbled up on an abandoned gas station. Full of trash and other debris scattered about here and there, he pulled around to the back. Checking his surroundings for the possibility of late-night crackheads in search of their next blow or greed-driven scrappers who might be lurking, Stackz turned off his headlights. Without fear, he then got out of the truck with his favorite throwaway in tow. Once more, he looked around to see if anyone was out and about. Seeing it was all clear, Stackz wiped the gun clean with not only a dirty rag but some Windex and tire cleaner as well.

As quietly as possible, he lifted the lid of the rusty industrial-size Dumpster. The big blue commercial monster was full beyond capacity with probably just about every discarded unwanted item from nearby residents and other businesses that didn't want to bother with proper disposal. Trying his best to not inhale the awful stench that leaped into his nostrils, Stackz spit twice. The way it smelled, a dead body might already be in it, so any other random person would definitely think twice about Dumpster diving and lucking up on discovering his gun. Stackz said his final good-byes to the pistol he'd been carrying since his release from prison and tossed it inside its new home. Using a stick, he then covered it up the best he could with the other rubbish. Casually, Stackz walked back to his whip as if he'd not just minutes earlier committed a murder and disposed of the weapon used to commit that felony. Starting the engine, he drove off.

Stackz did what was next on his list of things to do if he hoped to get away with murder: get ready to call T. L., his always-on-point cleanup man. Extremely loyal and trustworthy, Stackz knew he could count on his young dog. He was a soldier in the true sense of the word. Stackz been feeding and grooming T. L. since he was nine years old and his mama was out there getting high, addicted to crack, heroin, and popping pills. T. L. saw a lot growing up and had been through shit no kid should have to. Stackz and his little brother had stepped up and practically raised T. L. Stackz and Gee used to trap out of his mama's crib. When they saw the conditions he was subjected to, the two of them took him into their own home, treating him like a son, making sure he went to the best school, buying him everything a normal kid should have, and should have kept him doing right, but the streets were embedded in T. L.'s DNA. Having everything still couldn't quench the thirst for the street life out of him. So they kept "their son" close to them every day, teaching him so he'd learn how to think like a gangster and move like a boss.

They could count on him to get whatever task at hand done; quickly and efficiently. Still haunted by his mother throwing him away like garbage, T. L. was resentful at times and a known hothead when need be. However, he looked upon Stackz and Gee like the father figures he never had; he was their family. And he was willing to do anything to protect his kin; blood or not.

Now, T. L. was loved by many and feared by the shady-ass seedy side of Detroit just like Stackz wanted and needed a true hood warrior to be. T. L. could put in work and clean up the dirt he or Gee couldn't touch.

With one hand on the steering wheel, the other hand held his cell. Pushing the button on the side, he used the voice command to call T. L. In a matter of seconds, it connected the lines. The phone began to ring as Stackz caught a night air chill from the draft of not having a rear window. Looking over at his radio, Stackz saw the clock on the face read a little bit after three forty-five. Yet, it didn't matter how early or late it was. T. L. was on call twenty-four/seven always ready for action; good to go. For him, if it meant going to full-blown war at daybreak, he'd be as wide awake as if it was four in the evening.

On the second ring, T. L. answered. "Big bro, what up doe with you?"

"Yo, fam, what it do? I need you on deck ASAP on some real type of no-way-back-from-the-darkness business." Stackz seethed, still angry the three clowns had forced his hand into murder, even though it was self-defense.

T. L. was at his crib laid up with one of his many FFs, short for fuck friends. He grabbed the remote control to the flat-screen television and pressed mute. Having heard Stackz say "no way back from the darkness," T. L. sat straight up. He knew that was code name for someone had just got sent on their way. Intensely listening to his mentor run the evening down almost blow by blow, the eager-to-please goon got heated. Remembering he wasn't alone, he got out of bed with ole girl, not really knowing who she knew or could've been related to. She could be playing like she was asleep while ear hustling on the sly.

T. L. understood Detroit was the smallest big city ever, and if a nigga was trying to hide his black ass after doing dirt, unless you were as careful as him, Stackz, and Gee, that feat would be damn near impossible. Gathering his clothes, he got dressed while still listening to Stackz's game plan. "Yeah go ahead, bro. I'm on you. I'm throwing my shit on now and half out the door on my way." T. L. left the sleeping female in his bed, knowing she knew better than to touch a damn thing in his crib and risk getting her head knocked clear off her body.

"Okay, dig this here. I need you to shoot over to the spot where we always grab the food from."

"The spot with the food?" T. L. questioned, wanting to get the facts right.

"Yeah, the spot over from around the way," Stackz reaffirmed as he slowed down at a red light. "You know, where we hit up at when we come from the club. I had to turn up on these fucking clowns. I guess they was bugging and was sleep on a nigga thinking I was some sort of come up."

"Word?" T. L. quizzed, grabbing his car keys off the table.

"Yeah, your homegirl a cashier now up in that mother-fucker. Taking orders and shit."

"Who you talking about?"

"You know, what's her name? The honey with them funny cat eyes. The one you used to run with from the East Side. I saw her name tag, but that shit done slipped my mind."

From the description Stackz was giving, T. L. easily now knew who he meant. "Oh, yeah, Tangy."

"Yeah, yeah, that's her," Stackz replied, nodding his head. "She saw the whole play go down; her and the damn cook."

"Word?"

"Yeah, my dude. So you already know I need that surveillance footage. I can't risk making the news on some murder shit. You know I get banged on any more felonies, my ass is straight cooked."

"Naw, naw, say no more, bro-bro. I got this! I'm on it right now! I'm on my way out the door and en route as we speak." T. L. jumped in his car as his adrenalin pumped. "The way the police move in Detroit, I can beat them there and swoop up that tape."

Stackz knew he could count on his young dawg to handle things. "Good looking out."

"Come on now, fam, it ain't no thang. You know how we do. So I'll hit you back when I'm good with it."

"The way she was playing it with me, I think she up for helping us out. She seem street as hell."

T. L. laughed, knowing Stackz had hit the nail on the head. Tangy was street as hell; a little *too* street for him. That's why he stopped messing with her. She wanted to mean mug and skull drag every other female he knew. "She definitely about her coins, so I got a couple racks on me to ensure I don't hear 'I can't,' 'no,' or 'I'm scared' shit fly outta her mouth. You feel me? Money talks and potential cases get bought."

Stackz had one reply equally as clever and true as T. L.'s statement. "You already know real ones buy what they want, what they need, and what they please. Right about now, I needs that surveillance footage."

ORDER FORM
URBAN BOOKS, LLC
97 N. 18th Street
Wyandanch, NY 11798

Name: (please print): _____

Address: _____

City/State: _____

Zip: _____

QTY	TITLES	PRICE
	16 On The Block	$14.95
	A Girl From Flint	$14.95
	A Pimp's Life	$14.95
	Baltimore Chronicles	$14.95
	Baltimore Chronicles 2	$14.95
	Betrayal	$14.95
	Black Diamond	$14.95
	Black Diamond 2	$14.95
	Black Friday	$14.95
	Both Sides Of The Fence	$14.95
	Both Sides Of The Fence 2	$14.95
	California Connection	$14.95

Shipping and handling-add $3.50 for 1st book, then $1.75 for each additional book.

Please send a check payable to:

Urban Books, LLC

Please allow 4-6 weeks for delivery

ORDER FORM
URBAN BOOKS, LLC
97 N. 18th Street
Wyandanch, NY 11798

Name (please print):_____

Address: _____

City/State: _____

Zip: _____

QTY	TITLES	PRICE
	California Connection 2	$14.95
	Cheesecake And Teardrops	$14.95
	Congratulations	$14.95
	Crazy In Love	$14.95
	Cyber Case	$14.95
	Denim Diaries	$14.95
	Diary Of A Mad First Lady	$14.95
	Diary Of A Stalker	$14.95
	Diary Of A Street Diva	$14.95
	Diary Of A Young Girl	$14.95
	Dirty Money	$14.95
	Dirty To The Grave	$14.95

Shipping and handling-add $3.50 for 1st book, then $1.75 for each additional book.
Please send a check payable to:
   Urban Books, LLC
Please allow 4-6 weeks for delivery

ORDER FORM
URBAN BOOKS, LLC
97 N. 18th Street
Wyandanch, NY 11798

Name (please print):_____

Address: _____

City/State: _____

Zip: _____

QTY	TITLES	PRICE
	Gunz And Roses	$14.95
	Happily Ever Now	$14.95
	Hell Has No Fury	$14.95
	Hush	$14.95
	If It Isn't love	$14.95
	Kiss Kiss Bang Bang	$14.95
	Last Breath	$14.95
	Little Black Girl Lost	$14.95
	Little Black Girl Lost 2	$14.95
	Little Black Girl Lost 3	$14.95
	Little Black Girl Lost 4	$14.95
	Little Black Girl Lost 5	$14.95

Shipping and handling-add $3.50 for 1st book, then $1.75 for each additional book.

Please send a check payable to:

Urban Books, LLC

Please allow 4–6 weeks for delivery

ORDER FORM
URBAN BOOKS, LLC
97 N. 18th Street
Wyandanch, NY 11798

Name (please print):_____

Address: _____

City/State: _____

Zip: _____

QTY	TITLES	PRICE
	Loving Dasia	$14.95
	Material Girl	$14.95
	Moth To A Flame	$14.95
	Mr. High Maintenance	$14.95
	My Little Secret	$14.95
	Naughty	$14.95
	Naughty 2	$14.95
	Naughty 3	$14.95
	Queen Bee	$14.95
	Say It Ain't So	$14.95
	Snapped	$14.95
	Snow White	$14.95

Shipping and handling-add $3.50 for 1st book, then $1.75 for each additional book.
Please send a check payable to:
Urban Books, LLC
Please allow 4–6 weeks for delivery

URBAN BOOKS, LLC
97 N. 18th Street
Wyandanch, NY 11798

Name (please print):_____

Address: _____

City/State: _____

Zip: _____

QTY	TITLES	PRICE
	Spoil Rotten	$14.95
	Supreme Clientele	$14.95
	The Cartel	$14.95
	The Cartel 2	$14.95
	The Cartel 3	$14.95
	The Dopefiend	$14.95
	The Dopeman Wife	$14.95
	The Prada Plan	$14.95
	The Prada Plan 2	$14.95
	Where There Is Smoke	$14.95
	Where There Is Smoke 2	$14.95

Shipping and handling-add $3.50 for 1st book, then $1.75 for each additional book.

Please send a check payable to:

Urban Books, LLC

Please allow 4–6 weeks for delivery